MURDER

IN · THE

COLLECTIVE

BY BARBARA WILSON

THE SEAL PRESS

Library of Congress Cataloging in Publication Data
Wilson, Barbara, 1950-
    Murder in the collective.
    I. Title.
PS3573.I45678M8   1984   813.54   84-10330
ISBN 0-931188-23-7

Book design and cover illustration by Deborah Brown

Printed in the United States

10   9   8   7   6   5   4   3

My thanks to all those who read *Murder in the Collective* in manuscript form for their help, especially to Evelyn C. White, Jeanette Lazam, J.T. Stewart and Ruthann Robson. I am, as always grateful to Rachel da Silva for her enthusiasm and festive spirit, to Faith Conlon for her painstaking and inspired editing, to Deborah Brown for her designer's skill and sense of humor, and to WorkShop Printers, the collective that would not die. This book is dedicated to them — and to the people of the Philippines in their struggle for self-determination.

MURDER IN THE COLLECTIVE

1

I t was early June and raining hard. Outside the print shop where our collective was having its weekly Tuesday night meeting, the Northwest storm lashed against the brick buildings of Pioneer Square, driving the bums out of their doorways into skid road missions and shelters. Through the front window I could see dirty water rushing down the gutters, propelling the empty green Thunderbird wine bottles along the street. The weather forecasters had been gamely predicting sunshine and rising temperatures for days now; no one believed them. It was going to be another soggy Seattle summer.

"The point *is* . . . ." someone was saying.

I wasn't exactly bored. Just finding it hard to get into the spirit of things. But as facilitator of this week's meeting I was supposed to be on my toes, keeping one person from talking too much, another from trailing off before she/he had made her/his point; circumventing useless conflict while encouraging problem resolution. It was something I was usually good at: understanding what people meant even when they were floundering. I would have made a good speech therapist, my twin sister Penny used to say.

"You seem to be able to make sense out of total gibberish—you hear meaningful sounds when I just hear nonsense . . . it's amazing."

My sister, with the great sense of humor.

Maybe it was the weather, maybe it was just a symptom of the burnout common to all groups that are under-capitalized and over-idealistic. I was tired of hearing the same vague gripes over and over, but I didn't have the energy to do anything about it. Instead of gently but firmly cutting speakers off or trying to channel their complaints and charges into constructive criticism, I found myself just watching my co-workers as they talked.

First of all there was our twenty-five-year-old cameraman, Jeremy, rambling on about the poor quality of the new paper plates we were using on the press. He was small and thin, anemically good-looking with blond ringlets, earrings and torn tee-shirt revealing a skinny bare chest. He'd removed his Sony Walkman for the occasion, but the absence of music in his ears hadn't improved his coherence. "You know, I mean, it's like . . . those paper plates . . . they're just not up to . . . ." Not that he didn't have some good things to say from time to time, but his thoughts were swathed in such soft blankets of disclaimers and fillers that they usually died of suffocation before they were lifted out of the mental crib.

June, breaking in impatiently, was actually somewhat like Jeremy — in the way a 78 rpm recording is like a 33⅓. "Fine on the press. . . . What do you mean? . . . Color registration perfect. No complaints from this end *whatsoever.*"

June was Black, twenty-three, widowed, with two children. Her tough, little, flat-chested body and closely-cut Afro gave her an air of invincible efficiency; she was perfectly suited to the dangerous sports she loved: mountain-climbing, skydiving and white-water rafting. She also grew roses and wrote poetry and had helped all of us fix our cars at one time or another. She ran the press and she knew it inside out. "Those plates hold their position just fine!"

"Yes, but . . ." Jeremy persisted, shaking his curls and earrings, "I mean, June, come on . . . ."

I couldn't help sighing.

Four years ago Penny's and my parents died in a car accident while we were both in graduate school, leaving us Best Printing—a fully equipped print shop, a long lease and twenty years of business good will in the community. Instead of selling everything, as we were advised, and using the money for further studies (Penny was just starting a doctorate in biochemistry; I was finishing my Master's thesis on the Seattle General Strike of 1919), we decided to turn the shop over to a group of activists, to be used as a center for printing up political posters, flyers and books.

We hadn't meant to get involved at all.

Now, watching Penny writhe in her chair, and listening to June and Jeremy bicker about the paper plates, I still wondered why we had gotten involved, and whether we'd given up our academic futures for nothing.

Penny winked at me and blew out her cheeks like a pig, the same

BARBARA WILSON

trick that had made me smile for years.

According to our parents and to the evidence of early photographs, Penny and I had started out our lives as identical twins. But something had happened along the way, and by the time both of us reached our present age of twenty-nine and a half, we hardly even looked like sisters, much less women originally from the same egg.

Penny had short brown hair, cut punk and spiky, unlike mine, still nostalgically long and French-braided back from my forehead. She wore glasses with hot purple frames, that made the upper part of her face look both more sophisticated and more mischievous than mine, seriously bespectacled with wire rims. Perhaps because of the glasses our lower faces looked different too; my small lenses made my mouth seem wider, my nose longer and my chin more prominent, while Penny's top-heavy frames left only a little room for the rest of her face, with its small pointed chin and mouth curling up like a wisp of pink smoke.

Delightfully witty words could come out of that mouth, but also ferocious ones. She never scrupled when it came to laying the blame. For that reason many people professed to be afraid of her. Penny was the office manager and resident bookkeeper—some said resident Scrooge.

"This discussion is really useless," she was saying now. "We've got two boxes of the new plates to use up. It'll take us weeks."

"Yes, can we change the subject now?" Ray appealed to me impatiently. "We need to decide what to do about that flyer for the Nicaragua group. Are we going to let them have it for free or not?"

"At a discount," said Penny. "We can't just give away our labor all the time, no matter how deserving they are."

"But they're just getting off the ground, they don't have a dime," Ray burst out, and they were off.

I spaced out again. We must have had this same discussion fifty-two times in the past year and I knew the outcome already. If the group could come up with money for paper, we'd donate the printing. It was what we usually did, and probably the main reason for our financial precariousness. Penny always grumbled, "No one goes into the local alternative restaurant and says, 'Hi, I think the U.S. should get out of Central America—can I have a free bowl of soup, please?'," but for Ray every plea from a new organization was a personal soapbox issue, a forum for his own political beliefs.

"The U.S. is on the verge of invading Nicaragua, don't you care?" he was lecturing Penny. "This is a very politically progressive group, too. Not your usual mealy-mouthed leftist coalition. . . ."

"We're not a charity," Penny held firm. "Not yet, anyway."

I stayed out of it. Ray and I had been lovers for three years, estranged for ten months, and the collective had asked us please not to argue during meetings. So I looked at him instead.

He was wiry and slender, the bronze-skinned son of a Mexican father and a Japanese mother, both of them Red Cross doctors. He had a rich, persuasive voice, deep brown, slightly slanted eyes and a full black beard. Handsome, he was definitely handsome; his current lover, Zenaida, obviously thought so too, sitting beside him and listening too intently for my taste. Not that I had any *serious* regrets about Ray, but I hadn't expected him to get involved quite so soon—and with someone I had to see every day.

"I think Ray is right," she said in a vehement voice and with a loving look. "We have to support the revolution. That means using our own paper, our scraps, anything we have! I will help Ray work on it."

Zenaida, or Zee, as we called her, was Filipina, slender and fragile as a gold-leafed statue, with heavy, black, well-cut hair and a wardrobe of beautiful clothes. She came from a family of lawyers, most of whom were in the Philippines and some of whom were in prison for opposing the Marcos government. She'd originally come to Seattle to study nursing at the university and had stayed to pursue photography and politics, especially anti-Marcos politics. She worked with Ray doing layout and stripping the negatives in place.

"I think they've still got to come up with the paper stock themselves, don't you, Elena?" Penny said, appealing finally to the last member of the collective.

Elena shrugged indifferently. "It seems like we've had this discussion before."

Right, I thought, and you've only been here four months.

While every collective member made a qualitative change in the group, Elena had made more of an impact than most. She was a very out lesbian, who'd been to court to keep her children in a contested custody case. She'd won, but as a result of speaking around town and having her picture in the paper, she had been fired from her high school teaching job. She had also taken that to court. She was famous, not to say notorious, and she brought in a certain amount of business from people who just wanted to look at her.

On the other hand, she was the only one of us without actual experience. She'd first come to us about having some posters printed and had stayed to watch the press in action. Fascinated, and in need of a job while her case was being appealed, she'd asked to be taken on as an apprentice, at half-wages.

After some discussion we'd agreed, but things hadn't worked out as planned. First of all, everyone felt too guilty about paying a thirty-four year old single mother—and famous lesbian-feminist—only half of what we made, which was no fortune. So we'd increased her salary to equal ours. Unfortunately, this was tantamount to accepting her into the collective before she was properly trained. And, as a matter of fact, Elena hadn't yet been properly trained.

She found she wasn't good on the press, so she switched to the dark-

BARBARA WILSON

room. But Jeremy's charming vagaries got on her nerves after two weeks, so she came back out to the stripping area, so that Zee could teach her how to get the negatives ready for platemaking.

Elena was a little better at this sort of work, but after a month or so she began to complain that it was all too boring. What she was really interested in, she claimed, was the job of office manager. But here Penny drew the line. In her blunt, snappy way, she simply told Elena that she'd watched her go through too many people's time and energy in the last three months, and that wasn't going to happen to her.

As a result, Elena had been under my wing since then, doing whatever needed to be done. I was the general troubleshooter, no expert at anything, but able to do any of the jobs in the shop with some degree of competence. I was available when people were sick or overworked, or when we had a rush job or an emergency, both of which happened regularly once or twice a week.

Elena was pretty in an old-fashioned way, like the Breck Shampoo girl in a *Good Housekeeping* ad. Her face was baby pink, though lined at the forehead and around the mouth; she had a soft cloud of blond hair and her eyes were the color of milk chocolate. Her nails were chewed down to the quick of her thin, blue-veined fingers, and her manner could veer rapidly from the provocative to the indifferent to the hysterical.

It wasn't that I didn't like her. In fact, I found her, beneath the sometimes nervous behavior, fairly agreeable. She'd had a rough time the last couple of years. Becoming the media's favorite scapegoat for a whole movement just after you'd come out—with the consequent trashing in the movement itself for being a star—it couldn't have been any picnic. I could also understand why Elena, after the rigors of the custody case and the shock of being fired from a job she loved, would find the print shop a little dull. Printing is, for the most part, very routine work: a lot of measuring, adjusting, measuring again. There's not much intellectual stimulation to it, other than in the sense of being involved with words and images, and realizing the effect they can have.

Yet I still thought that Elena, if she continued working here, would probably be good for us in the long run. She'd already opened my mind to a whole section of the community I'd never known very well before . . .

With a start I realized Elena was talking to me. "Are you asleep or what, Pam? This is the second time I've asked you."

"What? No, I was just thinking . . . what is it?"

"I want to add another item to the agenda if we're finished with the other stuff. A proposal."

I looked around blankly at everyone's face, forgetting how intensely and strangely I'd been staring. Now they just seemed like the people I'd known and worked with for months or years: my little family, my collective. Too bad what they'd been talking about had passed me by.

"I guess I haven't been doing such a good job facilitating tonight," I apologized. "I'll try to do better. Any objections to Elena moving on to a new topic?"

Zee and June shook their heads; Ray shrugged; Jeremy scuffed his feet—he hadn't ever really taken to Elena. And Penny said, with the forced cheerfulness that comes from a long career of meetings, "Let's hear it."

Elena cleared her throat. She was very nervous suddenly, as if she were steeling herself for something unpleasant. A flush of red surged into her fair cheeks with their long creases around her mouth; she ran her fingers through her fluffy yellow hair, and I thought, with a start, how much she looked like Jeremy for an instant. With their coloring and blond ringlets they were certainly more twin-like than Penny and I.

"Let's hear it," said Penny again, with some impatience.

So Elena let us. "I've been talking to the women at B. Violet Typesetting and . . . ." She looked around at us quickly, almost challengingly. "I want to propose we merge collectives."

2

B Violet Typesetting was a lesbian owned and run typesetting and design business that had once been part of, as Penny liked to put it, a "co-ed" printing collective. It had been five or six years ago that the original women of Mobi-Print (named in honor of some anticipated mobilization of the Left back in 1970) had seceded. They claimed that since the men insisted on ghettoizing them in the typesetting room while they ran the presses, they might as well have their own business and make their own decisions.

The Moby Dicks, as the men inevitably and rather regrettably came to be called, fought it for a while (some of the women were their girlfriends, or had been), but eventually gave in and the collective split in two. It was a common story in the seventies. Mixed collectives started out having women's caucuses, then "women's spaces," then the women would either get the men to leave or leave themselves.

There were a lot of hard feelings in this case, especially since the new all-male Mobi-Print soon dropped like a great white whale into the unfathomable seas of bankruptcy. The women, who had regrouped and gained new lesbian members (or come out themselves), resurfaced as B. Violet Typesetting. They had wanted to call themselves Lavender Typesetting but were afraid they wouldn't get enough business. Violet was practically the same thing as lavender, someone reasoned, with the added advantage of sounding kindly and respectable, at least in the phone book. The story went that, later on, when customers asked to speak to "Miss B. Violet," the women would variously call out, "Barbarella, it's for you," or apologize, "Boadicea isn't here right now, but can I help you?"

To the disgruntled Moby Dicks, however, the women's collective was always known as "Be Violent," and through the years they had spread rumors about having been driven out forcefully by a bunch of man-hating, T-square-wielding Amazons.

While I'd never believed *those* tales I had been somehow negatively affected by the idea of a group of politically correct separatists trying to make it in the business world. We'd dealt with them on occasion, but it had never been particularly comfortable. Ray, who was usually the one to mark up the copy with instructions for the typesetter, complained that they pretended not to understand his handwriting, or ignored him at the counter if there were women waiting too.

I'd never quite admitted it to anyone, but I was glad B. Violet was on the other side of town. Obviously it was so much more convenient to go to the typesetters three blocks away from us, even if they were male capitalists.

Elena joining our collective made a difference, however. As soon as she found out what typesetting was and that there was actually a lesbian typesetting business in town, she was astonished that we didn't take all of our work there. She didn't go for the excuse that they were too far away, and as for Ray's difficulties, Elena shrugged them aside, saying that she was sure he was just imagining it, but if it *bothered* him so much to deal with women, then he should just send *her* or *Pam* instead.

All the same, there was something about Elena that both cowed us and appealed to our better instincts, as when she added seriously, "I think collectives have a moral and political obligation to help each other survive."

Who could argue with that? So I arranged that B. Violet should do our next typesetting job and took the copy over there myself.

The collective now had only four women, down from the six or seven they'd started out with, and some different faces. The thing that most surprised me the first time I went there was the neatness. All the typesetters and layout artists I knew worked in a rubble of sticky paper and tiny, lethal objects. But B. Violet was laid out as nicely as a piece of camera-ready copy. There were two modern photo-typesetting machines, two beautiful light tables, a small darkroom, lots of labelled shelves and even an area in front like a doctor's waiting room, with graphics magazines and women's newspapers on the table.

I didn't know the woman at the counter, but she was brisk and thorough and even friendly when she found out I was from Best Printing. She was a slowspeaking Texan, with a wad of gum, a pair of very long legs ending in scalloped boots, and movements as ropey as a cowgirl's.

BARBARA WILSON

Hadley was her name. We went over the type specifications together, and I was impressed that she seemed to grasp immediately what was wanted. She said she'd have it by the next day, and I went away very confident, pleased that Elena had pushed the issue.

But Hadley wasn't there the next day. Fran was; Fran, the oldest member of the collective and the one Ray had always complained about. If Hadley was the cowgirl out on the range, then Fran was the cactus she hitched her horse to: a tall thick barrel with a thatch of skunk-like black and white hair and a hidefull of stickers, all pointing straight at me.

"It's not done," Fran said immediately. "I don't know how you can expect it to be done so soon."

She looked harassed. But she also looked like the kind of person who enjoys looking harassed—just so you'll be sure to know how busy and important she is, and what an interruption your standing there and breathing is.

"But Hadley told me it would be done today."

"Well, it's Hadley's day off. I could have done it this morning but your instructions just weren't clear and I didn't have the time to call you."

She had a low, gravelly voice that in some circumstances might have been pleasant enough, and a strongly featured face that would have been handsome if it hadn't been so twisted with bad temper.

I could tell I was getting mad by the way my voice came out. Penny calls it the "robot-teacher voice": slow, overly well-enunciated, unemotional. "Bring out the copy," I said. "My instructions were perfectly clear and I'll show you."

And they were perfectly clear—as I had written them. But someone else, Hadley, I was afraid, had re-marked them so my meaning was confusing.

"If you'd used a red pen in the first place and hadn't changed your mind so much this wouldn't have happened," Fran growled, unwilling to take any blame at all.

The robot-teacher voice said, "I'm going now. I will be back at four o'clock to pick it up."

It got done, but with no love lost on either side. And these were the people, the incompetent, unpleasant women of B. Violet, that Elena was suggesting join our collective?

Penny spoke for me. "What? Are you out of your mind?"

"Are you going to let me explain or not?" Elena asked, over her nervousness now and seemingly imperturbable. It wasn't for nothing she'd been a high school teacher. She was used to getting around outright rejection and ridicule: "What? Me write an essay on Emily Dickinson, you gotta be kidding."

Everyone looked at her. I noticed that, unconsciously, arms had crossed and faces had set.

"Now, I know you all think I know nothing about printing and it's true, in a way, that I'm new and ignorant. But maybe, being new, I see some things that those of you who've been here longer don't see."

Stony silence. I wanted to tell Elena to drop it, at least for tonight. There were times when we could all stand a bit of lecturing, but now wasn't one of them.

Elena went right ahead, however, flicking back a curly blond lock from her forehead. "I think we waste a lot of time, and money too, not having a typesetting machine. Look at all those trips to the typesetters. And they make mistakes and you have to go back and get corrections. Or you suddenly need to add something else—one tiny word—and have to wait a day and a half for it. Isn't that right?" She looked at Ray and smiled. "Isn't it?"

Reluctantly he had to nod his head. No use pretending that he didn't sound off about the slowness or inaccuracy of our typesetters once or twice a week.

"It's a question of simple efficiency," said Elena smoothly. "Now I happen to know that B. Violet is in the opposite fix."

"What fix?" muttered Penny, but she didn't interrupt.

"They've got the equipment—two machines, a whole darkroom set-up with stat camera and everything—but not enough business. So you see, it's perfect!"

"Why don't they have enough business?" June asked.

"Hah," said Ray. "Go visit them sometime. You'll see."

Elena glared at him and said seriously to June, "The economy's failing and you have to ask why they don't have enough business?"

"Yeah," said June stubbornly.

"Yeah," repeated Penny. "Let's at least be business-like about this proposal. I'd want to see quarterly statements, a balance sheet, net worth, a bunch of stuff before I even consider the idea."

"Now, wait a minute," I said, remembering my duties as facilitator all of a sudden. "Elena has just brought up the idea. There are two questions to consider: would Best Printing be improved by having typesetting facilities is one of them. Can we discuss that?"

Elena looked at me with surprised brown eyes. I could see she hadn't expected to find an easy ally.

"No! We wouldn't be improved," said Zee energetically, shaking her smooth black head like a bell. "Definitely not. We have too many people around here already, too many problems just doing our own work. What do we need another business for? It's just another headache. That's what I think."

"I agree," said Ray. "You start getting people in here wanting type-setting and who knows where it will end? You can't do everything under one roof. Are we going to start binding next? And don't forget, Optimum Typesetters is just down the block. It'd be crazy to compete with them."

"That's a good point," I said.

"What do we care about Optimum?" snapped Elena. "It's just some man who owns it and pays his workers peanuts."

"That's true," I said.

"Stop trying to be so fair, Pamela," Penny said.

"I can't help it, I'm facilitating."

"Facilitating nothing. This is a pointless discussion."

Jeremy spoke for the first time, leaning forward with a narrowing, puzzled expression in his blue eyes. He forgot to look cute and spaced out and seemed almost angry. "Well, I'm against it. I mean, I'm a guy, right? I mean, and no offense, Elena, but what's to prevent these women from taking over and getting rid of me and Ray?"

"Oh Christ," said Elena, tense and suddenly close to tears. "What *is* your problem, Jeremy? Look, I never would have brought this up if they hadn't asked me to."

Penny was up in arms. "Why you? Why didn't they arrange a meeting with us, write a formal letter or something?"

"Yeah," said June, "how'd you get involved in all this?"

"Because I . . . because," Elena paused, unable to stop herself from turning bright red. "Because Fran is my lover now, that's why! Satisfied?" She jumped up and ran out of the shop, slamming the door.

We were all silent. I heard the rain pour down violently outside and said, "Well, I guess that means the meeting's over."

"Huh," said June. "You can bet we haven't heard the last of this."

After the meeting Penny and I went home to make dinner. We had a couple of roommates, Sam and Jude, but they were gone that night, and so it was just us, moving around the kitchen the way we had as kids.

No wonder.

It was the same kitchen.

It's funny—Seattle has become one of those trendy West Coast cities where every other person is from somewhere else. It's a little déclassé, in fact, to admit that you were born here. I mean, what do you have to talk about then? You can't be like the New Yorkers who miss the theater but love the slow pace, or like the Californians who bemoan the rain but admire the bus system. Sometimes it seems like every party you go to there are these little enclaves of expatriates: "Everybody from Manhattan take a seat; you from Pittsburgh, over there with the rest of them. Chicago, down front; Boston, upstairs. Seattle? No, nobody from Seattle here. Try the bowling alley."

But déclassé or not, Penny and I were born and raised here and seem to have a continuity that most people we know lack. Take the house. Even though we both moved out independently when we were eighteen and nineteen and didn't come back here to live until we were twenty-five, and even though the pink bedroom upstairs was now ivory and the bunkbeds were in the basement, the house was full of reminders of our youth. Scuffmarks, stains, broken things that had never gotten fully repaired; a door that hadn't been the same on its hinges since Penny had tied one of my front teeth to a string and slammed it (the tooth stuck to its gums); cracked cups, glued back together and still holding twenty years later; books with scribbled covers, wallpaper with the design filled in with ink; drawers full of scorched potholders, faded Girl Scout badges, burst necklaces.

It wasn't only our reminders either; our parents left their own—just not such violent ones. Our dad's Sunday paintings of cows and barns were still on the walls and Mom's collection of laughable and lovely cream pitchers still lined the dining room window sills.

People have asked us how we could want to live here after the accident. As if it were ghoulish or something. I think only those who were never close to their families at all could say that. Or maybe it's the way it happened. It's not like Mom or Dad grew into old age, became querulous and senile, or had a chance to take leave of their possessions and their memories. No, they simply vanished one day, smashed up in a head-on collision on the freeway, dead immediately.

I suppose our moving back into the house was one way of remembering them, living with them a little longer. Or letting them live. I don't find that macabre in the least.

And there were definitely advantages. The house was paid for and in good condition, except for the aforementioned scuffs and stains. We didn't have to buy a thing, and for two young women in the midst of disengaging themselves from scholarly pursuits in order to run a business, this was no mean relief.

We were happy there. At ease. It was obvious in the way we crossed and recrossed the kitchen, knowing the places of things, their history and meaning.

But I suppose the smoothness came from being twins too. I was working on sautéing the eggplant, just starting to think spices, when Penny swooped over with basil and oregano. "Let's add red wine to the sauce," she said, and then saw I'd already got the bottle out. It was always like that, but still we could marvel and laugh. We were different enough that outside our home we could sometimes forget our connection; inside, here, especially performing the familiar acts, there was something seamless, true.

"So does this mean the end of Elena or the beginning of a whole new chapter in the history of Best Printing?" Penny asked, tasting away and liberally adding more red wine to the spaghetti sauce.

She sounded more flippant than I suspected she felt. Elena's departure had left a sour, embarrassed taste in my mouth, that I hadn't been able to analyze yet.

"She seemed really upset, didn't she?" I said tentatively. "Like we were going to trash her or something."

"But Pam, if she'd just said that in the beginning, about being lovers with Fran . . ." Penny stirred the pot impatiently while I got out two glasses. As long as we were cooking with wine, we might as well drink it. I had a feeling that this discussion required a certain degree of inebriation.

"I don't think she really wanted that to be known—at least not so we'd be influenced."

"Of course we'd be influenced, now or later. It would have to come out. And we have a right to know."

"But *how* are we being influenced, that's definitely a question we have to ask ourselves."

"It would be the same if Fran were a man," Penny declared, draining her glass. "Worse, in fact. Because then you'd know for sure that he was using Elena to get into Best Printing."

"Penny! Is that what you really think? That Elena's being used?"

"Well." She looked a little ashamed. "Maybe not. But the alternative is that Elena herself is trying to cause trouble."

I poured us both more wine. "No, the alternative is that Elena thinks it's a good idea, and only happens to be lovers with Fran."

"Elena and her good ideas!" Penny burst out. "I'm sick of Elena and her good ideas. Ever since she came it's been nothing but 'let's do it this way,' or 'I think we should do it that way.' She doesn't give us any credit for having made decisions in the past about the best way to do things— she acts like we just fell into this."

"Well, didn't we?" I couldn't help laughing. Penny on her high horse was always inexpressibly funny to me. Her big purple glasses were steamed up from the water boiling in the spaghetti pot and her punk hair stood on end.

"Pamela." She looked severely at me. "There's no need after four years to pretend we know nothing about what we're doing. That's what women always do, act modest and dumb, don't take credit for what they've accomplished . . ."

"Oh, come off it. I read that book too. And besides, I happen to think that some of Elena's ideas *have* been good ones. Like having someone do a thorough inventory every week. If we're so smart, how come we never thought of that?—the way we'd run out of things and have to rush off and buy some more."

"It's not that easy always to anticipate what you'll need," Penny muttered defensively, dumping in the stalks of spaghetti. "Okay," she said suddenly, turning to face me. "*That* was a good idea. But what about some of the others—the filing system that meant buying a whole new set-up that turned out to be more trouble than it was worth, and Elena wanting to go to all those conferences at our expense so she could supposedly make job contacts for us—money down the drain. And that's what any association with B. Violet would be too—money down the drain, maybe even bankruptcy—" Penny flung out a hand dramatically, knocking over her wine. "But anyway, trouble," she said more calmly, mopping it up. "Hell, those women can't manage their own finances, they'd drag us down too."

As often happened, the more Penny tried to convince me, an already sympathetic listener, the more I started to pick holes in her argument. There's something graphic about someone who looks like you and who you've known all your life setting forth an idea so vehemently. You see how silly it looks. But then, I was always far less positive and self-assured than Penny. A carper from the word go. After Mom and Dad died I was completely set against the idea of working at the shop ourselves. All those boring weekends when we were kids, hanging around making paper dolls out of the scrap and sweeping up for a quarter— forget it, dump the business right away.

But Penny was against the idea too, and listening to her go on and on about what a mistake it would be to get involved, how much better it would be to hand it all over to other people, etc., I couldn't help but become convinced that it would be the best thing in the world for us to take the shop over.

We were always haggling back and forth, convincing each other and occasionally ourselves. It was so routine usually that it was like talking to yourself in the bathtub. But tonight there was something else in the air, something more than Elena's system of filing or her wanting to go to yet another feminist conference. Penny gave vent to it when we were halfway through our spaghetti and eggplant and more than halfway through our bottle of wine.

"Okay," she said. "Much as I think Jeremy put it badly tonight, there's truth to what he said. Why would the women from B. Violet, having left a mixed collective, want to join another one? What would that mean for us, and for Ray and Jeremy, or any other men who want to join?"

"We could have had an all-women's collective," I said. "Almost did. If I hadn't gotten involved with Ray about then and Jeremy hadn't walked in the door the day that Kay said she was quitting. . ."

"That's ridiculous," said Penny. "You know we didn't think like that. About being a women's collective. I mean, it's not that we're politically unsophisticated . . ."

She looked at me for confirmation. I shrugged.

"We're feminists . . ." she went on. "We know all about women woı.:ing together, creating their own spaces, taking control of their lives. I mean, we're two women who've known each other all our lives . . ."

"It would have been difficult not to."

"The point is, Pammy," she said with dignity, the dignity of half a bottle of wine. "*We* think it's necessary to struggle together—with men, not apart. We may get down on men occasionally, but we're not man-haters."

"That's not what I heard you say last week. And *I* think that straight women hate men a lot more. They have more reason and more opportunity."

"Doug and I are just having a cooling off period," Penny said, staring vaguely at the dregs of the empty bottle. "In fact, I was thinking of calling him tonight."

"You're better off without him, Pen."

"You would say that. But ever since Ray you just haven't made the attempt anymore."

"You make it sound like parachute jumping . . . Maybe you're not so far wrong."

"Seriously, Pam," (Penny was always using judicious adverbs like that. I never knew where she got it from.) "It's been almost a year now since you've been involved with anyone. You're not still thinking about Ray, are you?"

"No . . . though I can't help feeling a little dejected to see him with Zee now."

She sighed sympathetically, paused, and then, as if it had just occurred to her, jumped up. "I can probably get Doug now if I call. Before his class starts."

I got up and started rinsing the plates. I should have known their separation was too good to last. Doug was one of those thin, athletic types just this side of sports-fanaticism. He biked, he skied, he ran, he sailed, he'd been down to the bottom of the ocean and up to the tallest mountain tops. He worked at REI, the recreational equipment co-op, and he really got on my nerves. Penny found him terribly sexy, if a little lightweight intellectually.

I stacked the dishes, decided to leave them for later and started reading the evening newspaper. The New Peoples Army continued fighting hard on the island of Mindanao and Marcos was getting ready for his trip to Washington, D.C., in the fall. There was a photo of him looking like a wax mannequin and a caption saying the Philippines might have to return to martial law if the bombings continued. That was a joke—as if he'd ever really lifted martial law. I thought about Zee's uncle, imprisoned for ten years, since 1972, and about Zee. What would she do when her temporary visa ran out? I supposed she could always marry somebody in the States. Marry Ray, for instance.

Penny's laughter trilled in the hallway. She and Doug seemed to be on great terms again. I wished it had been as easy for me and Ray to make up. But just as it had begun, so had it ended. With fireworks. We'd managed to keep working together and now I guessed we were friends. We were civil anyway and once or twice, before he started seeing Zee, we'd gone out for coffee and managed to have an ordinary conversation.

BARBARA WILSON

But there was no way of ever going back. I didn't really want to.

He was always too glamorous for me, too intense. He wanted to stay up all night talking art and revolution; I wanted to go to sleep. He wanted to travel to Central America and work with the peasants; I wanted to stay safely at home away from the right-wing firing squads. He liked a sniff of coke now and then, elaborate sexual positions, driving all night, experimental music, calling relatives long-distance. I liked gardening, silence, having people over for dinner, reading Ruth Rendell and E. X. Ferrars in bed with a cup of tea.

He liked my "stability," the sense of home he had with me and Penny. I liked his looks, his background, the flair he brought to everyday life. We thought we could change each other, but I just got more stubborn, he got more exasperated. It was a mess in the end.

All the same, it had been a connection, an intimacy, that I now lacked. I hadn't made a conscious choice to draw back from a new relationship. It had just happened. I didn't seem to meet any new men; most of my friends were women, and the men I already knew didn't attract me. I'd started out wanting to live a simpler life, on my own again, trusting my likes and dislikes, away from the heat of romance and anger, and had found it so natural somehow that I didn't want to break the spell again.

And yet, I realized as Penny's voice got lower in the hall and I strained to hear, I was lonely. Lonely when any of my women friends fell in love and went off into the sunset with their cowboys. I knew it was normal, but I found it depressing.

The receiver clicked back in place and Penny returned to the kitchen grinning cheerfully. "Well, we're going to have a drink tomorrow night," she said. "And then, we'll see." She sounded extremely optimistic.

We talked about other things then: whether this heavy rain was going to continue and what that would mean for the garden; whether we pickled too many cucumbers last year; whether the fence would fall down if we didn't fix it this year. Homely household details. We didn't go back to the subject of B. Violet and Elena's merger proposal. I guess we just thought we'd wait and see what happened.

But something had already happened—to me, at least. In between the accusation of man-hating and the phone call to Doug, I'd begun to think I really did want to meet with B. Violet before completely dismissing the idea. I wouldn't mind seeing that woman Hadley again and finding out what she thought about all this. She might be a member of B. Violet but I'd still liked her, and besides . . . .

Actually, I suspect the most telling thing about my conversation with Penny that night, in retrospect, was that the word "lesbian" was never used.

Not once.

4
▼ ▼ ▼ ▼ ▼

A meeting with B.Violet was scheduled for the Tuesday evening of next week. I asked Elena if we could see their books in the meantime or at least a few quarterly statements. She called Fran and came back with the information that they didn't want to make any figures available until they'd been assured of some definite interest on our part.

"Just for security reasons," said Elena.

"Bullshit," said Penny, who'd arrived in the interim. "What do they think we are, the IRS?"

Elena only shrugged. "Maybe after the meeting, if everything goes well."

There was a tension in the shop that hadn't been there before. A new feeling of suspicion and uncertainty. I came across Jeremy and Ray muttering together and discovered June and Penny huddled in the same way.

Only Zee seemed to be outside it all; she was absorbed in her Filipino action group. They were getting ready to protest the Marcos visit to the States in September and were putting out a newsletter as well. Zee was responsible for its production, along with two men, Benny and Carlos. Some days all three of them were underfoot, acting like Best was the office of the *Manila Times*, talking in Tagalog, gesturing fiercely. All right I thought, so Marcos was a fascist megalomaniac who had ruined the economy and tortured everybody, but this was still a printing business, wasn't it? In America.

I remembered when Zee had first come to work with us last year how fascinated I'd been with her stories of the Philippines, its seven thousand islands, its blend of peoples, its history of struggle. She'd shown Penny and me slides one evening of Manila: Roxas Boulevard, Makati, the Wall Street of the city, Rizal Park on a Sunday with families everywhere, free concerts and picnics . . . and then, without warning, a series of horrible, falling-down slums full of swollen-bellied children, diseased beggars, child prostitutes—garbage and suffering flooding through the sewerless streets.

I'd been horrified and moved, and I'd admired Zee intensely; she was political but beautiful with her chic clothes and fine jewelry. American feminists were so deliberately tacky and utilitarian; I knew—I was one myself, in my overalls or jeans and tee-shirts, my sensible shoes and total lack of ornamentation.

Zee was like a tropical bird bringing news from another world, and I had liked her and been interested in her until the moment she became lovers with Ray. Then all of a sudden her jewelry was a symbol of upper class oppressiveness; her clothes were disgustingly feminine—look at those high heels and how *could* she work in a print shop without getting dirty?—and even her political enthusiasm was cause for suspicion. I told myself that Zee was a privileged woman from a highly-connected, though currently out-of-favor family in the Philippines. If Marcos didn't knock off any more of her relatives, someday when he was overthrown or dead of natural causes, Zee and the rest of the Oberons would be riding high again. They were lawyers, weren't they, not peasants or workers, and they owned a couple of sugar plantations in Luzon and real estate in Manila. Zee probably wasn't that serious about revolution; why should she be?

"I don't think you're being fair to her," Penny told me, after listening to me harangue one day. "Zee is incredibly dedicated to the newsletter and organizing in town. And her clothes didn't bother you—you know she makes them herself and everyone wears jewelry in the Philippines —before she got involved with Ray; you thought she was exotic."

Ashamed, I'd said, "I'm not jealous, really. Let's have her over to dinner soon. She and Ray. No, I really want to . . ."

But we'd never quite gotten around to it. In the early period of the collective's history we'd all spent a lot of time, maybe too much time, together. After Kay left, however, and Jeremy came, after Ray and I split up and Elena joined, we'd become more formal, less friendly. We were all so different. Sure, we had brunch meetings and an occasional beer after work, but June was really the only one Penny and I saw much of, and it was really Penny and June who were friends.

I never knew what Zee thought of me, whether she was sorry not to get to know me or Penny better. We were women, but we were white, and who knew what Ray had told her about me? She was always polite, but she was polite to everyone, polite and reserved, except about political questions. She sometimes looked as if she were waiting for something more from me.

But at this point I couldn't manage it.

By the time the meeting with B. Violet took place the following Tuesday evening the weather forecaster's increasingly timid prophesies had been realized. Not only had it stopped raining, but it was actually hot—seventy degrees and climbing. The air was at first steamy as a bathroom with the door closed; then the earth dried out and it began to feel like another climate had come to visit. Seattle reacted predictably. It called in sick to work, took off its shoes and sweaters and hit the glorious outdoors with sunglasses and fast tanning lotion. No one knew how long it would last. These could be the only sunny days all summer!

We met at seven-thirty in our shop. It was the first time any of them had been to Best Printing, and they spent the initial ten minutes walking around and commenting about the space. To my mind this smacked a little too much of tape measures and moving vans, and I felt my co-collective members rustling about uneasily in the background. Jeremy hovered protectively around the entrance to the darkroom, and June joined him.

At length, however, we all seated ourselves in a circle of chairs in the office, and finally I had a chance to look at everyone from B. Violet together.

There was Fran, sitting next to Elena: Fran with her thatchy white-striped hair smoothed down and her prickles temporarily out of sight. She was, in her way, a rather regal figure, a sort of Queen Victoria of dykedom, with her fleshy, handsome face, black-fringed light hazel eyes and ramrod posture. I thought she must be at least six feet tall. She sat with her legs far apart like a statue of some nobly unrelenting idea, with a notebook in her lap.

There was Margaret and, next to her, Anna. Both of them were light-haired and on the small side, wearing jeans and worn, striped shirts. Margaret had her sleeves rolled up and bit her nails sometimes; Anna had a black vest and noticeably large breasts. Otherwise they were remarkably similar. From the way they shot comments back and forth under their breaths, I guessed that they were very good friends, if not lovers, and from the way they shot glances of hatred at Elena I guessed that our favorite merger-urger was high on their shit list. I wondered how Fran had been able to talk them into participating in this meeting at all. She couldn't have initiated it completely on her own; therefore she must have had help from someone, namely Hadley, who sat there so nonchalantly, chewing gum, with her long legs stretched out to the limit

BARBARA WILSON

and her head thrown back as if she were enjoying the pattern of the ceiling's cracks.

There was something extremely likeable about Hadley Harper. Just her name and even where she came from—"Huyooston," she'd drawled in her slow voice when I'd asked. "Yuh, deep in the heart of Texas." She was all legs, almost hipless, with wide strong shoulders and elegant collarbones that bisected the deep V of her heavy blue gabardine shirt. Her medium-length hair, stuck carelessly behind her ears, was straw blond and prematurely gray; her eyes were a startlingly clear shade of turquoise blue, like that of a swimming pool in the desert at midday. Her speech, and her smile too, came more from one side of her mouth than the other, quizzical and amused.

I wondered, as we all settled ourselves, what some of the others in my collective were thinking about B.Violet—whether they'd already sized the women up or were waiting until they started talking to make decisions.

"So," said Elena, brightly and firmly. "Shall we get started? Decide on an agenda? And a facilitator? We should have a facilitator."

Everyone looked around at their own and others' shoes and sandals. After a pause both Hadley and June spoke at once: "I'll do it."

"Go ahead," said Hadley.

"Oh no," said June. "You do it."

"I'd rather you did."

"Christ," said Penny irritably. "Forget the facilitation. Forget the agenda. We just have one thing to talk about, and that's why B.Violet wants to merge with Best Printing."

"Wants to!" hissed Anna, crossing and uncrossing her arms over her large breasts, as if the charge were too much to bear. "Wants to!"

After that it was temporarily a free-for-all.

In retrospect I'm glad it happened that way. Oh sure, we could have been all nice and polite with an agenda of why and where and how and who, and a facilitator attending to the feelings of all concerned, keeping the discussion clear of roadblocks and making sure no one went off the deep end, but if it had happened that way I'm pretty sure it would have been uncomfortable and inconclusive. This way, at least, everybody got their feelings out.

And nasty they were too.

"If you think that B.Violet wants to join a bunch of males and straight women, and to be stuck in a little corner of your shop, out of the way, you're crazy," said Margaret, taking up where Anna's speechless denial had left off. Margaret had obviously brought her mental ruler to bear on our square footage and had automatically decided that they'd be relegated to the back if they moved in.

"There's nothing that says if we merged we'd have to stay in this exact space," said Elena, which drew a howl from Penny:

"You must be kidding—do you have *any* idea how much moving costs? Not to mention the cost of not doing business?"

"I'm sorry," Jeremy put in nervously, angrily, "But, like, you know, I just don't want to be apologizing all the time for being a guy. I'm sorry, but I just don't."

"You're apologizing now," snapped June. "You don't have to do that. Nobody should have to apologize for anything. We didn't start this," she added.

"I feel the same as Jeremy," said Ray. "I refuse to apologize, and I also feel that we have our own problems here that we're working on in terms of racism. We've finally worked some things out and now to have four new members, all white . . ."

Zee nodded vehemently, but said nothing. Margaret and Anna glared at her as if she was the male plaything incarnate.

"It's not at all clear to me," I said, "that B. Violet would have to become members of our collective. We might be able to work out an arrangement of sharing some facilities, but keep our own separate decision-making processes intact . . ."

Elena gave me an encouraging, even grateful look, which moved me to try to expand this idea that had only just occurred to me, but at that moment Fran, who had been gathering her forces like a hurricane cloud over in the corner, burst out in tones of wrathful contempt.

"You are *so fucking* unrealistic," she said, pointing directly at Margaret and Anna and possibly at the silent Hadley, too. "You're so determined to keep B. Violet—in spite of everything, no matter what—that you refuse to realize that nothing can stay the same. We can't continue as we are—on the Road to Bankruptcy . . ."

"I knew it," said Penny, her punk hair completely on end with horror. "You just want us to take over a failing business, sap us of our resources . . ."

"Kick out the men," Jeremy continued.

"And ignore the racism issue," finished Zee.

"Do I detect a note of hostility here and there?" put in Elena sullenly.

"You know," said Hadley. "You'd hardly guess it, but B. Violet isn't so *very* bad off."

It was the first time she'd spoken and for some reason it made an impression. It might have been the slow drawl of her voice, that sounded like we had all the time in the world to work this out; it might have been the ironic smile that put a curve in the right side of her face.

But whatever it was, it restored us, at least for the moment, to our senses. I wondered briefly how this calm personage had ever gotten hooked up with the wild-eyed Fran and the smugly hostile Margaret and Anna.

"We have assets," said Hadley. "No doubt about it. All the equipment is relatively new, in working order and, more important, paid for.

We also have some debts, not large but persistent; we're just paying the interest right now. We've also got a number of outstanding accounts receivable: local political groups whose fundraising events didn't cover their costs; feminists who think that business runs on slogans like 'Sisters pay last, if at all'; and even a few regular old companies who think that a business owned by women isn't really a business at all when it comes time to write a check."

Hadley smiled again and her brilliant eyes traveled around the room, stopping on Zee. "So it's hard times for us white girls. A lot of people are having hard times. And things might be better if we could join forces with you all—more traffic, more steady customers, more pressure on them to pay. But I do understand a merger would also create problems—for us and for you. Racism's a serious issue, and not one we've dealt with in a work situation. But there are other issues, like homophobia, that you all could probably stand to have your consciousness raised about, don't you think?" She paused and looked at June, who smiled diffidently.

"Well, thanks for your comments," Penny said briskly. "I think they helped us all settle down, at least. I recommend that B. Violet sit down and work out some kind of proposal so that our collective can go over it and decide if a merger is in our best interests—no pun intended."

I expected someone to challenge this, either someone from our collective who would feel that asking B. Violet for a proposal meant we were taking this idea seriously, or Margaret or Anna who would reject it summarily because they didn't want to put the energy into something that would only take place over their strong objections.

But no one said anything. The meeting had suddenly slipped into that catatonic state that sometimes occurs after strong feelings have been expressed and before any progress has been made, when members of the group will acquiesce to any delaying measure, just so they can go home and regroup their forces.

"I second Penny's suggestion," said Ray rather wearily, looking, for the moment, like a Samurai who's just laid down his sword in the cause of peace rather than justice. "We won't even know where we are until we have some kind of organized proposal."

Slowly Fran nodded her head. She, too, looked exhausted, even dazed. She glanced at Margaret and Anna, and seemed to draw some form of agreement from their lowered heads. "We'll do it," she said.

"So, are we finished now?" Zee's clear voice broke in. "I've got another meeting. An *important* one."

"Looks like it," said June, getting up and exchanging glances with Jeremy. "Coming?"

Penny looked at me. Was this something new? But suddenly all of us were on our feet. Chairs were pushed back, jackets and bags retrieved from the floor and the desks. Penny and Ray started talking about whether the new theater would accept our bid and how much credit we could give them; Zee ran out quickly, earrings flying, followed in short order by June and Jeremy, Margaret and Anna. I turned to say something to Hadley and found Elena at my side—Elena with her fluffy blond hair and soft, milk chocolate eyes.

"How about going out for a beer or something, Pam?" she asked me.

Out of the corner of my eye I saw Hadley approach Ray and Penny and start talking. "Well," I said to Elena, "I'm pretty tired." But then both my conscience and my better judgment smote me. Not only did I want to find out what Elena's role in this whole thing was, but I'd better find out, if things weren't to get completely out of control. "Sure," I said, "sounds good."

"Great," she said and then called over to Fran, who was already standing by the door. "Pam's coming too."

5
▼ ▼ ▼ ▼

S haring a pitcher with Fran was not my idea of an enjoyable end to the evening, but there was no way to get out of it now. Fran drove Elena in her VW wagon and I drove myself in my '67 Rambler to the University Bar & Grill. It was a pretty upscale place but I liked it because of its lack of hassle.

Fran had suggested Sappho's but had dropped the idea when I asked what it was.

As soon as I'd said it I realized it must be a lesbian bar. Sappho was a lesbian, right? I felt both stupid and defensive. Hey, it's not my scene, Fran, okay?

"Anyway," Elena had said quickly. "It's too noisy there. The Bar & Grill's fine."

Driving alone now I wondered what Sappho's was like. Dimly lit tables, a dance floor filled with bulky women like Fran, in jeans and flannel shirts, or silk blouses with plunging necklines and tall boots maybe, the way Elena had been dressed once when she'd been going out after a meeting . . . gyrating under the strobe lights or pressing close together in the dark.

My hands sweated lightly on the steering wheel and it wasn't just the warm evening. I felt a mixture of attraction, revulsion and fear, with the latter predominating most recognizably. Girl, I said to myself as I parked my Rambler, for someone whose scene this isn't, you sure are worked up by the thought of it. But why, all of a sudden?

I met Elena and Fran outside the bar and let them go in front of me. I observed them closely, in the interests of scientific investigation, and observed how they were observed by others.

I'd always thought Elena an extremely attractive woman. Conventionally pretty of face, she had more than a conventionally good figure: slim legs, narrow waist, full breasts. She wasn't tall but she moved as if she were, confident and upright. I tried, with others' eyes, to place her: an executive, a professor, a suburban housewife, a shop steward, a construction supervisor . . . she looked sure of herself, at any rate, and she fit in well with the crowd in the bar. There was nothing particularly "lesbian" about her, I thought, watching the appreciative glances she received.

Fran was a different story. She looked every inch the traditional dyke, with her flannel sleeves rolled up, her big, unbound breasts propped up on her full stomach. She strode through the room with the toes of her hiking boots turned outward and her arms swinging away from her sides; she was handsome but far too powerful somehow for the Bar & Grill, and I felt the trendy people turn away a little, amused or discomfited. For the first time I had an inkling of what had given Fran that prickly attitude of hers.

But also, perhaps, what Elena was drawn to.

We sat down and ordered a pitcher. Fran also asked for a shot of Jim Beam and when she got it, tossed it off in two gulps. Immediately she looked more relaxed.

"So, do you think it's all a lost cause?" Elena asked me, chewing on a finger. The air of confidence she'd worn crossing the crowded room had vanished. She watched Fran as if looking for cues.

"Probably," I answered as frankly as I dared. "I could see Penny and maybe June coming over to the idea with a certain amount of persuasion—it does make some business sense after all—but not the rest."

"But with you and Elena, that's four, that's a majority," said Fran. Her voice, after the bourbon, was husky, confidential, intimate. Her dark-edged light hazel eyes were warm now and she had a droplet of beer in the faint dark moustache over her full, well-formed lips. Her bulk and height gave her a presence that was hard to resist.

I said, with some stiffness, looking at the glass in my hand, "I haven't said what I think—that's the first thing. Second, we don't decide anything by majority but by consensus. I think it's important to realize, in the third place, who we're talking about: a couple of men who feel threatened and three people of color, all of whom have doubts. . . ."

"We're not racists," protested Fran, knocking back her beer and pouring herself another. "And as for the men, I don't think it would be that much of a problem, if we had separate work spaces. Hell, the typesetting would be separate anyway."

"I liked what you said, Pam," Elena broke in, "about maybe not merging collectives, but sharing some facilities. Maybe that's the way we should be going."

"Margaret and Anna certainly don't seem too pleased with the idea. Either way, merging or sharing," I observed.

"Margaret and Anna can go to hell," said Fran suddenly, pushing aside her second empty beer glass and calling the waitress over to order a double Jim Beam. Her voice had thickened still more, gone a little slurred. "I'm really getting sick of the way they treat Elena. I'm not going to stand for it much longer."

Elena looked at her nervously but laughed and poured herself another beer. "Margaret thinks I tried to become the star of the local lesbian scene. Anna's suspicious of me for working in a mixed collective. Hadley . . ." she glanced quickly at Fran. "But we can probably work it out."

I said, as gently as I could, "I don't think they're going to change their minds somehow—or Jeremy or Zee or Ray either."

Elena shrugged, drank, chewed on her finger. "Who knows?"

The waitress brought Fran's double. "We'll take another pitcher," Fran said. "Here. And keep the change."

Fran's face was flushed and her hazel eyes very bright, a little unfocused. Her voice was losing its intimate growl, becoming belligerent. It was happening very fast. Why didn't Elena stop her? But Elena was finishing off the first pitcher, pouring them both another beer. I put my hand over my glass.

Fran said, "I've always wondered, how come you don't have more lesbians in your collective? There are a lot of dyke printers, you know. Dykes go in for printing. I've been a printer myself, used to be anyway."

I shook my head. I felt the young professional couple at the next table looking at us. "I don't know."

"Don't give Pam a hard time, Fran," Elena said. "She could ask you the same kind of question. Where are the women of color in B.Violet?"

"They're in short supply," Fran laughed. "The ones who are out are in big demand. Black lesbians, Asian queers, Chicana dykes, everybody wants one to put in the display case."

"I don't much like that kind of talk," I said. "Even as a joke."

"Sorry," said Fran with a sneer. "I guess we've all got our sensitive spots."

I began to make motions to leave. "I've got a long day ahead of me tomorrow, guess I'd better . . ."

"No, wait," Fran said. "You think I'm getting drunk, but before you go I want to say something to you."

Elena reached out an unsteady, apprehensive hand. "Fran, maybe this should wait."

"Quiet," Fran said majestically to her. "My dad was a logger, not a professor like yours. I can hold it. And I want to say just one thing to Pamela Nilsen, that I know exactly what she's thinking when she looks at me, and when she looks at me and you. I know exactly what's going through her mind, her thinking I'm a fat, bad-tempered old dyke, and what do me and Elena do anyways, Elena who doesn't even look queer." The couple next to us were whispering and staring; I felt paralyzed. It was true what she was saying, but it still was all wrong.

"Pam probably thinks I beat up on you and maybe we're into S&M or something." Fran laughed loudly. "You know, whips and chains. . . ."

Elena was on her feet before me. "That's enough, Fran. We're going. You should go too, you know." In spite of her obvious anger there was a certain pleading tone to her voice.

"Forget it," said Fran. "Go on, get out of here, traitor."

Elena and I headed for the door. Someone I knew called out, "Hi Pam," but I ignored her. I wouldn't be coming back here for a while.

"Can you drop me by my house?" Elena asked when we got outside, adding miserably, "She's not really like this."

I said nothing. I felt shocked and pitying. I steadied Elena's shaking gait. She wasn't anywhere near as drunk as Fran but she was definitely on the way.

"She doesn't beat me and we're not into S&M," Elena said. "She's just trying to make me mad. We had kind of a fight earlier."

I wished I could believe her.

We got into my car and I turned on the ignition. I repressed the urge to make her confess. "You know, Elena," I said after a minute. "It doesn't have anything to do with you, but I don't think this is going to work, this merger thing."

Elena was sitting straight up with her hands in her lap, her hair a pale basket of flower petals in the refracted light from the street. I don't think she heard me.

"You should see her with my kids," she said. "They love her."

I got home to find our roommates Sam and Jude and Penny and the resurrected Doug sitting around the dining room table, having ice cream with Amaretto. They were laughing and talking about going hiking the coming weekend if the good weather held. Sam and Jude, like the sporty Doug, were big on wilderness. Much as I generally enjoyed their company, tonight the sight of all four of them put me in even a worse temper than I was.

Couples. Heterosexual couples. It was bad enough that we had to live with this happy pair, who'd been together for some outrageous length of time like ten years. But here was Penny with that creep Doug, planning to jump right back into the same maelstrom of love and hate as before.

"You want to come with us this weekend?" Jude asked. She was the bookkeeper for a number of alternative ventures, an orderly and idealistic person. Next to Penny she was my oldest friend and I usually felt I never got to see nearly enough of her. But I certainly didn't want to go traipsing off into the wilderness with all four of them.

"No thanks," I said, going past them into the kitchen and pulling the Swiss Almond Vanilla out of the freezer.

"Where've you been tonight?" asked Sam in an overfriendly voice. There had been a significant pause before he spoke. I could sense them all looking at each other, wondering what was wrong with me. I didn't care. I was still shivering over the scene in the Bar & Grill, but I was damned if I would tell them about it. I dumped two scoops into my bowl and then, judiciously, a third.

"Consorting with the enemy," I said, before Penny could. I came back through the dining room on my way to my solitary bedroom.

"So where'd you all go? The Bar & Grill?" Penny asked.

"No. To Sappho's. The lesbian bar, you know. Nah," I said, considering them coolly as I swept past the table and on up the stairs, "I guess none of you *would.*"

6

Perhaps because of the late-night sundae I slept badly that night, and my dreams were filled with dancefloor floozies who were the very opposite of the politically correct lesbians I knew, but who were quite provocative in their own way, with ruffled, deep-cut blouses and tight short skirts. I remember thinking in my dream, well if this is what goes on here what's the big deal? And being both disappointed and somehow cheered.

I'd turned off my alarm clock in my sleep and probably would have overslept if I hadn't heard the telephone ringing downstairs. I didn't feel able to get up to answer it, but it did have the effect of waking me up. I managed to struggle to a semi-sitting position as I heard someone's steps pound down the stairs.

I was still semi-sitting, pondering my dreamlife, when there was a knock at the door and Penny came in. She was wearing her own peculiar form of nightdress—tee-shirt and socks—and her spiky hair stood up like a fence on her head. I was about to remark that she'd better dip her snout in the shower before she let Mr. Olympic catch sight of her, but something in her face stopped me.

"What's wrong?" Since we were both here and our parents were both dead, I knew no immediate family member had come to grief, but that didn't mean there weren't plenty of other people who might be in trouble. "What happened?"

"That was Elena," said Penny. "She's down at B.Violet. She came there looking for Fran because she didn't come home last night."

"What happened to her?"

"Elena doesn't know. She says she found something that shows Fran might have been there, and there's a little blood or something, but what's happened is . . ." Penny suddenly sank down on my bed. "The place has been completely vandalized."

"What?"

"The two machines are smashed, and the copy ripped into shreds. The negatives cut up. A hammer through the big light table. Everything."

We sat staring at each other.

"Who could have done such a thing?" Penny said.

I kept thinking of Fran sitting at the table in the Bar & Grill. The suppressed violence in her voice. If she'd continued to drink, could she have, for some reason, gone back to B.Violet and smashed everything? In anger at Elena, me, herself?

"I just hope to God it wasn't anyone from our collective," said Penny.

I stared at her open-mouthed. That possibility had never even occurred to me.

Penny and I said little on the way to B.Violet. Any conjecture was far too frightening. We arrived to find a cop car out front and two cops, a man and a woman, in the doorway, along with Hadley and Elena. Anna and Margaret were on their way, Elena said, but there was no sign of Fran. Elena seemed glad to see us but otherwise she looked awful, with ashblue rings under her eyes and a haggard, dustmop-against-the-floor look to her blond curls.

Hadley, on the other hand, just looked confused, like any late-sleeper somehow set on her feet before the gears are clicking. She kept stumbling, which actually wasn't so odd, considering the amount of stuff on the floor now.

B.Violet occupied a pleasant storefront in North Capitol Hill, on a street that was more residential than business. It consisted of three rooms: the office/waiting area, the typesetting and design room, and the tiny darkroom. But everything was in shambles now; it looked like the set of a TV sit-com after a free-for-all scene. The office wasn't so bad—just a chair or two knocked over, some files pulled out and strewn around. But inside the second room there was complete havoc. The tabletop Compugraphic was on its side on the floor; the freestanding one had its screen dashed in and gummy rubber cement poured through the keyboard. The big light table had been shattered by some sharp object so that the glass top swirled out in fern patterns; the smaller light table had been pushed to the floor and part of its glass was missing. Scattered over everything, like wet black leaves in autumn, were cut-up bits of phototype fonts and negatives. In the darkroom there were more torn negatives and plates, and the plastic bottles of developing fluid and photographic fixer had been opened and overturned. The smell was lethal.

"Don't anyone light a match," Penny muttered to no one in particular.

Otherwise, no one could say much of anything for a minute. Even the cops seemed overwhelmed by the viciousness of the attack.

Then the male cop spoke. "Any idea who did it?"

"You said on the phone you found some blood," added the woman cop. According to her tag her name was Officer Alice Hawkins. She was a well-muscled Black woman with skin like shiny walnut wood and the heavy, wide-legged walk of the holstered cop.

Elena nodded and, not quite trusting herself to speak, led the way to the office. In a dark corner was the missing glass from the light table, sharp as a surgical knife. Along one side was a line of coagulated blood; there was a small stain of it on the carpet as well.

"I saw it when I went to the telephone to call," said Elena, in a shaking voice, fumbling in her pockets like an old cigarette smoker for some comfort, and then catching herself.

The boyish, husky male cop, Officer Bill Rives, pulled out his pad. "What time did you get here to work this morning, Ma'am?"

"Well, I . . ." Elena half-searched her pockets again and darted a quick look at me and Penny. For the first time I began to see how complicated this could be—not just in the usual ways that dealing with the law is if you're "living an alternative lifestyle" ("*How* many people live in this house, did you say? And *what* is their relationship to each other? And you say you all work in an ice cream collective?")—but complicated also in that none of us knew exactly who was involved in this and whether we should be trying to protect anybody, or in what way.

"Well," said Elena again, nervously. "I don't actually work here. I mean, I wasn't coming to work exactly. But I got here around seven. About ten after seven, because I left my house at seven and it's about a ten-minute drive away . . ."

"You don't 'actually' work here?" Officer Alice prodded.

"Elena has been helping us out," said Hadley, speaking for the first time, and in a firm voice. "She works with these women over here, in a printing business," she gestured to me and Penny. "The two businesses are thinking of merging, and Elena has been doing some of the groundwork." Hadley made it all sound quite normal and above-board.

Officer Alice asked, "Do you think that someone . . ." her eyes flickered around the room, "might have been against this merger?"

"It's quite possible," said Hadley calmly. "It wouldn't surprise me at all."

I wished I could be as matter-of-fact as she was. My mind was racing with possibilities. Zee had dashed off to a meeting, she said. But could she have come here? What about Jeremy and June? Jeremy seemed far too wimpy for something like this, but who knew about June? Maybe she'd just been acting persuadable to fool us? Ray? I couldn't imagine it. Yet he wasn't in favor of the merger and I doubted he ever would be. I knew where Penny had been all night, Hadley was out of the question, and as for Elena—just look at her, how upset she was, she must be suspecting Fran too.

Officer Bill had walked back into the typesetting room and was looking around again. His heavy boots echoed on the wooden floor. "I'm going to call another team to do the fingerprinting," he said, and then, as if to himself, "Sure as hell looks like somebody went crazy in here."

Elena blanched, hearing him, and I knew she was thinking of Fran, wildly drunk, crashing and smashing her heart out here last night. That had to be the explanation.

Officer Alice was getting our names and ages. I was surprised to find out Hadley was thirty-six. She looked younger in spite of her graying hair.

"You can't be twins," Alice said when she came to Penny and me. "You don't look a thing alike."

"It's our hair . . . our glasses," Penny and I said in unison. We were used to it.

Margaret and Anna arrived about the same time as the fingerprinting team. The first thing I noticed was that Margaret had a band-aid on her index finger. Officer Alice saw it too.

"That a recent cut?"

Margaret shrugged. "Last night," she said and looked around. "Goddamn, look at this place. Why wasn't I invited to the party?"

"She did it slicing onions," Anna added. Anna seemed nervous, and not as surprised as she might have been, considering that her place of work had been put out of commission in such an ugly way. "God," she kept saying, but not very convincingly.

Well, and why not? I thought. Anna and Margaret had been vociferously against the merger last night; they may have felt that they had nothing to lose by wrecking B.Violet, if it would save them from working with us.

The fingerprinting team were dusting and lifting off impressions around us. I could see Elena starting to twist and wring her hands. Hadley noticed her too, and asked if they could be excused for a moment. They went outside and sat on the curb. Hadley put her arm around Elena's shoulders and I saw Elena break down in tears.

Margaret said casually, "Where's Fran? Why isn't she here?"

"Is that another member of the business?" asked Officer Alice.

"The only founding member left," said Margaret. "And she will *lose* it when she sees this place." For some reason the thought seemed almost to amuse her. Anna looked at her and laughed.

Elena and Hadley came back in. Hadley looked thoughtful. She said to Alice, "You know, we don't want to rule out the possibility that we were vandalized by someone in the community who didn't like our half-tones, or even by some weirdo from the Moral Majority, but if this *did* happen because of the merger, then I doubt that we'd want to press charges. I think we'd prefer to work it out among ourselves."

"I hear you," said Officer Alice. "But you know you're goin' to have to tell the insurance company something."

"Our policy lapsed last month. Fran forgot to renew it," said Margaret, and there was that same smug amusement in her voice that made me look at her index finger and wonder all over again. Why would Fran have destroyed B.Violet anyway? She'd worked here for years; she wanted it to survive.

"Well then," said Officer Alice. "I think you still might be glad to have the report and the fingerprints on file down at central. You never know. All the talking in the world doesn't bring back your equipment."

"We got the fingerprinting down," said Officer Bill, coming back into the front room. "Now if we can just get yours, too."

"No," we all said in unison, perfect children of the seventies. "No fingerprints."

Officers Alice and Bill looked at each other.

"I get the feeling it's internal, Bill," said Alice.

Only Anna laughed.

7

Hadley, Margaret and Anna stayed at B. Violet in order to assess the damage and see if there was anything that could be salvaged from the mess. I hoped that Hadley was planning on having a serious talk with Margaret and Anna.

Penny and I took Elena home with us for breakfast. We probably wanted to see how much she really knew about what had happened too.

But all she wanted to discuss was her relationship with Fran, right from the beginning. We got her to wait until we'd at least had a cup of coffee and then, while Penny broke eggs into sizzling butter and I made toast, we prepared ourselves to listen.

It had been when Elena was fighting her firing from the high school that they'd first met — six months ago. Fran was scmebody's friend and Elena hadn't paid her much attention. One of those people you just see around, say hi to.

"I was actually a little put off by her," Elena confided. "She really seemed butch, I mean, she'd been in the Army and had never been to college, worked at odd jobs, driven trucks, had a motorcycle. A real bar dyke. And who was I? A teacher, a housewife, a mother, living in Belle-vue, realizing that I was turned on by the woman next door. And the salesclerk at Safeway. And some of my students. If I hadn't been so idealistic and told my husband I couldn't live with him anymore, if I hadn't become a raging lesbian-feminist when he told me he was taking me to court for custody of the kids . . . I'd probably still be back in Bellevue, taking off my clothes with the woman next door, but enjoying all the privileges associated with class and heterosexuality . . . I'm talking privilege.''

Penny flipped the eggs indifferently. "So what brought you two together then?''

Elena was animated now, drinking coffee, gobbling toast as if she were starved, and with each bite gaining new strength. "It was the kids! Garson and Samantha latched on to her right away. It was really funny. We were all at someone's house, in a big discussion about the court case or something and I say, 'Where's Sam and Garson?' and find them upstairs, in the middle of some complicated game, string and cards, and having a wonderful time. With this woman I hardly knew, and was slightly afraid of . . .''

"Let me guess," said Penny, serving the eggs. She gave me a glance as if to say, How long are we going to have to put up with this *Love Story* business, but I was oddly moved and interested. For one thing, the image of Fran, child-friend, didn't jell with the Fran I knew: drinker, bruiser and possibly crazy.

Penny's sarcasm was lost on Elena, who was leaning into her coffee cup with a dreamy expression. "They just love her, the stories she tells them, the jokes. When she's over it's like a party, it's like family, the way it should be. We watch TV and make popcorn, play games. On weekends we take them places. . . .'' Elena trailed off and then came back to reality. "I can't tell you the number of women I've been involved with over the last three years—as friends or lovers—who've thought that children were nothing but a big, fat drag. 'Can't you leave them at home?' 'They just make a mess. . . .' ''

I looked away guiltily. My sentiments exactly.

"So what's the problem then?'' Penny asked, wiping up her plate and leaning back in her no-nonsense way. Even with her big purple glasses and short, shocked hair, she still managed, at times, to look like the vice-president of some multi-national corporation—ruthless, suave, impatient.

"Class,'' said Elena. "It's a class difference between us.''

I thought about Fran's S & M hint last night and the way she laid into the Jim Beams and beers and wasn't so sure. "Do you think Fran might possibly have a drinking problem?'' I asked.

"We're all the same, we all lay down our middle-class values and expect everyone else to follow them. . . . Fran's accustomed to drinking a lot. It doesn't bother her. I mean, it doesn't affect her in the same way it does you or me.'' She paused, and I recalled that she'd had her fair share last night too—trying to keep up, to prove that she wasn't a nice housewife anymore?

I didn't press her, though perhaps I should have. Instead I asked,

"You think there's any chance that she ran amuck at B.Violet?"

"You said this morning that you thought she'd been there, that there was something . . ." remembered Penny. "What was it?"

Elena put down her toast and I could almost see a half-chewed piece of it sticking in her throat, unable to go down. "It's so hard for me to believe," she said. "I know there must be some explanation. She's not like that, even when she's drunk. Verbally hostile, but not destructive. She loves B.Violet; she's worked there six years. She helped start it."

"What was it you found of hers?" Penny pushed.

Elena gave up. "Her car keys."

"Maybe they were an extra pair."

"I know she only has one pair. And we drove together to the meeting at Best. And you drove me home, Pam. So unless something is totally crazy, I guess she must have been at B.Violet last night."

There was a long silence. Elena put her head down on her arms. "I don't know what to do," she said, muffled. "I *had* her car keys in my hand, but somehow I lost them."

"Just now? I mean, at the shop?"

Elena nodded. "Now you'll never believe me."

I couldn't figure out whether she was trying to protect Fran or to accuse her. "If the keys are there someone will find them."

"That's what I'm afraid of," Elena said.

It was after ten-thirty by the time we got to Best Printing. Elena wasn't with us; she'd decided to go back to Fran's apartment to see if she turned up. I told her to call if she needed moral support and she pressed my arm gratefully as she got out of the car.

"So what are you now? The Lesbian's Home Companion?" asked Penny.

"Knock if off, sis."

"Sorry," she said. "It's that jerkface Doug. In a way I'm just as glad the phone rang and everything happened this morning. Kept me from thinking about him. He didn't stay the night, you know. There we were, having ice cream and everything. Sam and Jude had gone upstairs and things were getting cozy. 'What time is it?' he says all of a sudden and jumps up. 'Why? Got a date?' I say. And you know what? The asshole did. Shit, was I pissed. You don't do that to people, eat their ice cream—Haagen-Dazs is expensive you know—and get them all horny, then leave to go sleep with someone else."

"That *is* low," I agreed. I couldn't deny, however, that I felt a little pleased. Jealousy isn't good for the soul and that's definitely what I'd been feeling last night upstairs with my three scoops of Swiss Almond Vanilla.

"So you went to a lesbian bar, huh?" said Penny.

I'd forgotten my little lie. "Uh, well, not exactly. They wanted to, but you know me, too chicken. We ended up at the Bar & Grill."

"Too bad," said Penny. "I've always wondered what Sappho's was like."

"You've heard of it?"

"Sure."

Even your own twin can surprise you sometimes.

At Best we were greeted with attitudes ranging from loud scorn to apparent indifference. So we thought we could just stroll in any old time, did we? We were just lucky that it hadn't been that busy. Before we told them about the sacking of B.Violet, I tried to notice whether any of them seemed different—more tired, more hysterical, more subdued, more guilty—and whether any of them had bandages on their hands. But if any of them were wounded, it wasn't in obvious places. And even to my practiced collective eyes, everyone seemed much the same: Jeremy vague and spacey; June zippily cheerful; Ray irritated and concerned; Zee—but in some ways I didn't feel I knew Zee well enough to see a difference, if there was one. She was gloriously turned out this morning as all others, in thin red-and-black-striped pants that were tight around the waist and ankles and full around the knees. With them she wore a short-sleeved red shirt and a black sweater knotted around the shoulders. With unusual silver earrings, many rings and bracelets, her smooth heavy black hair arranged faultlessly as ever, she looked as if she were working at *Vogue*, not at Best.

We told them what had happened. About the vandalism, about the cops and the fingerprinting and non-fingerprinting, about Fran being missing and Margaret's cut finger. The only thing we didn't mention and I don't know why, was that Elena had found Fran's car keys. And lost them.

"They must be feeling so bad," said Zee quietly. "To lose everything. What will they do?"

"Well, I hate to say it," said Ray, "but at least we don't have to worry about the merger question anymore."

He looked at me somewhat defiantly, but also in apparent innocence that these words might be taken wrongly.

No one contradicted him. No one seemed to be worried, or to find it odd that B.Violet had been destroyed just after a meeting to discuss a merger with us. Clearly they all thought it was an inside job, internal sabotage, either by Fran or by Margaret and Anna.

Well, wasn't that what I thought myself?

Elena called later to say there'd been no word from Fran. She was still at Fran's, having written a long letter, and was preparing to go back home to be there when her kids got home from school.

"I don't think you can do anything more, Elena," I tried to assure her.

"I think it would be better if I got angry," she said. "I'm starting to feel like a fool."

"Save it for when she turns up," I said. "You have a right to be anxious now. Just don't let it get you down."

Hadley also called later and was to the point. "How'd you like to buy a light table, cheap? With a new top it'd be fine. . . . That's about all that's working here. The rest of the stuff is junk. They even ripped up our accounts books."

"You don't think it was someone who owed you money, do you?"

"I'm sure we could have worked out some other payment plan," she said in her long drawl, then she turned business-like. "If you're free tonight I'd like to talk to you a little more about all this, get your ideas and bounce some theories around. I'd love to rule out the possibility that either of our collectives was involved, especially ours."

"I don't think anything can be ruled out until Fran turns up."

"The more I think about it, the more I think that Fran couldn't possibly have done it."

"Even though her car keys were there?"

"I'm sure there's an explanation."

"How about Margaret? Did you notice her onion breath?"

"Let's discuss it over dinner tonight. We'll hash it all out."

"In that case I recommend a good hashhouse . . . Ever been to the Doghouse Restaurant?"

"No. I've seen it though. Over by Seattle Center?"

"Yeah. Bring your ten-gallon hat, Tex."

8

▼ ▼ ▼ ▼ ▼

The Doghouse Restaurant (Max. Cap. 250) had been around since before WWII and hadn't changed much in decor, menu or service since then. It had big soft booths you could lose yourself in and capable older waitresses wearing black skirts and vests and white shirts. The cocktail lounge had framed portraits of various canines all over the walls and Dick Dickerson nightly on the organ. It was probably the last restaurant in Seattle to still have plastic plants, toothpicks holding together the sandwiches, paperwrapped straws served with drinks, and Worcestershire, A-1 Steak Sauce and catsup on the table, every table. Both the placemats and a giant mural over the counter (with its towers of pie racks and constantly filled coffee cups, its smokers and its newspaper readers) displayed the motto "All Roads Lead to the Doghouse." In one corner of the picture was a harridan with a rolling pin; in the other a sad-eyed pooch in the doghouse; and in between a hilly course strewn with signs that read "Matrimony," "Blonds," "Private Secretaries," and "Boozers."

Hadley was waiting for me, without a cowboy hat but still recognizable behind the tall menu, with her graying hair and slightly furrowed brow. No beauty certainly, but a solid sort of person. Dependable. Or so I needed to believe.

"Hey there, Pam," she said, looking up, looking pleased. "This is quite the place."

"Our parents used to bring us here on Sundays sometimes—as a treat."

"They were nice, I bet. Your parents." She said it factually, in a way that caught me in the chest. Yeah, they'd been alright.

"How about yours?" I asked, while skimming for form's sake the menu. I already knew what I was going to have: a Bulldog, hold the onions.

"My dad's into oil and my mother's into archaeology. She's in Turkey now, I think, excavating."

I tried to conceal my surprise. I wouldn't have figured Hadley for a wealthy background. As if she read my thoughts Hadley smiled her one-sided smile and said, "Fran's biggest dream was that the old man could be persuaded to bankroll the lesbian revolution."

"Well, couldn't he?"

"I'm thirty-six, honey. I've been away from home a long time."

The waitress, a favorite of mine named Sally, came over. She wore harlequin glasses and a watch pin. "Long time, no see, sugarplum," she told me, and then to Hadley, "I've known Penny and this little gal here since they were knee high to ladybugs."

"I think it's grasshoppers, Sal."

"Never you mind those old ugly grasshopping things. Nice young ladybugs is what you and Penny are. Now, what are you and your friend having, Miss Pam?"

We told her and watched her go back to the kitchen with a swing in her step, a firmly-built woman in her sixties with a wigfull of auburn sausage curls.

"I've been wondering a lot about older women," said Hadley, watching her. "My hair started going gray all of a sudden last fall. I don't know what it was, maybe just the hair genes kicking over all at once, but it sure gave me some sense of what it's all going to be like. Forty years of being called Ma'am and Mrs. Harper started last year."

"You look good in gray," I said, then blushed. But Hadley came back easily, "Thank you, Ma'am."

"That's Miss Pam to you."

"You don't fool me," she smiled. "You've got a little experience under your belt too."

I blushed again.

I was grateful that Sally brought our coffee just then. At some point I would have to explain to Hadley that I was straight, not at all wavering, and that I didn't feel attracted to her, but just wanted her for a friend, even though I'd never had a lesbian friend before and had no idea if you even *could* . . . but fortunately we had other things to talk about now.

"If you had a list of suspects," she said, "would they all be from B.Violet?"

I nodded and tried to defend myself. "Margaret and Anna seemed to hate the idea so much . . . and if you'd seen Fran drinking and how worried Elena is, after finding the car keys—well you've *seen* Elena. Fran *must* have been there."

Hadley sighed. "And I have a disinclination to trust Ray and Jeremy, just because they said so little at the meeting—and because probably ninety-nine percent of the violence in the world is done by men."

Bristling, I said, "Ray would never destroy anything . . . and Jeremy—he's just a little wimp, if you knew him."

"That's the thing. I don't. But he kind of gives me the creeps, the way he hems and haws all the time. It seems forced somehow. Is he really as young as he seems?"

"He's twenty-five and wishes he were ten years older like all his heroes. I think he had older brothers and sisters or something who used to lock him out of the garage where they smoked dope and played Jefferson Airplane in the sixties. He's spent his life trying to get in that garage."

Hadley laughed. "There are some of us who've spent our lives trying to get out of it."

"But he's harmless, really, and he does care about politics; he's learning to, anyway. I've been noticing that he's getting involved with June. I think it will be good for him."

"Tell me about her, tell me about all of you," Hadley said, digging into the monstrous Chef's Salad Sally had just brought.

"June? She's always been a little more Penny's friend than mine. June likes danger, and so does Penny, in her rational way. They've done some amazing things—whitewater rafting, kayaking, they go skydiving together if you can believe it. As for me, I'm a total physical coward . . . anyway, June's about the same age as Jeremy, but *what* a difference. She grew up in Seattle, went to Garfield High and got married right after. To a nice guy, I guess, a really nice guy. But he was shot, in one of those weird freak accidents. June says a bunch of them were fooling around, they were still teenagers, someone had an 'unloaded' gun and somehow it went off. I think June was holding it, though she's never been able to say it."

"Christ."

"There wasn't a trial, just a hearing. No one was blamed . . . but June was left with a one-year-old and then found out she was pregnant again." I paused to take a bite of my burger. "She worked days, went to school nights and did a printing course. She's been working with us for three years, almost since the beginning."

"Well, count June out of the sabotage. Zenaida too. I can't imagine her wanting to scratch her fingernail polish."

"Don't underestimate Zee. She's a cool character. Sometimes I wonder if she hasn't got more guts than any of us. But she's working with the anti-Marcos group and has more important things on her mind.

She wouldn't have time to think about B.Violet."

"She's got a thing with Ray, am I right?"

I nodded without saying anything. I still didn't find it easy to talk about somehow, but Hadley didn't notice. She said, "What about him? He's definitely physically capable of wreaking havoc. Where's he coming from?"

"Straight from the arms of pacifism. His parents are both doctors for the Red Cross. His mother's Japanese, her parents died in Hiroshima. His father's Mexican-American, but one of those people without a strong national identity anymore. They moved around a lot, Ray with them sometimes, in school in California other times. I know he's got a temper, but he's heard enough about violence and destruction to last him a lifetime."

"He didn't want a merger though."

I tried not to remember Ray's comment earlier about 'Now, at least, we don't have to merge,' and defended him. "You heard his reasons. It wasn't misogyny, but the racism issue, the starting all over again with a bunch of white women. He's had to do a lot of educating—he likes having Zee and June there . . ."

Sally filled our cups for the fourth time with the dark, bitter brew. I was beginning to get a nervous, unpleasant buzz—a reminder of why I didn't seek out the Doghouse more often.

"I hear you," nodded Hadley. "I guess I don't really suspect him, but then . . . ?"

"There's always me and Penny."

"Or Elena."

"Elena was the one who suggested the merger in the first place. And Fran's her lover. You could never get me to believe that Elena would destroy B.Violet."

"Stranger things have happened," said Hadley, but without conviction.

"But Margaret and Anna could have," I persisted.

"Now let me do my defender bit," Hadley smiled. "I've known Margaret for about six years. We've worked on a lot of issues together, put out a newsletter once for two years, lobbied for gay rights in Olympia, spoke on lesbian topics all around town. Margaret is absolutely true blue. Sarcastic sometimes; bad-tempered occasionally, but not violent. It's impossible, I can't picture her touching anything at B.Violet."

"But isn't she, aren't she and Anna, you know, separatists?" I asked, wading into dangerous water. "I mean, more than you?"

"Me?" Hadley laughed, mocking a southern belle. "Why, I just *love* men, honey."

I pursued it doggedly. "That's what's behind this whole thing somehow. That's what I think. Margaret and Anna might have preferred to wreck B.Violet rather than merge. To punish Elena and Fran maybe."

"They'd only be punishing themselves."

"Why did they seem so gleeful then this morning?"

Hadley shook her head. "I wouldn't exactly call it gleeful. I mean, it's true they and Fran have had their differences, but . . ."

She still hadn't addressed the issue, I felt. My urgency increased. "Well, *aren't* they lesbian separatists? Don't they just want to work with women?"

Hadley wasn't smiling now. "Your voice is raised, Miss Pam. Very unbecoming. I also detect a note of hostility to your own sex—maybe even lesbian-baiting—also rather impolite."

We stared at each other, neither willing to risk a further exchange. I felt sure that she was hiding something, protecting Margaret in some way. I didn't know what she thought, but there was a distance between us that hadn't been there before.

"Shall we go?" she said.

For some reason I felt close to tears. "Ready when you are."

We figured out the check, said good-bye to Sally, paid the cashier and went out into the balmy evening without saying much more than "So long." Only as we reached our separate vehicles in the parking lot did I hear her voice.

"Hey Pam. I'm sorry. I hurt your feelings."

I turned and saw her tall figure silhouetted against the Doghouse sign.

"Me too," I said. I heard my voice carry strangely in the suddenly still evening air. "I guess I was, you know, baiting."

Her truck door closed. She was crossing the parking lot, and her boots made a light firm clacking on the asphalt.

"I want to tell you something," she said when she reached me. "I *have* known Margaret a long time, but Margaret and Anna together is a different story. They've gotten funny together about some things, reinforced each other's ideas. The merger is one. I'm sure they didn't wreck the place, but I wouldn't be completely honest if I didn't say that they seem sort of pleased about all this. It's true too—they only want to work with women and they haven't gotten along with Fran for months."

"Listen," I said. "It's early." I looked at my watch. "Not even eight-thirty yet. And I think we need to talk through some of this stuff. I'm glad you said something. I didn't mean to be such an asshole in there."

"I guess I could go with a beer or something after all that java." Hadley smiled a bit wickedly. "Ever been to Sappho's?"

I gulped a little. "No, but I'd love to."

"Great," she said, turning back to her truck. "Just follow me."

"Wait," I said. "Could we go by Best first, just for a minute? I want to raid the petty cash until tomorrow."

"Oh, I've got plenty," she said, but she seemed pleased when I insisted. "Okay, see you there in a minute."

That's funny, I thought, pulling up in front of the print shop on its quiet sidestreet near the Kingdome. Who in hell left the light on in there? I couldn't imagine that anyone was working late. The whole week we'd been short of business; there were no rush jobs of any kind. Besides, it wasn't the front light, but one way in the back. It made a dim red glow. The darkroom, the goddamn darkroom. When was Jeremy going to learn?

The door was locked. Just as I put my key in, Hadley pulled up.

"There's a light on," she called out.

"Yeah, Jeremy left the darkroom light on, I bet. He's done it before."

"I'm going in there with you." Hadley leapt out, holding a softball bat. I couldn't tell if she was joking or not.

"Don't tell me you play ball," I said.

"Hell, I'm the captain of the team."

"Okay, okay," I said, unlocking the door and striding boldly in. "All saboteurs out in the open."

It was quiet. Everything was in its place, of course. There was only the red glow coming from the darkroom, through its partially opened door.

"I'll kill Jeremy," I said. "When the fuck is he going to learn?"

I went to the back and opened the door to the darkroom wide. Whatever Jeremy was supposed to learn was unnecessary now. As was my threat to kill him.

Someone had done it for me.

9

▼ ▼ ▼ ▼ ▼

A red light is used in the darkroom so that you can see to develop your film without exposing it. Jeremy had apparently been developing negatives, for the pans of different chemicals stood in the broad sink, the water was still running, and square and rectangular pieces of film had been hung like tiny negative laundry on a clothesline to dry; some pieces still had droplets of water clinging to them.

The red lightbulb gave an extra dimension and feel to the small room, making it seem both warmer and more sinister. Jeremy, lying cross-angled on the floor, his eyes open blankly and his mouth twisted in a deplorably silly grimace, was as if bathed in red blood, though there was only a small sticky hole in his temple.

Hadley and I stood clenching each other's arms without saying anything at first. Then I started to sob. He looked so young lying there, with his angelic blond curls and empty wide eyes, skinny as an orphan. His Sony Walkman was still attached to his belt, but the earphones had fallen, loose and soundless, to the side.

"Why did he do it?" I cried.

"I don't think he did," said Hadley.

Her normally relaxed voice came out dry and breathless. We clutched at each other again. The shop suddenly seemed to vibrate with our fear. We were all nerves, in the state when any noise will make you jump a mile.

The office door in front swung open with a bang and Hadley and I both bit down hysteric screams.

"Who's there?" I shouted.

"I saw your truck, Hadley, and I wanted . . ." The voice walked unsteadily towards us. It was a loud, shaky, deep voice that I almost recognized, but not quite. Hadley knew it, however; she turned as if to protect a view of Jeremy, but she wasn't quick enough.

Fran came barreling through the door screaming, "Elena."

She'd thrown herself down by the body's side before she realized it was Jeremy. "Oh god," she said, scrambling up heavily again. "I thought . . ."

Like Jeremy's, like ours, Fran's face now had a softening red glow to it. It seemed like we were all moving in a film where clay models were used. Spatial distance was different and facial expressions dramatic and simple.

"Did he kill himself or what?" she asked, stupefied.

"We don't think so, we think . . ."

". . . murdered? But who would?"

"Why did you think he was Elena?" I asked.

"I don't know, the hair, I guess. In this weird light." Fran shrugged me off, gradually preoccupied with another thought. "But that means the cops will be here, and oh, goddam it. What am I going to do?"

"What are you talking about, Fran?" Hadley asked sharply.

"Last night. B.Violet," she said impatiently. "It was *him*."

"Jeremy trashed the place out?" I said. "Jeremy? No."

"I'm telling you, I fucking found the guy there last night. After you and Elena went and left me, I decided to go back down to B.Violet and get something I forgot."

"What was he doing, Fran?" Hadley asked. She was calm but worried now, and trying to draw us out of the darkroom's red light.

"He was in the back. Most of the damage had already been done. He was cutting the type fonts into little pieces."

We'd moved into the other room and I'd switched on the office light. The fluorescent illumination didn't make the situation any more real. I kept thinking, we have to call the police, we have to call the police, but Hadley was trying to get Fran's whole story.

"The little wimp tried to get away; he was terrified. I said I was going beat the shit out of him for what he did to our shop and . . . then . . . I think I picked up a piece of glass and . . ." Fran shook her head. In the cool white light of the office she looked exhausted and old, with bloodshot dazed eyes and a tremulous shake to her hands, one of which had a cut between the index finger and thumb. "I just don't remember. When I sort of came to myself again, I had some blood on my hand and he was gone. I guess he knocked me out. I didn't know if I'd done anything to him or not . . ." A big flannel shoulder jerked towards the darkroom door. "But I sure as hell didn't do that."

I wasn't so sure, but the very thought of it gave me the creeps. "If you didn't do it, why are you afraid of the police?" I asked.

"I'm not afraid of them," said Fran venomously, while beginning to back away to the front door.

"Listen, Fran, let me get this straight," Hadley put a restraining hand on her arm. "You went to B.Violet last night. Around what time?"

Fran shook her head.

"We left her at the Bar & Grill about ten-thirty, I think . . ." I said.

"So it was probably between eleven and twelve, closer to twelve, maybe, when you found him there."

"Look, what is this? Just leave me alone," Fran muttered. "Isn't it bad enough that our whole fucking shop was destroyed? He deserved what happened to him." She looked frightened at what she'd said. "I don't mean that. Oh god, if the cops figure out I was there with him, they'll think I wanted revenge."

"You probably passed out or were knocked out before you touched much of anything but that piece of glass, but you did leave your keys," Hadley said.

Fran flinched. You could tell she'd been desperately worrying all this time about what had happened to them. "And the cops have them?"

"*I* have them," said Hadley slowly. She reached into her pocket and drew them out, tossed them with a tiny clink to Fran. I wanted to tell her no, Fran had to be here when the cops came, so she could tell them about last night, but Hadley and Fran seemed locked in a private stare.

"I'm getting out, I've got to," mumbled Fran.

"Wait," I said, but Fran was already headed out the door, and Hadley didn't try to stop her. "Hadley, why'd you let her go? They need her information."

"Cause she's drunk," said Hadley. "Talking to them wouldn't help her or the cops."

"She didn't seem drunk now. That was last night."

"When Fran gets drunk, she stays drunk for awhile. You probably saw her in her offensive my-father-was-a-logger stage. But she's got others. I'm telling you, she was drunk yesterday, drunk last night, and she's still out of it today. She'll keep on for the next few days probably."

"Except for last night, she hasn't acted it."

"If you knew her, you'd know that's how she acts."

"But why isn't anybody helping her then, if it's that bad?"

"You don't think anybody's tried?" Hadley looked both bitter and amused.

"You mean Elena?"

"In case you hadn't noticed, Elena's a bit that way herself, attached to the bottle, I mean. That may be the source of their attraction."

I couldn't understand her attitude at all. "How can you be so . . .

BARBARA WILSON

calm about it?''

"Calm!'' she laughed abruptly, looked at me as if I were crazy, then said, "Don't you think it's time we called the police?''

They arrived remarkably quickly, while I was still on the phone to Penny, trying to explain what had happened.

"Now, start again, you're completely worked up, Pam. Jeremy was in the red light and Fran didn't remember what had happened. But Jeremy, Pam, is Jeremy all right?''

"I have to go now," I said. "It's the sirens.''

"Pam, is Jeremy all right? I have a reason for asking.''

"Can you just come down here, Penny, please?''

"I'm coming, I'm coming.''

I couldn't bring myself to tell her.

Horror has a way of settling in layers, like dust in an old house that you can't brush off just once. Delayed shock, I guess, the body's way of softening the blow. It amazes me in retrospect that Hadley and I were so cool, first at finding Jeremy and then at dealing with Fran, especially since I did suspect her of being more involved than she let on. I didn't think she "murdered" Jeremy, but that was partly because I wasn't thinking "murdered" any more than I could help it.

I hadn't brushed off that final layer of dust called death.

The six cops who turned up (three patrol cars full) were a lot different from Officers Bill and Alice this morning, just as homicide is quite a different crime than breaking and entering. They were all men and all enormous, striding with their heavy boots into the office, into the back of the shop to the darkroom.

I began to feel confused and very tired, after my burst of adrenalin. They wanted to know so much, they were everywhere. Outside, through the open door, the blue lights of their cars turned in quick pirouettes and you could hear the crackling, mysterious authority of their radios.

I showed them the darkroom. They asked me to turn off the red light, turn on the white, and I did so immediately, without even considering if there was any film or photographic paper that might be exposed. In the harsh brightness of the 100 watt, Jeremy looked even more pathetic. The cop was asking me what his name was, where he lived, who should be called.

"Jeremy Plaice. P-L-A-I-C-E. He worked here, yes, in the darkroom. I don't know why he was here so late, it's unusual . . . He lives in the U-District, on 18th, in an apartment, I can get the exact address . . . He's got a family in California, I'm pretty sure . . .''

The cop was turning Jeremy over gently, searching for a wallet. He pulled out keys, rolling papers, and a small tin of grass from one pocket of his jeans. From the other one came a wad of bills and some change. There was no identification.

In the other room I could hear a cop interrogating Hadley. "Did you notice anything different when you came in? Just the red light on? About what time was this? Did you touch anything? Any idea who might have . . . Did you hear a shot, see anyone?"

One of the cops in the darkroom was counting the bills. "He sure carried around a lot of money," he said noncommittally. I saw the flash of a hundred-dollar bill. Jeremy, with money? But before I could mull it over, another cop was asking me, "Any reason you can think of he might have been killed? Trouble with a girlfriend, married woman, a triangle? Was he involved in dope dealing or any other funny business?"

"Are you sure it wasn't, you know, suicide?" I asked.

The cop looked at me. "People don't usually put a revolver to their head and then manage to get rid of the gun."

I winced, and suddenly I had to get out of there before I threw up. I knocked past a cop with a camera, past another dusting the sink and door with powder. I rushed into the other room, past Hadley and her questioner, out the front door and straight into the arms of my twin.

"What's happening here, Pam?" she said. "I got a call from June, she was practically incoherent. She said she'd had a fight with Jeremy and . . ."

I tried to put my hand over her mouth, but it was too late. Hadley's cop was at the door. "What's June's last name?" he asked professionally. "And how can we get in touch with her?"

10

They arrested June that night. No doubt they'd punched one of their computer buttons and found that four years ago a husband of hers had been accidentally shot in the forehead by his wife.

As soon as we got home Penny started to look up lawyers in the phone book. It was almost midnight but Penny didn't want to wait.

"Why the fuck did I have to say that, put my foot in it? I can't believe it, I'm so stupid."

"It's my fault. I should have told you on the phone that he'd been killed. It just seemed so brutal."

Penny finally remembered Marta Evans, the lawyer who'd worked with us some years ago on restructuring our business.

"Murder?" Marta said sleepily. "You said someone was *murdered* at Best Printing?"

"It was Jeremy, no, you don't know him, but he was shot in the head in the darkroom—and they've taken June Jasper in for questioning."

"Goddamn. What time is it? Okay, okay, I'll do something. I'll call them or go down there." She paused, trying to remember. "Isn't June the Black woman?"

"Yeah. And Marta . . . June accidentally shot her husband four years ago. And she was involved with Jeremy . . ."

"Okay, I'm on my way."

Penny and I looked at each other in relief. "Now," I said. "You've got to tell me what June said to you."

"Well, first of all, did you ever know June and Jeremy were involved?"

"Only suspected it a couple days ago."

"They've been hanging out together for a month."

"Now that's discreet. In our collective too."

"They wanted it that way. After what happened between you and Ray . . ."

"Hey," I said, nettled. "I didn't plan it."

"Well, June just said they both wanted it quiet. That's why they got on each other's backs at work all the time."

"And I just thought they disagreed," I said, ready as usual to twit Penny, but suddenly choking on the thought that Jeremy, laid-back, good-intentioned Jeremy wouldn't be around to disagree with any more. "Go on."

"They've been more or less living together, June said. And that's how this argument started. He wanted to give up his apartment and move in with her. That or else give up everything altogether and get out of town. Travel."

"Travel?" I sputtered. "June and her kids? And what about us, Best?"

"That's what June said. She didn't want to go anywhere. And she didn't want him to move in. She only liked him living there, being around all the time, as long as he still had his own place."

"Good thinking."

"I guess they'd been discussing it for a while and then June just couldn't take it any more and told him to fuck off last night, to clear out and go travel somewhere, to Antarctica, the farther away the better. You know how hot-tempered she can be. She says she threw a cup at him or something. And all of a sudden Jeremy just erupted. She'd never seen anything like it. Screaming that he didn't need her fucking attitude any longer—she wasn't the only scene in town. And anyway, things were changing for him, he was on a good streak but he was running out of patience, he didn't have to stick around listening to her shit and on and on . . ."

"Jeremy . . ." I stopped. I couldn't believe it. But I couldn't not believe June either. I didn't know what to believe. And suddenly I thought of Fran's story that Jeremy was the one who destroyed B.Violet. I'd thought she was lying, but now . . . and what the hell had Jeremy been doing with hundreds of dollars in his pocket? He wasn't that big a dealer.

"Penny, there are a few things I haven't told you. Like . . . Fran. Fran was there tonight. She came in just after we found Jeremy, she came rushing in and flung herself down, thinking he was Elena—the hair, I guess. And she told us that Jeremy had sabotaged B.Violet last night. That she found him there.''

''She did what?'' exclaimed Penny. ''She found him at B.Violet and she didn't say anything? Why didn't she stay around for the cops tonight?''

''Maybe because she made that up about Jeremy,'' I said. ''She may have had some kind of alcoholic black-out and destroyed it herself.''

''Or,'' said Penny calmly, ''she realized that her motives for offing Jeremy would look too good to the law.''

''Or,'' I said, but didn't finish. The possibility that Fran had actually offed Jeremy became real to me for the first time.

''But if she didn't,'' said Penny, ''who did?''

There was a hushed but persistent banging at our front door. My heart mimicked the sound instantly.

''I'll go look,'' I said. I sneaked up to the peephole and announced, ''It's Zee.''

Zee was, for the first time since I'd made her acquaintance, less than perfectly turned out. Her sculpted black hair was pulled back into a ponytail, leaving her wide-angled, rather flat face as free-floating as a light gold balloon. She was dressed simply in jeans, running shoes and a dark sweatshirt, and she was out of breath.

''Penny, Pam, let me in,'' she was whispering urgently to the doorknob when I opened the door. She bounced in and grabbed each of us by an arm. ''Something awful has happened. At the shop. There were policemen carrying out a body.''

I couldn't help shuddering. We'd turned away from that last horrible sight.

''I know,'' I said, as gently as I could. ''It's, it was Jeremy.''

She burst into frantic tears, grinding her eyes with the balls of her hands. Her body was trembling like a fish out of water. Penny put her arms around her and I stroked her hair. It was heavier than it looked, stiff and shiny as a lacquered basket.

We led her to the sofa and Penny asked, ''How did you happen to see it, Zee?''

At that she only cried more hysterically. Penny rocked her back and forth, murmuring ''Now, now,'' but I couldn't help thinking, What was Zee doing in Pioneer Square so late at night? She didn't have a car and she lived way up on Beacon Hill. For that matter, what was she doing in our Ravenna neighborhood at midnight? Why hadn't she asked the cops what was going on? Why had she come here instead of calling us to find out, and why had she been sure we'd know what had happened?

I pushed these thoughts away temporarily and got up to make us all a pot of tea. When I got back from putting the kettle on, Zee was a little more coherent.

"Thank you Penny and Pam, now I am better. I'm sorry I was so crazy. Now I think I'll go, now."

"You're not going anywhere," said Penny with surprising firmness, turning her cradling movements into restraining ones.

"Please, I'm just going to Ray's house in the next few blocks."

"Let him sleep, for god's sake," I said harshly, and Penny gave me an irritated look. "I mean, don't you want to know what happened to Jeremy?"

"Yes," said Zee slowly, almost reluctantly. "I want to know." She half-sat up; her pale ochre face was splotched with red, her thick hair fell into her eyes. "What happened . . . to him?"

I told her how Hadley and I came to find him in the darkroom, and how Fran had burst in thinking he was Elena. That fact didn't seem to register with her.

"He was working in the darkroom," she repeated. "He was developing something?"

"Yes." I remembered the small negatives hanging up to dry. I hadn't bothered to look at what they were. Now it struck me that they couldn't have had anything to do with Best Printing. I took a stab in the dark. "Were you supposed to be meeting Jeremy there, Zee? Say around ten or ten-thirty?"

Her jaw dropped, then snapped closed again as tight as if it were stapled. Penny looked at her, surprised and worried. "Zee, was something going on between you and Jeremy? You can tell us, we won't tell Ray."

The staples flew apart like magic. "With Jeremy, with that little weasel? I wouldn't be caught dead, I mean . . . how could you ever think of me and him . . . No, only for one reason was I going there, the same reason as always . . ."

She stopped, stared wildly at us and jumped up. "I'm going to Ray's, I don't care. Ray will understand, Ray isn't like you! He trusts me!"

And with that she was out the door. Penny and I let her go. The teakettle was whistling. From upstairs came a weakly irritated cry, "Turn that fucking thing off!"

Penny and I went into the kitchen and complied.

"Well," she said, "I'm not sure I'm cut out for the amateur detective business. At what point do we call the number they gave us at the station?"

"Who are we going to point the finger at?" I asked glumly. "They've already got June there. I suppose it's possible she followed him down there and shot him, but I find it really hard to believe."

"What if Ray did it?" tried Penny. "Found out about Zee and Jeremy and with typical Latin passion . . ."

"No macho herrings, please. You can't honestly be thinking of Zee and Jeremy getting it on in the darkroom, can you? The thing she was interested in was the negatives . . . why?''

Penny pumped the tea ball up and down in the pot before removing it. "But Fran. Why was Fran there? She was the one with the motive, of course.''

I sipped my tea carefully. "I'm not ready to tell the cops anything yet. Let's wait and see what happens.''

Penny nodded wearily. "I think we've had enough excitement for one night.''

"More than enough," I agreed.

The clock was striking one when something clicked in me. "What if," I said excitedly, "just what if it wasn't Jeremy they meant to kill at all?''

"What are you talking about, Pam?''

"What if, because of the red light . . . and because Jeremy had his head bent, rinsing the negatives, they couldn't see his face?''

"Who else could they think he was?''

"Elena, of course. Elena.''

11

The most immediate problem the next morning was to make sure June was out of the clutches of the police. Penny and I woke up early, called the station and got the run-around. They'd either never heard of her or she'd been released sometime during the night.

There was no answer either at June's or at Marta Evans's. This wasn't altogether surprising. It was only seven; anyone who'd been up all night might not be inclined to answer the phone.

Sam was up too and, while we ate granola and he drank what he called a pep drink—milk, yeast, lecithin, eggs, strawberries, yogurt and honey, along with his usual four cups of coffee (he liked to cover all bases)—we filled him in on the recent events.

"What does the group think of all this?" he finally asked. He always called the Best collective "the group," an old-fashioned hipsterism that made me feel like we were a jazz ensemble. I was fond of Sam, but he got on my nerves the way Jude never did. Without her around he always seemed a little dull and technical, with a helpless air of never knowing how to respond. The recent studies of male/female languages were direct illustrations of Sam's conversational skills. He was perfectly enthusiastic when discussing a topic he'd brought up—floppy disks for instance—and to the extent that Jude's feminism had influenced him, he was civilized enough to listen, without interrupting, to you spouting off about your own passions—the overthrow of the white capitalist patriarchy, for example—but as far as giving off any little reassuring "umms" or "oh reallys" or showing any sort of facial reaction while you talked—you could forget it. He'd listen to you with the politeness of a doorknob and then, after a silence just long enough to disconcert, he'd come out with a question that missed the point entirely with its innocuous brevity. Thus, "What does the group think of all this?"

"You mean the plot to knock off all the men in the collective?" I said, "Well, I've heard Ray is hiring a bodyguard."

Penny gave me a look. She didn't have the same reaction to Sam. She thought of him as a "very sincere guy."

"We're the only ones who know, Sam," she said in a hushed voice.

"June knows," I pointed out. "And Zee. And Zee must have told Ray when she went over there. Jeremy, of course, doesn't need to know. So that just leaves Elena. I guess we'd better call her before she gets down there."

Penny nodded. "What about the Bee Vee's? Let 'em read it in the paper—or on a warrant?"

"Hadley was with us," I reminded her. "I'm sure the topic will come up."

"Oh god," Penny suddenly started crying. "We're talking about it in this flippant way—as if it didn't really happen, as if it weren't Jeremy who'd died."

I felt tears springing to my eyes too, and I was ashamed that I hadn't liked him more, that I had so many new suspicions of him, that I even had the fleeting queasy feeling he may have done something to deserve it.

"Well, see you," said Sam, getting out while he could. "Uh, hope you find the murderer."

"We're not the ones looking," I said through my weeping. "Thank god."

But of course we were.

At eight there was still no answer at June's, so Penny and I decided to make a personal visit. In the meantime, Jude had come downstairs and had compensated for Sam's lack of response by a positive waterfall of questions and humming, clicking and ohing. I realized more than ever what had made her develop this almost exaggerated mode of urging other people's words out. In the beginning of her relationship with Sam she must have had to use a pick and hammer. Strange how you never noticed it when they were together—they'd perfected a pattern between them.

Hadley also called.

"How're you doing?"

"Sleepy, sad in a way, thinking about Jeremy." I almost told her about Zee's late night visit, but decided to save it until I'd thought about it further. "Have you seen Elena . . . or Fran?"

"Elena's here with me now. No sign of Fran."

Hadley seemed as constrained as I. Elena was probably listening. I wondered if I should mention that Elena could have been the object of the bullet. Last night it had seemed like a revelation: this morning it just seemed stupid. Besides, if Elena were already completely freaked out about Fran and the destruction of B.Violet, how would she react to a suggestion that she may have just escaped being murdered?

"Tell Elena," I said, and paused. Tell Elena what? To lie low for a few weeks? To leave the country until it all blew over? "Tell Elena that she shouldn't come in to work. No regular business hours today. Penny and I are going over to June's now to see what she knows, if anything."

"Okay," said Hadley. "Call me later, okay? Maybe we can get together."

"All right. See you."

And suddenly, I really wanted to.

No one seemed to be at home at the apartment where June lived with her kids on Capitol Hill. A sixties-built block on stilts with parking underneath, the whole place had a somewhat deserted air. Curtains were drawn and windows were closed, even though it was the beginning of another hot day.

We knocked for a few minutes, and Penny called out cautiously, "June, you there?" but no one came to the door. She was either deep asleep or she hadn't wanted to come back to the place she and Jeremy had shared—if she'd even been released. We decided to drive over to her mother's and see what she knew.

Mrs. Rich lived with June's married cousin and her husband in the Central District, in a rambling two story green house with rose bushes all around. They were luxuriantly in bloom this summer morning, still fresh with dew.

"She's sleeping," said her mother when she answered the door. Mrs. Rich was a big-boned woman, lighter than June, and with the same snappy energy. Her eyes were brown and slightly almond-shaped under the red and yellow turban she wore. She didn't look very friendly now, even though the last time we'd been there—to the cousin's wedding—she'd hugged us like family.

"We just wanted to find out if she was okay," said Penny.

"Who is it, Mama?" called June from one of the back rooms.

"Penny and Pam," Mrs. Rich boomed back. "You sleep or ain't you?"

"No, I can't sleep no more," said June. "Let them in, Mama, I'm coming.''

We were seated on the couch when June walked into the living room. She looked exhausted and wired at the same time and her usual jaunty look was shot through with anger and pain. "How 'bout some coffee, Mama?'' she said, and to us, with a shrug of a smile, "No way I'm going to get my beauty sleep today, I guess.''

She sank onto the couch beside us and Penny put an arm around her. "They didn't keep you there too long, did they?''

"Nah. Not really. What could they pin me with, I mean? So the guy was my boyfriend and so we had a fight and so about an hour or two later he got offed.'' June's voice was dully ironic. "So why should they accuse me of anything?''

"But they didn't keep holding you or put you in jail, right?'' asked Penny. I could hear the guilt in her voice. After all the cops had heard about Jeremy and June's fight through her.

"Oh yeah. Just asked a few questions. Like 'How long you been fuckin' that white boy, girl?' and 'Where'd you get that gun?' And 'Shore nuff look like you got a thang against these mens, to be shooting 'em like this.' They gave me a Black cop, see. Get the truth out of me. Someone from my own 'culture,' knows about us Black girls' murderous instincts.''

Mrs. Rich came in with coffee. "Makes me so mad I could spit, the way they treat her. Like she was some old piece of trash. There's nobody thinks what happened before was nothin' but an accident. My baby's no killer, no way, and you know I never liked that boy one bit.''

"Ever since last night I've been getting the idea that none of us ever really knew Jeremy,'' I said.

"Huh,'' said June, sipping her coffee. "You're telling *me*. I never thought I'd see the day some white guy would try and walk on my face, but I saw it last night. I never want to see it again. Or I *will* kill somebody.''

"Fran said that Jeremy was the one who destroyed B.Violet. She said she found him there smashing and ripping things up.''

June took this in. "Someone maybe killed him for that then? Like that big bulldagger Fran? She could, I bet.''

"Don't know. She's sure been drunk enough lately not to know what she's doing. Who knows if she even saw Jeremy wrecking B.Violet or if she did it herself.''

"I couldn't give him an alibi that night even if I wanted to,'' said June. "We started out together after the collective meeting, but then he had to do a dope deal, he said.'' June shook her sculpted black head. "My opinion was he was screwing around on me. That's what we were fighting about last night. He wants to get out of town fast, he says, move on out. When I said, no way, I'm not going anywhere with these two kids and you and your roving eye, that's when it started. All his talk about *attitude.* That's the first thing they start on when they're fucking someone else.''

"June, shush now," said her mother.

June's round, nut brown eyes filled with tears. "He had someone else, he was just using me. He pretended to be so nice and sweet and liking the kids and all but he was a goddamned motherfucker and I'm not sorry he's dead!"

She stalked abruptly from the room and her mother went after her. Penny and I continued sitting, at a loss. I kept thinking about Zee and her appointment with Jeremy and what all that meant. I found it impossible to believe that Zee could have been involved with him, but what else had all that stuff Jeremy threw in June's face been about? I sure didn't feel like telling June about Zee's visit last night.

Mrs. Rich came back out. "Time for you girls to go," she said. "June's tired, real tired."

"Is there anything we can do?" Penny asked.

Mrs. Rich smiled bitterly. "Just find out who killed that boy and thank them for me."

12

▼ ▼ ▼ ▼ ▼

After leaving Mrs. Rich's house Penny and I stopped for another bolstering cup of coffee and a donut, then went on down to the shop. Neither of us had much to say; we both felt too bad about June.

The sun had begun to smolder in the sky like a cigarette burning an orange-red hole in a bright blue tablecloth. Another scorcher, said the radio announcer, mildly hysterical. May reach ninety. I was glad I'd worn a halter top, sorry I didn't have on shorts. Maybe we should just take the day off and go swimming?

"So what's the big idea?" said Ray when we got to Best. He was stomping around in a rage and lit into us like a flying piece of machinery. "No note, no nothing. I get down here early to start the big job and where is everybody? Zee's not here, Jeremy and June aren't here, Elena's not here, you're not here. Is this a holiday I don't know about maybe? The sunshine festival? Is it a wildcat strike? No one answering the telephone and no one coming in. It's almost eleven, and *no one's here but me.*"

"Didn't Zee tell you last night?" Penny said, holding up a hand to stop him.

"I didn't see Zee last night," shouted Ray. "Tell me what?"

"But she said she was going over there," I stuttered.

"Never mind, Pam," said Penny. "Ray, listen." Her voice got quiet and funny. "Something happened here last night. An awful thing. Someone shot Jeremy."

"Shot Jeremy," he repeated, uncomprehending. "Where is he then? In the hospital?"

I shook my head.

Penny shook her head.

"Not dead, no!" Ray sat heavily on the sofa. "Those goddamned women," he shouted.

Penny opened her mouth and then closed it. She sat next to him on the sofa and put her arm around his shoulders. He started sobbing, inconsolably, like a small child, like the way he had when we'd had our first fight. It was the first time I'd seen anyone really cry *for* Jeremy, because they cared. It embarrassed and shamed me that I couldn't cry in the same way, that my tears this morning, like Penny's, had been more from the horror of the thing, the idea of murder, than for Jeremy the person.

I couldn't comfort Ray either; the time had long passed when we could help each other get through anything. I left him to Penny and went back towards the darkroom.

The more I thought about it the stranger I found Zee's visit last night. She'd been distraught when she heard about Jeremy's death, but she hadn't asked for the details. She'd been overly concerned about the negatives he'd been producing and had as much as admitted they were supposed to have met here sometime that evening. And she'd been so frantic to go to Ray's, claiming that he would understand. But if she hadn't gone to his house, where had she gone?

I stopped at the door of the darkroom. There were no lights on inside, either red or white. It gave me a chill to be here again. All too clearly I remembered the sprawl of Jeremy's thin body last night. I turned on the white light and poked my head in. Everything was normal, quiet; there wasn't even a stain of blood on the floor. I glanced toward the line where the negatives had been hung to dry.

Not a single one was left.

I called the company whose job we were supposed to be starting that day and cancelled the whole thing. Better have them mad at us now than frustrated for days while we struggled to catch up. I told the production manager the truth, that our cameraman had died suddenly, but he wasn't much appeased. "Couldn't you send the camera work out?" he wanted to know.

The wheels of capitalism never stop.

Penny had taken Ray in hand and was going to drive him home. She told me that she wouldn't be coming back either. "Last night's caught up with me. I'm about ready to drop."

After they left I sat alone for a while, listening to the telephone but not feeling like answering it and trying to think. Eventually I unplugged the phone jack. The sunlight poured hot and strong through the windows. How had everything gone so wrong, so suddenly? Last week all I'd had to worry about was my lack of interest in men—this week it was destruction and murder served back to back. Things weren't supposed to happen like this—not to people like us . . . .

I must have slumped over asleep at the desk because I burst out shrieking when someone tapped me on the back.

"Oh, it's you," I said weakly when I made out Hadley's face. I settled my glasses back firmly on my nose. "Was I sleeping or something?"

"I got worried when I didn't hear from you," she said. "And then I tried to call . . . ." She held up the disconnected telephone cord, laughing, "Just nervous, I guess."

"Perfectly understandable," I said. We smiled at each other and I shook the sleep from my eyes.

"Listen," Hadley said, after a pause. "You want to go have a picnic?"

"What, now?"

"Well, it's lunchtime after all, and a gorgeous day to be outside. We could go over to Gas Works Park, lie on the grass, talk it all over. Pam, it'd be great."

"It's not as if I'm exactly getting any work done here," I said, sighing and looking around.

"Fantastic. Come on, lock up."

She had a picnic basket waiting in the passenger seat of her truck, along with a huge Chinese kite shaped like an octopus: oblong, with tentacle streamers. It was purple and green and red, a beauty.

"A present," Hadley said, opening up the door and handing it out.

"Thanks!" I was dumbfounded for a moment at her generosity. "Is it symbolic? I mean—an octopus?"

"If there's not enough wind we can use it as a sunscreen," Hadley smiled. "Hop in."

Gas Works Park was Seattle's first post-industrial recreation spot. They hadn't moved the machinery; they'd simply painted it in bright colors and landscaped hills and paths and playgrounds around it. It looked across Lake Union to downtown Seattle, where the new skyscrapers were changing the line of the city.

Hadley's picnic basket contained fresh rolls and chèvre and tomatoes and strawberries, and a bottle of Calistoga water to wash it down. After eating we launched the kite from the ridge. The same breeze that was sending the white-sailed boats scudding around Lake Union kept the kite up at a low, but respectable distance. We sat back and sighed in unison. For me, it was as if all my anxieties had been attached to that octopus kite—they weren't gone but they were now safely at a distance, sailing and bouncing about in the blue sky.

"You want to bring me up to date?" asked Hadley. She was sitting with her long legs drawn up to her chin like a kind of enormous cricket. Her hair shone silver and her eyes were brighter than the sky, so bright I couldn't quite look into them.

"Well. To begin with. Last night after Penny and I went home, around midnight, Zee comes knocking on our door. She was all worked up, said she'd seen a body being removed from the shop. She wanted to know whose, but when we told her Jeremy's, she seemed somehow like she knew or suspected already. Then she asked about some negatives in the darkroom, wanted to know if he'd been working on anything. I said I'd seen some negs hanging up. And then I wanted to know if she was supposed to be meeting Jeremy there for some reason. At that she got all hysterical, said she was going over to Ray's and left. This morning we find out that she didn't go to Ray's—he was at the office when Penny and I got there and he didn't know what the hell was going on—he got all emotional—the first person to really cry for Jeremy."

"Poor guy," said Hadley. I nodded, omitting to tell her Ray's remark about the goddamned women. For all I knew he was right.

"So I went to the darkroom—and the negatives were gone."

"You think the cops took 'em? As evidence?"

"Wouldn't they have to tell us? I mean, we were there until the very end. If they'd gone back to investigate they would have had to have a search warrant."

"So Zee might have gone back there last night . . ." Hadley echoed my own suspicion. "Those negatives were proof maybe . . . ."

"Of something she and Jeremy were working on together."

We watched the kite dip and sway, dip, dip. I got up hastily and ran back and forth a few times along the ridge, trying to find the breeze to lift it again. Sweating, but temporarily successful, I sat down again next to Hadley.

"What about June?" she asked.

"Don't ask. They gave her a really rough time, the bastards. The lawyer got her released. I hope to god they don't arrest her again. I suppose they'd need some evidence—a witness or the weapon or something."

"You don't think," Hadley said carefully, "that there's any possibility . . . ."

I shook my head. "I can't believe it, I just can't. I know they had a fight, but June's not crazy."

"Well, I've been spending the morning with Elena. *She* was totally hysterical when I told her this morning."

"Did you call her?"

"No, she came over looking for Fran at some ungodly hour. If I'd thought about it more I might not have told her that Fran was around last night and that I'd handed over the car keys. But my first thought was to reassure her that Fran was at least among the living."

"Unlike Jeremy. What reaction did she have to his murder?"

"She shuddered. She shrieked."

"Do you think she thought . . . that Fran had done it?"

"I didn't think of that."

"You know what I wondered—it's far-fetched, but still . . . It occurred to me that Jeremy might not have been the intended victim at all. That Jeremy and Elena look a lot alike in some ways . . ."

"And someone thought he was Elena? But that's even more impossible. Who would want to kill Elena?"

She looked at me closely. "You're not thinking that Margaret or Anna wanted to bump her off, after they'd destroyed B.Violet?"

It sounded ridiculous aloud on this sunny afternoon. I mumbled, "Well, what about her ex-husband? She had to fight him on the custody case; maybe he wanted revenge. And what about all the hate mail she got after the school firing? Or some of the feminists who'd probably like to stuff a sock in her mouth sometimes. Elena's aroused a lot of opposition in the last couple of years."

"But *murder*, Pam."

"There may have been as many reasons for Elena to be murdered as for Jeremy."

Hadley suddenly shivered and jerked at the kite. "If that were true then Elena still wouldn't be safe."

"Where's Elena now?"

"She went back to her vigil at home, waiting for Fran."

We looked at each other. "I guess I'm just more sympathetic to lovers than you, Pam," Hadley said.

"Huhmmph."

After that we didn't say much, just lay flat watching the kites. I started yawning and forgetting the direction of my thoughts. They swirled and fluttered like the bright nylon and paper shapes in the sky. Fran, Elena, Ray, June, Zee, Margaret, Anna. Bobbing and bouncing, evading each other, soaring, dipping down. One of them must have done it, but which one?

Sometime later I woke with my face pressed against the sweet-smelling grass and my body burning. Hadley was asleep too, breathing with her mouth slightly open. Her half-clenched hand still held the ball of string, but our kite had settled somewhere far down the slope. It was a peaceful moment and I didn't wake her.

I wished we could go on lying there as if nothing at all had happened.

13
▼ ▼ ▼ ▼ ▼

After Gas Works Park Hadley and I went to her house for a cup of coffee. My face and shoulders were sunburned and my brain felt like a small hot roll in an oven. The surface of my skin was tenderly feverish to the touch, erotically feverish. I kept wanting to say something about it to Hadley; instead I leaned my head out the window to cool it.

Hadley lived in a huge collective household in a rambling old mansion overlooking Lake Washington. The living and dining rooms were paneled in dark walnut and papered in yellow roses. There was a jungle of plants along the bay windows that any tropical country would be proud of. Here and there were the regulation political posters: some left over from long ago Vietnam days—doves and raised fists—some advertising women's dance groups or free clinic benefits. In some ways the house, like most of those that had survived the seventies, was a minor museum of the changing counterculture: old *Ramparts* in the bookshelf next to *Co-Evolution Quarterly* and *Runner's Magazine;* a hash pipe lying serenely on a shelf beside a bottle of B-Complex, high stress tablets; a copy of *Lesbian Nation* side by side with *Managerial Woman.*

Hadley led me upstairs—three flights—to a huge attic bedroom with romantic dormers and a skylight. The floor was sheathed in oriental rugs, the white painted rough stucco walls covered with masks and carvings, archeological by-products of her mother's career, I imagined.

Hadley filled and plugged in a small electric espresso coffee maker and got out two fine china cups, setting them on a round, heavy walnut table with clawfeet next to one of the dormer windows. The view was of the back garden with its rows of new vegetables coming up, and of several horsechestnut trees, cooling the house with hundreds of fresh green fans.

"It's really sunny and nice here in the morning," Hadley said.

I couldn't help glancing at her bed, right under the skylight. The mattress was covered with a turquoise and black handwoven spread and looked firm and bouncy on its brass bedstead.

"It must be nice to look up and see the stars at night," I said.

"Oh yes."

She looked embarrassed and I suddenly swallowed hard and then the espresso pot boiled over and Hadley rushed to save it, laughing, "I always fill it too full."

Although my heart was beating too fast I decided to continue the conversation about her room as if it were a normal subject. I mean, it *was* a normal subject, wasn't it? "It seems like you have the best of both worlds up here," I said, sitting down at the table. "Company when you want it, but peace and quiet too." I was thinking—I wonder who she's involved with? I wonder who sleeps with her up here? My limbs were heavy with heat and lust; a more sensual fluid than blood coursed through them, almond oil perhaps, overpoweringly heady.

Hadley nodded, busy with the little machine. Her face was flushed with the steam. "Yes, it's nice to have a place to escape to. I've lived in collective households where every time I so much as stepped out of my room I had to hear what someone's therapist told them that day."

She set the espresso in front of me and sat down herself. Through the dormer window the sky breathed in, full of the scent of horsechestnut leaves. It was about four o'clock. I felt very weak. I thought, what if she asks me point blank: Are you interested in me? Have I made a decision? It's a life-altering decision . . . I was focused on her face like a drugged person.

Hadley was indeed looking at me with a question in her eyes but it wasn't the question I imagined.

"How can we find out if Zee and Jeremy were involved in something?"

"What?" I hastily gulped some of my coffee to get my mind functioning again. "I mean—we could ask her, I guess."

"Would she tell us?"

"Maybe. Maybe not. Depends on if she trusts us . . . I don't think she does." I swallowed more coffee, great doses of it like a bracing medicine. What had I been thinking, after all, that Hadley and I would . . . right now . . . no, of course not.

"You know where Zee lives, don't you?"

"Beacon Hill. With her aunt. But Hadley—we can't just burst over there, demanding to know things. Let's look at our own position, I mean, are we detectives or what? We're not really qualified; we might really screw things up."

Hadley looked at me as if disappointed. She hooked her gray-blond hair behind her ears. "But what's a detective except someone who wants to find out what happened? Don't you? I do. We have a stake in all this. And I want to find how all of it links up, what it all means. We're certainly more qualified than any old male detective they'll put on the case. Hell, Pam, we know these people, don't we?"

I held my head in my hands. "No," I said. "I feel like I don't anymore. There are too many people involved in this whole thing; I can't keep them straight!"

"That's what my mother says about collectives," Hadley laughed. She removed my hands from my head, one after the other, and held them. Her fingers were long and dry and cool. I felt a change go through them when we touched.

"Murder's nothing to play around with," I said weakly. "I haven't known you long enough to want to see you bumped off for snooping."

"Pam," she began, but then her head cocked, as if listening. From someplace far below I heard her name being called. "Had-leeee . . . telllllll-aphone."

"Be right back," she muttered, letting go of my hands abruptly and disappearing.

There was a pad of paper and a couple of pens on the table. In order to stop myself from rushing madly about looking for traces of her life and loves in the disgusting way my new passion urged me, I began to make a list. An orderly list entitled:

MOTIVES FOR MURDER

(I think I had seen this in a book somewhere; if not, it was still a good start for a person who tended to arrange her shopping lists in categories: Vegetables; Staples; Sundries.)

A. Revenge for sabotage of B.Violet (Fran, Margaret, Anna)
B. Result of fight between Jeremy & June (June)
C. Collaboration between Zee and Jeremy—why? (Zee)
D. Jealousy—male (Ray)
E. Wrong person killed—Elena (?)

"You know," I said to Hadley when she returned. "I can't help but think we may be going at this ass backwards—trying to figure out the murderer before we know who destroyed B.Violet. They happened in sequence. They've got to be connected." Then I noticed Hadley's face. "What happened? Who was that on the phone?"

"Elena. She says she just got a call from Fran. She says she might have some information that would shed some light. She asked if I wanted to come by. What do you think? Do you want to come?"

"Is Fran coming?"

"No, Elena says she's still lying low somewhere."

I was unable to restrain a last quick look at the turquoise and black bedspread. I folded up my list and said, "Let's go."

Elena lived about twelve blocks from Hadley, on the poorer side of Capitol Hill. She rented the lower half of an old frame house. It was the most ramshackle of the homes I'd visited today. Part of it had to do with the natural chaos children under ten bring to a house—bikes, toys, dishes and clothes littered the front porch—and part of it had to do with the state of the building itself—the tar-like shingles were peeling off the outer walls at a great rate, the porch was rotting underneath and the door had ominous black scorches along one side.

It was a depressing place, that not even the new striped curtains at the windows or the pink and purple rhododendrons out front could cheer. It reminded me again how poor Elena had become since she'd lost her teaching job, and almost lost her kids. Once, when we first met, Elena had showed me photos of where she'd grown up, in a college town in Indiana. She'd been standing, an angelic child of six, with her dog, in front of a huge white house with a deep, screened veranda.

Elena saw us before we could knock, and flung open the door. "I'm so glad to see you." Her blond curls were greasy and her chocolate eyes rimmed with red. Two kids tumbled out at her feet.

"Where's Franny, where's Franny? I thought you said this was maybe Franny?" said the little girl, Samantha. She was about six, with her mother's blond curls and turned-up nose. The boy, Garson, tall for eight, dark-haired and dirty-faced, hung back sullenly at the sight of us.

"How're you doing?" Hadley asked, taking Elena's hand. "Did you sleep at all today?"

"Couldn't," Elena said, trying to smile and motioning us inside. "I was so worried, and now this phone call."

It seemed dark in the living room, perhaps because of the brightness outside. Gradually the furniture took shape—a cast-off couch and chair set, slipcovered, a couple of tables piled with crayons and fingerpaints. There was an unframed Vermeer print on one wall and a Lesbian Mothers' Defense Fund poster on the other. The rug was scattered with jigsaw puzzle pieces and Legos that made a scrunching sound under our feet as we followed Elena to the kitchen. Samantha and Garson went back to watching TV.

Elena pulled three beers out of the refrigerator.

"Not for me thanks," I said, trying not to sound too disapproving. It occurred to me for the first time that Elena might have been drinking a good part of the day. Her movements were rapid, broken and sloppy; her voice was a little slow, as if she were being careful about her pronunciation.

I looked at Hadley for possible confirmation—hadn't she said last night that Elena had a drinking problem too?—but she was opening her bottle and asking, "Why don't you start from the beginning, Elena? What did Fran say?"

"Well, she was drunk," said Elena precisely and scornfully, oblivious of her own state. "She started out talking about last night, how she thought I was dead but it was Jeremy. She said . . . a lot of stupid things . . . she . . ."

"Like what?" I interrupted.

"It's not important," Elena shook her head. "The important thing is that she's afraid of being arrested about his murder because he wrecked B.Violet. She doesn't want to turn up until they've found the murderer."

"You believe her then?" Hadley said. "That he was the one who did it?"

"Who else?" Elena looked away and I saw her hand tighten on the beer can. "Of course I believe her. I just don't know what happened when she discovered him."

"He was still alive the morning after the sabotage," I put in.

"Tell me again about last night," Elena turned to Hadley. "What did she say, what did she act like, when you saw her?"

Hadley must have been over this with her several times before. She repeated calmly. "She thought Jeremy was you, then she realized that if Jeremy had wrecked B.Violet the night before and she'd seen him, then she was a likely suspect for his murder. She was drunk but she was fairly coherent. That's why I gave her the keys. Plus, you know, I was a little out of it myself, what with seeing the guy dead and all."

"Who got offed?" asked Garson interestedly, coming into the kitchen.

"No one you know," said Elena.

"When are we going to eat, Mom? I'm hungry."

"When I say so," Elena snapped. "Now beat it."

Garson walked out slowly, his shoulders and head expressing the most wounded feelings.

Elena apologized, "I'm not myself, I . . ." She sagged back into her plastic kitchen chair and tears formed in and fell from her red-brown eyes.

"Maybe the kids should go somewhere for the evening," Hadley suggested, putting an arm around her. "Especially if there's any possibility Fran might turn up. It'd make it easier."

"I could drive them," I offered. "I'd be glad to." I'd be glad to get out of there, actually. Elena drunk and self-pitying was not an attractive sight. How could Hadley be so sympathetic—to both of them?

Elena fought to get a grip on herself, nodding to show she thought it was a good idea. "Take them to Jill and Marie's," she said finally. "They'll understand."

"Can you remember anything else Fran said," persisted Hadley. "You said on the phone . . ."

"She said—she was probably making this up, you know—that Jeremy was an informer."

"An informer?" I repeated. "An informer for whom? What was she talking about?"

"She said he was being paid by someone, she saw him being paid . . . don't ask me," Elena stopped abruptly. "I know it sounds stupid."

"A spy at Best Printing? Employed by one of our rivals?" I couldn't help laughing. "Or maybe hired by someone to scope out B.Violet? And Fran discovered him in the act of investigation. Oh, Elena," I said. "Jeremy, an informer? That's ridiculous! How could she know? Where did she see him?"

"I don't know, I don't want to talk about it anymore. Oh god, where is she?"

Elena put her head down on the kitchen table and sobbed.

14
▼ ▼ ▼ ▼ ▼

I t was just after six when I dropped the kids off with Elena's friends.
Hadley had explained the circumstances on the phone and Jill and
Marie asked no questions, simply unleashed Samantha and Garson into
a herd of kids running around the back yard. We exchanged a few per-
functory remarks and then I was on my way again, driving Hadley's
truck. She'd said she'd just walk home from Elena's and I could give it to
her later. I started home for dinner, then abruptly changed direction.

I suddenly decided to drive up to Beacon Hill and see what Zee was
doing.

Zee's aunt's house was a small neat one overlooking the freeway.
The lot had recently been planted with a new lawn; there were stakes
and strings all around and a fresh green was just coming up. The drapes
were closed and the porch light was on, though it was quite early still.
Otherwise the house was perfectly ordinary. I'd only been here once
before, to drop Zee off. She'd asked me to come in and I'd stopped for a
minute. Her aunt was a beautifully dressed, plump, black-eyed woman.
In the Philippines she'd been married to a union lawyer who'd disappeared early in the seventies and was presumed dead. She too had
been held for questioning, but had managed to leave the country. She
had been in the States for six years and worked as a nurse at a large
Seattle hospital. That day she'd offered Zee and me tea and cookies;
when she'd gone to get them I'd seen she walked with a slight limp.

I knocked. There was no answer. Knocked again. Louder.

A neighbor woman next door poked her head out her window. She was Chinese, maybe Korean. "No there. Ladies no there. Go away."

I thought for a minute she was telling me to move on and stared at her in surprise, but then I thought more about it and asked, "They went away where? Do you know where they went away to?"

"No here, no here. They go morning, they have bag. They go taxi. Go home."

"Home? You mean, the Philippines?"

"No here, no here. Go away, go home," the woman said and disappeared behind a curtain.

"Well, Detective Nilsen," I muttered to myself. "What now? Check the passenger list for the morning flight to Manila?"

I looked more closely at the house. There was no doubt about it. In spite of the new lawn, the drapes were tightly closed and the house had that indefinable air homes get when their owners plan to be gone for a long time.

It was always possible, of course, that the two of them had simply gone off somewhere for a vacation. But the timing was a bit awkward, considering Jeremy's demise, and there was also the fact that Zee hadn't mentioned anything about a trip last night.

There was more to all this than met the eye—more than was meeting my suddenly sleepy eyes, for sure. I decided the very best thing for me would be a nap.

Sam and Jude were in the kitchen making dinner when I walked in. "Penny's asleep," they told me.

"That's just where I'm headed."

"Don't you want anything to eat?"

The fish stew smelled inviting but I was too tired to be hungry. "Save some for me. I'll be up again in an hour or two."

But once I lay down I was out for good. I hadn't had more than a few hours last night and today's sun as well as the feeling of deepening mysteries had knocked me out. I fell quickly into such a deep and dreamless sleep that it was a long while before I was aware that someone was shaking me awake.

"Pam," my sister was saying. "Pam, come on, wake up. Something important. Wake up."

"Ughnngh," I groaned. "No, no."

She kept shaking my shoulder. "Pam. Pam. Come on."

"Goddamn it," I said suddenly and clearly, my voice infused with the fierce and irrational anger that comes of being dragged into consciousness again. "What the fuck is it?"

"Zee," she whispered.

"Zee what? I could use some more zees."

"Shhh," she said. "Not so loud. Zee's here."

"No she's not, she's taking a vacation, she went away," I muttered. "What the fuck time is it, anyway?" I sat up. The room was dark and so was the window. I must have been sleeping for hours. I felt awful.

"It's midnight," she whispered. "I don't want to wake Sam and Jude. Look, Pam, I need your help. Zee and Ray are here and she wants to tell us some things. She wants us to hide her."

I was more awake with every sentence. "But she and her aunt left on a trip, the neighbor said. . . . She's here? With Ray?"

"That's what I'm telling you," Penny said patiently. "Now are you awake or aren't you?"

"I think so," I said, getting up and stretching. "Unless I'm still dreaming." I discovered, to my surprise, that I was dressed and ready to go. On my feet I didn't feel so bad. "She wants us to hide her," I suddenly said, taking it in. "From what?"

There was one lamp lit downstairs in the living room and Ray sat, black hair and beard glittering like tar, under its glow. Zee was shadowed in a corner, legs curled under her on the big chair, fingers twisting a button of her short-sleeved silk shirt.

"Zee, what's this about?"

"I . . ."

Ray broke in. "Zee needs a safe place to stay for a while." Irritable, concerned, a little too masterful, he was addressing himself to Penny rather than me. "This is the best place, I think."

"Why not let her talk for herself?" I said. "Zee, what's going on? Your next door neighbor told me you and your aunt went away, with suitcases, in a taxi."

"My aunt has gone to stay with relatives in New York for a little while." Zee's face was composed now and she spoke quietly. "And no, it's not a coincidence. But all the same, she wasn't involved and shouldn't have to answer any questions."

"Questions about?"

"About me and Jeremy."

I expected to see more of a reaction on Ray's face. If not teeth-baring angry jealously, then at least wounded pride. But he was smiling at Penny, who had just yawned uncontrollably and wrenchingly.

"Then June had a right to be jealous," I said.

"No, it wasn't that way, it wasn't that kind of involvement," Zee said quickly.

"But you were planning to meet Jeremy last night at the shop for some reason."

"That's true," said Zee. "I was." She paused and looked at her feet, as if wondering where they had taken her. "I had gotten there early. I thought, if Jeremy hadn't arrived perhaps I could do . . . something . . . on my own. We should have been meeting at eleven. I got there at ten and saw the police cars everywhere. I went into a doorway across the street and just watched. Finally I saw you leave and then they brought a stretcher out. That's why I came to you last night, to find out what happened."

"But you didn't go to Ray's afterwards."

"No. I didn't. I . . . had to go back to the shop."

"To destroy something," I suggested.

"No," said Zee firmly. "To save some things."

I looked at Ray. "Do you know what this is all about?"

"I trust Zee," he said. "I think we've all got to trust Zee."

Out of the corner of my eye I saw Penny yawning again and suddenly turned on her. "Are we boring you? I suppose you've already figured out the whole thing."

She yawned again. "It's physiological, dear, not a measure of my interest. And yes, I think I do have an inkling."

"What then?"

"You were the one who suggested the idea to me. Noticing the negatives hanging to dry and also noticing that they'd been taken down the next morning. Zee asked about them specifically last night. Therefore, I deduce that both Zee and Jeremy had an interest in those negatives and probably a joint interest." She paused and ran her fingers through her cockscomb hair. "I don't necessarily deduce from that that Zee had anything to do with his murder."

"But what were they—what were *you*," I looked at Zee, "doing with the negatives?"

"Forging," said Penny and Zee in unison and Zee continued, "We were forging documents for illegal aliens."

She had met Jeremy, Zee said, through Best Printing, but she'd also seen him once or twice at a demonstration and once at a benefit for the anti-Marcos group she was involved with. She'd judged from that that he was a sympathizer. One day, over lunch, they'd gotten talking about the current situation in the Philippines. He was really shocked; he said he'd had no idea it was so bad there. He asked if there was anything he could do about it, anything to help out. Well, maybe Zee had confided more than she ought. She had said there was a big problem now with people like herself, students who had gotten involved politically or who came from politically inclined liberal families, and who were now afraid to go back home, who wanted to stay in the States. They couldn't get papers to stay, most of them. Not for working, not for further studies. She already knew some who had gone back home and immediately been put in jail.

It was Jeremy's idea, yes, he had suggested it. What kind of papers did they need, he wanted to know? Work papers, green cards, certificates. Wouldn't it be possible just to make them? Duplicate them, fill them out, and sign them? After all, they worked at a print shop.

When did all this start? Six months ago, maybe seven. It had taken them a while to come up with the information and the best way of producing the documents. Now they met, had met, once every two weeks. The negatives on the line last night had been for some new forms the government had started using.

Over the course of half a year they had gotten new papers for twenty or thirty people.

"I suppose they paid pretty well for the documents," I said, thinking of the roll of bills in Jeremy's pocket.

Zee looked surprised. "Not much," she said. "Jeremy and I didn't take anything, just the cost of the materials and a little bit more. It was for political reasons."

I said slowly, "Elena today suggested that Jeremy was an informer, that Fran told her she saw him accepting money or something. . . . Maybe he was spying on B.Violet, she said."

Penny snorted, "Elena is one of those half-baked lefties who always think they're being infiltrated. Jeremy's been with Best for almost a year and this merger idea only came up last week. How could he have been investigating B.Violet? How come he wasn't investigating us?"

"Maybe he *was* investigating us," Ray said.

15
▼ ▼ ▼ ▼ ▼

I t was three in the morning before I got to sleep again. I'd spent an
hour hearing the whole story from Zee and another two thinking it
out for myself. Penny had fixed up a bed for Zee in the attic and Ray had
finally gone home.

I lay in bed watching the street lamp through the window and realized that my attitude toward Jeremy had changed drastically in the past
forty-eight hours. Before his murder I'd had only pleasant, if sometimes
impatient, feelings about him. He had called out the familial in me,
rather than the romantic, even though I acknowledged his good looks.
He was too skinny, too pretty, too young; he wore too many earrings,
smoked too much dope. Yet it had been fun to horseplay with him sometimes, to shake my (elderly) head over his naive remarks. I'd always
been more lenient with him than with any of the others; I'd made jokes
about his spaciness but had still accepted it with an "oh well," a shrug.
Jeremy's forgetfulness, his slow tentative smile as he asked you to repeat
something or as he apologized, they were just his way.

But what if they hadn't been "his way"? What if Jeremy's sweet
boyishness, his puzzled vagueness had been all put on? What if the real
Jeremy was the one who told June she wasn't the only scene in town, the
one who had hundreds of dollars in his pocket, the one who forged
identity papers—the one who was an informer—for someone—about
someone?

It was hard to believe. I thought back to the day Jeremy had come by the shop last year. Kay had been doing our camera work then. She'd been a hard person to get along with, testy, with a flaring temper, and in recent months there'd been a lot of fighting. She'd finally announced she was leaving. Fine, we said, while wondering what to do now. That same afternoon a young blond man with earrings and ringlets had stopped in the doorway.

"What's all this? Oh wow, a collective printshop. What a great idea, far out. Hey, I studied printing and camera in California. You don't need anybody, do you?"

An FBI informer would never have had such good luck. An FBI informer would have been seen through months before. An FBI informer wouldn't waste his time on Best Printing. It wasn't like we were some ultra-left group fomenting revolution. We just did printing.

Automatically, memories of different jobs passed through my mind. Benefit posters and flyers for bookstore collectives, for food and bike co-ops, pamphlets for anti-war groups, brochures for feminist businesses, a few books every year on subjects like rape, racism and cultural genocide . . . it was true that almost every leftist feminist or progressive group had dealt with us at one time or another. . . .

A sudden chill passed over me and I huddled deeper under my covers. It had just occurred to me that a print shop might be the ideal place to keep tabs on the various groups in town. No need to go and hunt them down, they would come to you, flyer copy in hand, earnestly explaining their politics. You'd know of every benefit before it was announced, read every bit of literature before it appeared in the mail. Aside from that you could hear a fair amount of gossip as well—which group wasn't speaking to which group, for instance; the ins and outs of various party lines; who was coming to town, who was leaving, who was here.

And what a bonus being in the darkroom, able to develop all those negatives—one for you, one for them—not to mention the photographs you could take—with your secret camera—of everyone who came to the shop.

It was a nightmarish thought and one which, I stubbornly continued to feel, was impossible. Not Jeremy, not Jeremy. We would have known.

And yet, what had we really known about Jeremy? He talked freely—but about nothing in particular. He lived in a small apartment by himself in the University District, he had a few friends who called him up from time to time, he'd had a girlfriend once, I remembered . . . had those people suspected? Had they been FBI agents or informers too? And what would the FBI do now that he was dead? Would they be investigating? The very thought was enough to make me scrunch up into the tiniest ball I could. I hadn't frightened myself so thoroughly since the day after my parents died.

The next morning I felt, at least temporarily, much better. The sun was shining through the kitchen windows and buttering the counters and floor with its light when I came down to make some coffee. It was about ten o'clock and no one else was around. There was a note on the table from Penny:

"Pam—didn't sleep too well and got up to go down to the shop. Don't want to let things get too much out of hand there. Hadley picked up her truck, said not to wake you. Will call you later about alphabetizing."

Alphabetizing? I stared at the word a few minutes before realizing that Penny was referring to Zee up in the attic. XYZ we'd sometimes called her for a joke. God, I'd forgotten about her. She was going to roast up there if she stayed the day. Was it really so necessary to hide her? In the light of the morning it seemed very cloak and daggerish.

I made two cups of coffee and took them both to the small door upstairs, across from the bathroom. It was locked.

"Zee. It's Pam. I've got some coffee."

I heard her coming down the stairs inside, then the door being unlocked.

"Do you really think that's necessary?" I asked, handing her a cup.

"I don't know. But I do it anyway."

She turned and I followed her up. The attic had at one time been Penny's and my favorite playing place, and it still held happy associations for me, even though it was now little more than a storage area for trunks and boxes and old mattresses, skis and sleds, hoola-hoops and roller skates. It wasn't so warm up here as I'd thought, not so early in the day.

Zee sat down on her mattress, and sipped the coffee thoughtfully. Barefoot, without make-up and with her hair pulled back, she looked far more serious than usual. Younger, too.

"Are you going down to the shop, too?" she asked.

"I haven't decided. I know there's work to do but it kind of gives me the creeps to be there. Everything has been so up in the air the past few days, too. I don't know what to think. I feel like I could put it all together if I had some time."

"Don't get too involved, Pam, not if it's going to mean trouble."

"You tell me not to get involved, when we're hiding you up here and you're involved. . . . What are you scared of, Zee? You think the cops will figure out you and Jeremy were helping illegals to stay?"

She nodded without meeting my eyes.

"But you took the negatives. And there's nothing to connect you to Jeremy, is there?"

Zee paused. "No," she said. "But all the same, some funny things were happening the last few weeks. They make me nervous. One guy, a guy we helped with a labor certification, got turned down from a job he wanted, he didn't know why. They kept his papers. Lucky they were under a false name and we got him new ones, but this keeping the certification, it's unusual, it's frightening."

"Have all the people you've helped been political? I mean, anti-Marcos?"

"Anti-Marcos, yes, but we mean a lot of different things by that, you know. Lots of people in the Philippines are anti-Marcos now, but not everybody does anything about it. Well, and they can't always," Zee added, looking over at me as if wishing I could understand. "It's very dangerous. Thousands are in jail, and some of them because they did just one little thing, maybe only talking back to some local mayor or something. One old guy I heard of, he just went and asked for his pension, the pension that was owing him, and they put him in jail, they beat him, you know, and put him in jail. That's the way there now."

"But the Filipinos you know in America, are they anti-Marcos too? Do they care if they're not living there?"

Zee looked at me curiously, as if trying to gauge the extent of my interest.

"Well, you've got to remember," she began slowly, "there are different kinds of Filipinos here, different groups: first wave, second, third. They say the first wave is the ones who were brought over and who came over to work in the fields in California. You know Carlos Bulosan, the writer? No . . . well, he wrote about that life, a very beautiful novel, you know—*America is in the Heart.* These men, they were mostly men, sometimes went back, sometimes stayed, and brought over a girl, married, had families. They've been here as long as lots of immigrants from Europe. . . .

"The second wave, they were those guys, from the war, you know." When I looked puzzled she explained patiently, "The Filipinos fought for the United States in the war; they thought that because they were governed by the U.S., had treaties and like that, the U.S. would protect them from the Japanese. Oh no, the Japanese invaded, killed thousands; Manila was the worst-bombed city in the whole war, you know, worse than Warsaw. You didn't know that, did you? No, Americans don't know that. . . . But after the war Congress passed a bill saying that all the Filipinos who fought in the war could become citizens. So they did, and they came over here, to have the good life. Everything they wanted—car–house–television, that's what they heard. We all hear that, all our lives, how great life is in America."

"And the third wave?"

"It's mostly professionals—doctors and nurses, engineers, computer programmers and things like that. It's not hard to come if you have some money and some relatives—almost everybody has some relatives

BARBARA WILSON

here—and a skill. Or you're a student. Marcos doesn't care so much if professionals leave. Because the Philippines can't support them, and they just get liberal and dissatisfied. And besides, everybody sends money back home. He doesn't lose much."

"What about the students, the radicals?" I asked. "Aren't they some kind of fourth wave?"

"If we were truly so radical," Zee smiled a little bitterly, "we would stay in the Philippines and join the guerillas. You," she made a sweeping gesture in the direction of the downstairs, "have your own special ideas about what is radical. But listen, okay," Zee's voice got hard. "We have been years and years under American imperialism and we hate it. Hate the Coca-Cola and the soldiers and sailors and air force at Subic and Clark, hate the way our women are prostitutes and our men are black marketeers or the way we have to work for your companies in factories making little pieces of things, not even the whole thing! But we come to the U.S. anyway when we're in trouble or to study, because where else can we go? We come here, we can stay with relatives or go to school— your nice, your such nice universities with their student centers and swimming pools—and we can sit in the library and read all the Marx and Fanon and everybody we want to, and nobody is going to bother us, you know, cut our toes off one by one or put electrodes on our genitals or anything . . ."

"Zee," I said, putting my hand on her arm. "Zee . . ."

She shook me off. "We come to America because we are middle-class or upper-class and we don't know how to fight wars or if we want to, and because we *can* come here." And she was crying now, holding her arms close to her sides. "But if you do anything here, the more visible you become, the more you can't go back. You just have to keep staying. You don't influence the Americans, because they don't hear you, they don't believe you when you talk about what's happening in the Philippines. You just stay, you just stay. And gradually you lose touch, and it's a little unreal to you, too. You live in a country like this, and you forget; it starts to seem impossible. You don't believe it either."

The morning sunlight was falling now in a straight path over her shoulders and my legs, as we faced each other, both crying now.

"You've never really liked me, Pam, have you?" she said, after a minute.

"I . . . I'm sorry Zee, how I've been. Can we start again?"

"Yes," she nodded and put her hand out.

We shook on it, a little solemnly, then couldn't help laughing.

Zee said, ". . . You know, Ray and I, it's not . . ."

"I don't want to hear about you and Ray. I don't mind, really, I don't mind at all. I'm happy for you, and embarrassed about my bad manners. But that's really the least of our worries now."

"But Pam, really . . ."

Then the doorbell rang.

16

▼ ▼ ▼ ▼ ▼

I went to the window of the attic and looked out. I didn't see a car I recognized in the street, only a plain navy blue sedan. I couldn't imagine who it was.

"I'll lock the door after you," said Zee.

I went downstairs quickly and got to the door as the bell rang again. I opened up on a man in a polyester suit, the same color as his car. Oh Christ, the FBI.

"Ms. Nilsen?" he asked, showing me his card. Fred Parker, Lieutenant Detective, Seattle Police Department.

"One of them."

"May I come in? I have a few questions to ask about one of your employees, Jeremy Plaice."

I motioned him inside. He was a tall, fair man with a clean-shaven, friendly face. He moved dragging one leg a bit and compensating with his other, as if it were an old injury.

We sat down in the living room. I felt as if I were entertaining a distant relative or friend of my parents.

"Tea or coffee?" I couldn't help asking.

Lieutenant Detective Parker shook his head politely. He'd taken out a small pad and pencil.

"Pam or Pamela?"

"Pam. Penny, my sister, is at the shop."

"Yes, I know. I've seen her."

He got up early. I hoped Penny had acquitted herself well. It made me nervous, though, that she hadn't called to alert me. What if our stories clashed?

"What can I do to help you?" I said less than eagerly. "I already had my statement taped that night."

"Let's start by going over the events the night of the murder. Can you tell me first what you were doing earlier in the evening and then what you saw when you arrived at the shop?"

"Well, I worked at the shop until about six, along with Ray Hernandez. He was there too. Then I left . . ."

"Was Mr. Hernandez still there?"

". . . Yes, he said he'd close up later." I tried to sound firm rather than hesitant. I'd forgotten Ray was working on a job he wanted to finish. "So, anyway, I went and did a couple of errands—dropped something off at the cleaners, picked up some film I'd had developed—and at seven I met Hadley Harper for dinner at the Doghouse Restaurant. Sally Gassett, the waitress, will remember."

He was writing all this down in shorthand. He asked me, "Ms. Harper is a friend of yours?"

I nodded. I didn't feel like going into the merger business any sooner than I had to. I continued, "So we ate and everything, and then about eight-thirty we came by the shop. I wanted to borrow ten dollars from the petty cash. I, we, saw a red light from the darkroom and went in. Jeremy was lying on his back, but sort of crumpled, on the floor. He had a hole in his temple, there was some blood."

"So this was about eight-thirty?"

"Around then, maybe a little later."

"The call to the police came at 9:02."

"Oh well, it must have been later . . . I didn't have a watch."

Lieutenant Detective Parker's eyes flicked automatically to my wrist. If he'd lifted the watch face he would have seen skin that had never been touched by sunlight. Never lie to the police, I'd heard over and over again. But I didn't want to tell him about Fran, to have to get into that whole thing—she and Elena and the merger—it was too messy.

Lieutenant Detective Parker said only, "There was no one else in the shop? No one else came in after you?"

"No," I said. There it was. Perjury or whatever they called it.

He switched the subject. "How many employees at Best Printing?"

Hadn't Penny set him straight? Or was he just testing me? "We don't have employees. It's a collective."

He didn't write that down, I noticed.

"The papers are in your and Penny Nilsen's name," he said.

"Yes . . . but we all share the profits and the work."

"How many of you are there?"

"Didn't Penny tell you?"

He just looked at me, neither patient or impatient. "It's only a formality—to ask different people the same questions."

I bet, I thought. I was beginning to sweat a little. He no longer seemed quite the innocuous friendly fellow he had at first.

"There are, were, seven. Ray Hernandez, Zenaida Oberon, Penny, me, Elena Perrault, Jeremy and June Jasper—you must know June, she was pulled in that night for questioning." I got angry thinking of it, but Parker just nodded.

"Can you tell me about their movements that evening?"

"No, I don't know where any of them were."

"What can you tell me about Jeremy himself? What kind of person was he? Is there anything he was involved in that might have contributed to this . . . event?"

"I've heard," I paused deliberately. "That he was an FBI informer."

Lieutenant Detective Parker didn't raise an eyebrow. "Oh, that's interesting . . . You think he might have been killed because he was informing on you?"

"Well, I didn't say that. I don't know for sure either. You should be able to find out from the FBI though."

"It's not always that easy." Parker gave me a surprisingly frank smile. "Informers go by aliases, and sometimes report to just one man . . . we'll see what we can find out though. . . . So you don't think it was a lover's quarrel," he changed the subject abruptly. "No jealousy, nothing like that? What was his girlfriend so mad about?"

I shook my head. "June would never murder anybody."

"Except her first husband," Parker said smoothly.

I bit my lip with anger, but I had to admire his technique. Ever since he'd come he'd kept me constantly on edge. I had no idea what he really thought.

"What about the others?" asked Parker. "Zee, Ray, Elena? How did they get along with Jeremy?"

"Fine," I said, a little dully. "Jeremy was really very easy to get along with. A little scatterbrained but likeable. As long as he had his stereo earphones on he was happy." And his daily joint.

"We've had a hard time tracking down any friends or family," Parker said.

"Oh, he's got a family, parents, brother, sister, he was always talking about them. They're in southern California someplace. He was planning to go visit them soon. Fullerton, I think."

Lieutenant Detective Parker wrote that down. "Thank you, Ms. Nilsen. That will be all. We'll contact you if we need any further information. If anything else springs to mind," he glanced at my watch, "don't hesitate to call me." He gave me his personal card.

I was surprised somehow that he was leaving. I had expected to be challenged, at least to have him ask if I had any ideas about who murdered Jeremy. He hadn't asked who told me that Jeremy was an informer or what he would have been informing on. Was he stupid, or was I?

"By the way," he said, as I showed him the door. "We haven't been able to locate Ms. Oberon. The neighbor said she and her aunt had gone away. Any idea where?"

His eyes were suddenly piercing straight through me. I was totally unprepared.

"An emergency," I stuttered. "I don't know anything, just a note." I stopped. What had Penny told him, not told him?

He waited a moment for me to continue, then smiled pleasantly. "I'm sure we'll be contacting you again, Ms. Nilsen," he said as he went out the door. "Good-bye. And have a nice day."

"Bye," I nodded miserably.

Bastard. Well, you haven't found out anything yet.

I waited a good ten minutes to be on the safe side and then went back up to the attic door and tapped. Zee let me in.

"Who was it?"

"A cop. A detective."

"A detective."

"Don't worry," I said. "I didn't keep looking guiltily upstairs. But . . ."

"What?"

"He is looking for you. He just wants to ask you some questions. The same as the rest of us."

"What did you tell him?" Zee was pacing back and forth across the one cleared patch of floor, hands in her jeans pockets.

"Nothing much. I certainly didn't make his job easier, that's for sure. He'll probably be back. God, why did this have to happen? Who killed Jeremy, Zee? And why? Could it have been someone you know? Someone Jeremy was blackmailing or something?"

"No," she said. "It was all done through me. They didn't speak to Jeremy."

"But he knew who they were, didn't he?"

She looked unhappy.

"The detective didn't seem all that surprised when I said I'd heard Jeremy might be an FBI informer. How do you find things like that out, I wonder? Write and request our files?"

"Be careful, Pam. Please be careful. It's maybe more dangerous than you think."

She had stopped pacing and was now standing with her back to me, staring out the window. An eerie impression that we were in a kind of prison, a cell, passed over me, disappeared.

I said suddenly, "Zee, what really happens to people who go back to the Philippines, people who've been active here?"

She turned slowly, as if pulling herself out of a trance. "I could tell you about Benny's brother. He went back. You know Benny, Benito—yes?—the boy working with me on the newsletter? Yes. Well, he and his brother, Amado, were both in the student movement in the Philippines. Amado was one of the leaders of a demonstration, an illegal one, some years ago. Then he came here to school. He was going to the University of Washington for a civil engineering degree. He was also active here. He was the one who started the newsletter—and he traveled around talking some. Well, one day this spring he finishes his degree and says he must go home. He says maybe it's dangerous, but he's never been bothered by anyone in America, so maybe they don't know much or anything about his activities here and they don't remember what he was doing in the Philippines before . . ."

Zee was sitting on the mattress again with me and had taken one of my hands. Her own were very cold and soft. It was as if by the force of her will she wanted me to understand the exact significance of what she was saying.

"Benny said, we all said, don't go. But we didn't really know what goes on there in the Philippines anymore. Sometimes all of a sudden there would be an easier time, you know, like a warming up. Not so many arrests, maybe some promises, a little more hope. It was that way when Amado decided to go back. You see, Marcos had said martial law was over last year."

Zee's beautifully shaped lips curled bitterly.

"Can you imagine that any of us would be taken in like that? But we were, we wanted so much to believe. . . . And so Amado went back, in April, I think, April fifth. We had a party for him. A week later Benny got a telegram: Amado is dead."

Her hands closed like cold iron vises on mine. I couldn't speak.

"He was tortured, his body was found . . . no, it's awful. Benny, he couldn't believe it. He went around like a crazy man, he wanted to go there and murder Marcos personally. Such a waste, Pam, to think of Amado killed like a dog and thrown out on a pile."

"But what did they arrest him for? How did they know?"

Zee wasn't crying, but her pale ochre face had gone paler; her black eyes were filmed with grief. "We don't know, we never know how they know us, why." she said.

"But that's why we don't want to go back."

17
▼ ▼ ▼ ▼ ▼

I decided, after all, not to go in to the shop, but to work on the garden in the afternoon. With the recent hot weather and lack of attention, things were starting to get out of control among the kale and the lettuce. The garden, at least, was one place I could have an effect that counted. I was badly shaken by what Zee had been telling me; one more country in the world to worry about; one person dead there, how many others?

I hoed and weeded, watered and thinned. After a couple of hours I began to feel better, my bare feet digging deep in the brown earth, my fingernails black, sweat on my forehead and back. I breathed in and out the smell of green, overwhelming green, until I was dazzled by it and had to sit down.

The phone had rung twice that afternoon but I hadn't let myself be interrupted. Around four, however, after a shower, I decided it was time to answer it. Hadley, of course, how had I forgotten about her?

"Hi," she said. "What's new?"

"Not much. I was interviewed by a detective."

"Yeah, me too."

"Fred?"

"Yeah."

I wanted to ask if he'd caught her on the time, the mysterious lapse between 8:30 and 9:02, or if she'd mentioned Fran, but caution prevented me from using Fran's name on the phone. For the same reason I didn't want to mention Zee. And then, too, Zee had said not to tell anyone.

"But that's not what I called about," Hadley continued.

"Oh?"

"Nah. I called to see if you want to see some softball tonight. My team's playing."

"Sounds great. What do I wear? My old song girl's outfit?"

"Don't tell me. The baton-twirling twins of Roosevelt High?"

"Just kidding. We were both ugly and studious."

"That's a relief."

"Not at the time. Where and when?"

She gave me the details, then I started dinner. It would be a vegetable medley tonight, fresh garden produce, sautéed in sweet butter and herbs over rice.

I put the rice on, cut up the vegetables, then went up to check on Zee and to bring her a pitcher of iced tea. The attic was sweltering now. Zee lay on the mattress in her bra and pants, surrounded by newspapers.

"Someday we're going to recycle those," I apologized.

"They make interesting reading," Zee said. "It's sometimes incredible to me how things get reported in the American press. They are so open about some things, so closed about others, always judging. It's what I never understand about the U.S., I guess."

"What?"

"The selfishness, like babies have. You don't ever realize that the rest of the world is obsessed with you. The Manila papers, since I learned to read, are full of editorials—every day—on what America thinks, what America does, what is our relationship to America. It is like a love affair, you know, or something—we hate you when we feel rejected, we love you when you look at us, like you take us seriously. Imelda and Ferdinand, they live from day to day like wives, or really like prostitutes, highly paid ones, you know, who pretend they are free, that they have someone in love with them—when in fact they are being used. Like the rest of us."

The attic was as close and hot as a sauna, painfully pressing on my sunburned skin. I took off my sandals and mopped my tender brow, trying not to hyperventilate. My Norwegian ancestors had only passed on genes to withstand freezing temperatures while digging potatoes or herding reindeer. I'd never make it in Manila.

"Yes, whores!" Zee continued. "The U.S. uses the Third World like a man uses a prostitute, did you ever think of that? Flirts with her a little, you know, pretends she is human, maybe spends a little money on her to make her pretty, then, when he has got what he wanted—the natural resources, control of the economy, a dumping ground for useless commodities, complete subservience, in other words—he treats her like a whore and pretends to feel sorry for her while he kicks dirt in her face and makes sure she can never get up from the ground. And all the time the woman hates him but she still wants him to marry her, hopes that he might . . .

"Do you know how many women in the Philippines are prostitutes?" Zee asked. "How many thousands live in tiny little rooms outside Subic Bay and Clark Air Force Base? They come in from the country, you know, their families have no money—maybe they've had their land taken away by some relatives of Marcos, who knows? They start out as hostesses, in Manila maybe, in the high rise hotels, with the businessmen from all over the West. Six months or a year later they are dancing topless at a lousy bar near one of the bases. They fall in love with a sailor who says he will marry them, they have a baby. He goes home without saying good-bye. They give the baby to their parents, they go back to work, maybe at not such a nice place, maybe just on the street somewhere . . . ."

I felt as if I were going to faint. "Zee, why are you telling me this?"

"Because you are a feminist, aren't you? An American feminist. You should know how the rest of the world lives, how the women live. If they are not being used for their sex they are pushed into factories and ruin their eyes looking through microscopes, making computer chips for Hewlett-Packard, IBM; they are making thirty–forty cents an hour, you know, and then they are laid off when they are twenty-five because they are old, they are blind, they might want more money or cause trouble . . . And you should care, you should care, because it is *your* country doing this and it is *women* who are suffering."

I *was* hyperventilating now, not just with the heat however, but with the suffocating feeling of being responsible. And I didn't want to feel responsible; it hurt too much, it wasn't comfortable. I could hear myself almost gasping for breath. So many many times I'd sat in pleasant surroundings, watching films or hearing speeches on the horrors and sins of imperialism, nodding like a little marionette when the right strings were pulled. Oh terrible, so awful. Here's a dollar for the hat and let me put my name down on the petition, the mailing list. And then out into the evening air again, for coffee, for dessert, the brief moment of guilt and acknowledgement quenched. There was a painful justice now in being so physically uncomfortable. I didn't like it one bit. And I couldn't move.

Not until Zee suddenly laughed and broke the tension. "You can do me a favor if you want . . ."

"What? Of course. Anything!"

"Get out of here before you collapse. You're red as a beet!"

"Zee . . . I mean, I'm glad you came to us."

"That's why I came, because I trust you. You and Penny both."

We sat smiling at each other, then I remembered my rice cooking. "Sam and Jude will be home soon. I wish you could come downstairs. It's so hot up here . . . Are you sure you need to be worried about the police? I mean, we're all implicated in one way or another . . . ."

"It's too dangerous. Too much important is involved."

"But won't it make them more suspicious if you don't turn up?"

"Maybe. But it's better this way, Pam, believe me. For now."

"Okay, well . . . tell me if you need anything, or Penny. I'm going out tonight, but maybe . . ."

"Don't worry," she said, smiling, patting the newspapers. "I'm only up to 1980."

"We really have to recycle those papers some time," I sighed.

Penny came home and into the kitchen. She was tired but more cheerful than I'd seen her in a few days. "The paper delivery arrived, the typesetting's all done, we'll be ready to start tomorrow. Ray said he'll send out the camera work . . ." She took a carrot and started chewing.

"Did a Lieutenant Detective Parker come by?"

"Yes. I just gave him the story. How you called and I came down to the shop." She seemed reluctant to talk about it. "You know, Ray says he's going to take the shop portfolio around tomorrow and see if . . ."

"I know, but didn't you have a funny feeling about that detective, that he didn't believe you, that something else was going on. He wondered about Zee and he didn't seem that surprised when I said I'd heard Jeremy was an informer . . . ."

"Pam," Penny turned and faced me squarely. "I decided today that I don't want any part of this, this, detective business. I mean, trying to find the murderer ourselves, keeping things back from the police, any relevant information. I didn't know what to tell him when he asked where Zee was, I said she had an emergency and left with her aunt . . . ."

"Thank god," I sighed, but Penny went on:

"I wish we hadn't told Zee she could hide here." Penny's eyes rolled up in the direction of the attic. "I don't know why she had to involve us."

"She's a woman, she's in trouble of some kind, she's one of our collective, she's a woman," I repeated, trying to disguise my sense of betrayal; Zee had said she trusted us and now Penny was withdrawing her support.

"I know, I know, I'm not asking her to leave. But all the same, I don't want to be any more involved than I am now. I guess I'm saying I'd prefer not to deal with her while she's in hiding, while she's feeling the need to hide, because I don't know what it means. I'll leave it to you."

"And Ray."

Penny looked suddenly vulnerable. "If you want my opinion, Ray doesn't want to be involved in this any more than I do."

"I don't care about your opinion," I snapped. "I'm not sorry we're protecting Zee, I'm not sorry that I happen to be concerned about a murder in our very own darkroom. And as for Ray, he's even more of an asshole than I thought he was, abandoning his lover at a time of crisis."

"They're not lovers anymore. And he's not an asshole," Penny said heatedly.

"What do you mean they're not lovers anymore? How do you know?"

"He told me." Penny turned to the sink and began rewashing some radishes.

"Since when are you and Ray Hernandez such confidential friends?" I said, advancing on her.

"Oh, leave me alone, Pam," she said. "And why don't you drop your grudge against him while you're at it? It's about time."

I was too furious to speak and instead slammed out the front door. She could fucking well finish dinner by herself, eat it herself too. Turncoat. Sucking up to Ray now, was she. Goddamn bitch, leaving Zee in the lurch, doesn't even care who murdered Jeremy, doesn't want to be involved, never wants to get involved, a sucker for a male sob-story.

I ran around the block once and then up to the park. By the time I returned I had calmed down considerably.

Penny had just finished sautéing the vegetables and was sitting down to eat in the kitchen. She looked rather forlorn, with her chopsticks, paper towel and glass of water. Her spiky hair looked droopy and a couple of tears were still on her cheek.

"Sorry Sis," I said, coming over to hug her.

She held me tightly. "Me too."

But we didn't talk about it. And that was a mistake.

18

▼ ▼ ▼ ▼ ▼

After dinner I took another shower and put on clean jeans, fresh socks and a tee-shirt that said "U.S. Out of Central America." I re-braided my hair in a dissatisfied way, turning from side to side in front of the mirror. I couldn't get the image of Zee's face as she talked about the prostitutes and factory workers out of my mind. I felt large, white, over-bearing. I wanted to hack off all my hair, start again, do something. I pulled my braid completely away from my face. Exposed, open—but not bad, not bad at all. I peered and preened until Jude banged on the bathroom door.

"Hot date tonight, Pam?"

Well, maybe.

The softball game was between two women's teams, each sponsored by a women's business. Hadley's team, as she'd told me, was the Heats; the opposing team was nicknamed Lesbian Lightning. It was a Friday night game at a small North End playing field, and the few rickety bleachers were packed with ardent women fans, shouting encouragement and giving advice before the game started.

Hadley was instantly recognizable by her height; she stood in the midst of her team, giving them a last-minute pep talk, pushing her gray-blond hair back over her ears with rhythmic intensity and smiling her one-sided smile. Her turquoise eyes glittered even from this distance.

The Heats suddenly split to all corners of the field, taking up their positions. Several of them looked familiar to me, and I recognized Margaret on third and Anna playing catcher. If they saw me in the crowd they gave no sign, but Hadley waved and smiled. Then she took her place on the pitcher's mound.

It came as no shock to me somehow that Hadley would be good, but I was surprised at the skill of both teams. The Lightnings weren't slouches when it came to knocking back Hadley's varied pitches. They got a woman on first right away; the next player did just as well. Hadley struck the third batter out, but the fourth had a bruiser of a swing and belted a low one out into right field. No outs on that one; bases were loaded.

Hadley was putting a lot of concentration into her pitch; she lifted her shoulders, took a couple of steps back and forth, measuring the batter with narrowed eyes. Then she pitched a straight low one right over the plate. Strike. The batter looked more determined. The next pitch came a little higher, a little faster. The batter swung, missed. Strike. Hadley bent down, straightened up, stared concentratedly at the ball, and let fly.

Crack. The ball arched up in a perfect half circle, a sure catch, but the batter and every woman on base got ready to peel out, just in case. A moment of suspended animation—and the outfielder missed it. Shouts, screams. The first batter made home, the second was rounding third and down the stretch for a slide when Anna caught the ball and tagged her out in a dusty flourish. Then, before any of the spectators could blink, the ball sped over to Margaret on third where she quickly caught a Lightning player sneaking on to base. Three out!

The bleachers were palpitating with excitement and so was I. And this was just the first inning. I heard someone remark on the way the Heats had improved since Hadley started pitching; someone else was talking about the inspired combination of Margaret and Anna on third and home, wiping out all those runs.

I saw that I would have to reconsider my suspicions of Margaret and Anna in the light of their softball skills. Could two great ballplayers be murderers, or even saboteurs? Well, it was always possible. They both had a tight-lipped concentration and a connection between themselves that verged on the obsessive. What if they really had believed themselves threatened by the merger, forced to combine with a straight collective against their will? Were they capable of such a strong grudge against Elena that they'd want to off her, believe that they were offing her? Or maybe they'd known it was Jeremy all the time, maybe they were just getting back at Best Printing because B.Violet had been wrecked. Maybe they hated men so much that. . . .

The Heats came up to bat. Hadley was nothing special—a little too loose-limbed maybe for the necessary speed. She hit a good one, but was later tagged out between second and third. The Lightning's pitcher wasn't much more than adequate, but the team had quick outfielders and worked well together.

Once again, Margaret and Anna were the Heats' stars. Anna especially was fast and daring. She was on first before the ball had barely zipped past the pitcher; she stole her way to second, then tore past third to home in the time it would take an ordinary woman to bump into the short stop. Margaret was almost as speedy, and she had a strong swing as well. She hit the home run of the game and nobody acted as if this were unusual.

And if occasionally I thought of Zee in the sweltering attic while I sat outside in the warm summer evening, surrounded by women laughing and shouting and jumping up and down with excitement over the quintessential American game—it was less with guilt than with some renewed sense of hope. After this whole thing had been resolved, Zee and I would become friends. I'd find some way to help her, work with her, support her cause. It didn't matter about Ray; thank god that stupid jealousy was finally over.

The Heats won, 13 to 7.

"Goddamn," I said to Hadley as she pulled off her glove afterwards and rubbed her sweaty face with a towel. "You were great, you were just wonderful. How'd you get so good?"

Hadley swung an arm around Margaret who was passing by. "Dunno. How'd we get so good, M.B.?"

"This is the best we've ever played, I think," said Margaret, smiling at me happily. "We were really hot tonight."

Anna came up, caught sight of me and withdrew a little, but couldn't keep it up. She was jigging in delight. "I'm so up. I'm not one bit tired. I gotta keep moving, keep going."

"Let's go dancing," Margaret suggested and with unforced courtesy turned to me. "Want to come, Pam? To Sappho's or someplace?"

Anna picked up from Margaret that something had changed in my relationship to Hadley, that maybe I wasn't so straight as I looked. "Yeah," she said, hardly missing a beat. "Let's go dancing. Come on, you two."

Hadley paused a moment, looked at me and smiled. "Are you interested?"

I said I could probably be talked into it.

We went by Hadley's first so she could get some fresh clothes and then stopped at Margaret and Anna's so the three of them could shower. Margaret and Anna lived in a house with two other women and their two kids. I had some beer and played a game of checkers with one of the children and talked about the softball game with whichever one of the three didn't happen to be in the bathroom. I still felt a little awkward with Margaret and Anna, but not much. They were really trying now to be friendly and to include me. At first it seemed for Hadley's sake, but more and more it seemed for mine.

About ten o'clock we turned up at that den of iniquity, Sappho's— my first women's bar. Actually, it wasn't such a big deal after all. Dark and loud and full. I'd thought it would feel like an initiation into something subterranean and alluringly perverse, but it was pretty much like any other mixed bar, except that it wasn't mixed.

"You look a little disappointed." Hadley smiled while pulling me out to the dance floor, leaving Margaret and Anna with a pitcher of beer and various acquaintances in a booth at the back.

"Just that I don't play pool."

"Don't play pool, don't play softball, how do you meet anyone?" she laughed, as we joined the others on the floor under the red and blue lights.

The disco beat had turned into a slow Supremes.

The big speech I'd intermittently been working up in my head—how I wasn't a lesbian, but I was sort of interested, but I didn't know, but I sort of wanted to find out, but I couldn't be sure, but I really liked her, but maybe just as a friend—vanished at the touch of her hands at my back, at the feel of her hips against mine. She was tall enough so that her breasts fit neatly into the hollow of my neck. She smelled of some piney soap.

"Oh, I, ah, meet them at meetings, murders, things like that."

Hadley laughed. She bent her head so that her breath touched my ear, but she didn't say anything. My knees were going a bit weak. If Penny could see her twin now. What was happening to me? For a moment my mind spun with theories, fears, desires, then, like a washing machine at the end of its cycle, it rumbled to a comfortable stop. At the bottom of every theory was Hadley's voice, touch, smell.

"Oo-oo-oo, baby, baby . . ."

It was the last slow one for a while. We danced hard and fast, smiling and making jokes, then went back and joined Margaret and Anna.

The sympathy and warmth on Anna's face as she looked from me to Hadley was almost funny. While I felt it wasn't fair of her only to like me as a prospective lesbian, not as myself, I also found myself opening up to her and Margaret, feeling community, a desire to share my discovery, see that it was real.

"You make quite a couple," she said, as Hadley turned to talk with some friends. "You're both good dancers, it's fun to watch you together."

Margaret slid over, nodding in a friendly way. "Have you found out any more about Jeremy?"

I returned abruptly to the present. "We'll leave it to the cops. What about B.Violet?''

"We were there this morning," Anna said. "Still cleaning up. It's almost a lost cause. I wish Fran would turn up so we could discuss what to do about the mess."

"You haven't heard anything? Have you talked to Elena?''

Margaret and Anna shook their fair heads, looked at each other. "You'll probably think I'm off the wall," Anna said. "But I wouldn't be surprised if Elena or Elena and Fran had something to do with the wrecking. Maybe even the murder."

Hadley turned around. "Let's not start that again. Come on, get out there and dance. Anna, you said you wanted to dance and you've been sitting guzzling beer for an hour."

"Nag, nag, nag," Anna said. "I just found out how tired I am, that's all. It's nice to sit."

"It's the beer making you tired," Hadley said. I noticed she'd hardly touched her glass.

"Nah," said Anna stubbornly. "I'm exhausted. I think I just want to go. Margaret?''

"Me too."

"Want to stay a little longer, Pam?" Hadley asked.

"Just a little. I know it's Saturday tomorrow but I've got a lot to catch up on."

"Try another slow one," Anna suggested with a wink, getting up.

Hadley waved her off. When they were gone she asked me seriously, "Did they embarrass you?''

"No. Well, maybe a little. I guess because it's true."

"Shall we follow Anna's advice then? It's a slow one."

After the slow one there was another slow one and then another and by the fourth slow one I was practically a puddle on the floor.

Then the series broke up in a blaze of disco and Hadley said, "Ready to go now?''

"I want to come home with you," I said unsteadily but bravely.

"That's what I want too."

I'd left my car at Margaret and Anna's but decided to leave it until the next morning. In her truck Hadley and I raced up Capitol Hill. It was only when we were on her street, near Elena's, that she spoke. I was so caught up in my fantasies and fears that at first I didn't get it.

She repeated herself. "That *is* Fran's car. She's back. And Elena's light's on."

From her tone I sensed that detective work had suddenly gotten the upper hand of romance. Well, I was interested in what Fran had been up to as well.

"It's after twelve," I said. "But who knows how long Fran's planning

BARBARA WILSON

on sticking around. This may be our only chance."

"My sentiments exactly," she said briskly.

Love would have to wait a little.

19

▼ ▼ ▼ ▼

A t first I didn't think Elena was going to open the door, even when she peeped through the tiny hole and saw it was Hadley and me.

"It's okay, Hadley," she said through the scorched wood. "Everything's okay now. Fran's here and everything's okay."

"I want to see her," said Hadley.

"Well, she's asleep. She's asleep and she's exhausted."

"I don't believe you, Elena. Come on, open up."

She opened up. Fran was sitting resignedly on the sofa, drinking a cup of coffee.

"Hi, Had," she said and nodded to me, "Pam."

She looked tired but relatively tranquil. Her black, white-streaked hair was smooth and her strong forehead gleamed like coated paper. Her eyes were a little bloodshot, but not much. She didn't turn away from Hadley's scrutiny. "Here you see me," she shrugged. "Back in the land of the living."

"Not everyone is, anymore," I put in. "Jeremy, for instance."

Hadley said, "Would you mind telling us where you've been all this time and what you know about what's been going on?"

The gentleness and intimacy of her tone took me aback; what a way to question our star witness. Elena, who'd been fidgeting over to one side, broke in.

"Can't it wait, Hadley? Fran has been through a lot. We've spent the last two hours just getting things straight between us. *Why* do we have to talk about Jeremy and the rest of it now?"

I thought Elena looked worse than Fran, like she was the one who'd been out on a binge. Fran just appeared tired, but Elena was strung out like a nervous cat. Her hair was still greasy and a muscle moved in her slender cheek. There was a slightly rank smell to her, as of too many suppressed feelings. Emotions, like the garbage, should be taken out and dumped once in a while.

I would have given in, gone home, but Hadley was implacable, in spite of her gentleness.

"You can go to bed anytime, Elena. It's Fran's story I'm interested in."

Elena didn't budge, but shot Hadley a look of despair and dislike that astonished me. I'd thought they were friends; what was all this about?

But Fran was speaking, in deep, measured tones, as if her speech were rehearsed. "I know I've put you through a lot, all of you. I can't really say what started it. I remember just feeling angry, at you, Pam, and at Elena, in the Bar & Grill. I get into these things, these drinking things, with the excuse that I'm allowing myself to feel, allowing myself to get in contact with how I really am, bad and strong and not afraid. And I want to lash out." Fran's deep voice had gotten flat now, almost expressionless. "There's a fatalism to it, as if something builds up and then just has to work its way out. I feel it, I don't understand it. And lately, you know, of course, it's been getting out of control. It's scared me to face giving it up though. It's been the only way I've known of getting rid of myself for a while. That's the hardest thing, knowing that without drinking I'd have to be myself all the time."

Elena made an agonized gesture towards her, but Fran brushed it away. "One thing I did today was call AA. The woman I talked to, she really helped me. I've been there, she said, and I knew she had. So I guess I'm going there tomorrow, maybe every day for a while, see if I can stop . . . I am going to stop, I'm going to." She looked around at us wryly, as if she were standing on the other side of a river and looking back. "I'm not asking for congratulations, you know. It's a hard thing to admit you're an alcoholic, like publicly saying you're a failure, you have no control. I wouldn't do it if I weren't so scared." She laughed briefly and smiled at Hadley. "We both have drunks for fathers, Had. How come you didn't turn into one too?"

"I've got my problems too," Hadley said, smiling back with real affection. "Like, I'm queer, you know."

"Yeah, but I'm queer too."

Elena suddenly burst into tears and ran from the room. Fran started to rise, then sat down again. "This has all been hard on her . . . But I guess you came here mostly because you wanted to find out what I know about Jeremy's death, didn't you?"

"Start from the beginning," Hadley said. "You were at the Bar & Grill, and Elena and Pam left around 10:30."

Fran shook her head, rueful. "Let's leave out the time element for now," she said. "If I was wearing my watch I don't remember ever looking at it. I don't remember how long, really, I was anyplace. I do remember being angry, and drinking, and then leaving the Bar & Grill. I don't remember driving. I remember going to B.Violet and seeing a light on, going inside and finding Jeremy."

"What was he doing when you saw him?"

"Cutting up negatives. The office and workspace were already destroyed."

"Weren't you scared?" asked Hadley. "Like he might be off his rocker?"

"Fortunately, I was off mine," Fran said, "so I just went right for him, picking up the first thing I saw, that piece of glass from the light table. The next thing I knew it was morning."

I asked, "Why didn't you call the police? To report him?"

"Because at first I didn't remember anything. I was just lying there surrounded by B.Violet, with an awful headache, and I had no idea what had happened. I didn't remember coming there and smashing up everything, but I was immediately convinced that I had. My only thought was to get out of there as fast as I could, before anybody came in. I couldn't find my car keys, so I just started walking. I walked down the hill to the Arboretum and slept for a while, discovered I still had some money in my pocket and went and had breakfast. It was while I was eating that it started to come back to me . . ."

Or was it then that you began to concoct your story about Jeremy, I might have said—yesterday. But tonight I was trying hard to put myself in Fran's place, to understand, if I could, the frightening world she must have been living in—a jigsaw puzzle gone smash, with pieces everywhere.

Hadley was gentle, but firm. "What did you do after breakfast?"

"Threw up, felt better. Ate some lunch. I walked around some more, thought about calling you and Elena a few dozen times." Fran nodded to Elena who'd come silently back into the room. "I should have, I know . . . . Instead I went and had a beer. I thought it would clear my brain a little, steady me up, make me remember. It did, at least the first couple of beers did. I knew I hadn't done the sabotage and that Jeremy had, and I wondered why. Was it because he hated women so much, because he was so afraid of the merger? Another couple of beers and I decided to call him up and confront him, then I decided it would be better if I went to where he lived and tried to find out the truth, maybe beat him up or something . . ."

"Did you think about anybody else during all this?" I couldn't help bursting out. "Think that your friends might be worried about you, that the rest of us might be getting suspicious?''

Fran shrugged defensively. ''Not really, maybe a little guilty about not letting Elena know where I was—but even that had disappeared after a while. I started to feel sure that I was on to something. The more I thought about Jeremy, the more belligerent I felt. Coming and wrecking B.Violet, he deserved the worst kind of treatment . . . short of death,'' she added, glancing at me. ''I'm only trying to explain how I felt. I never did confront him that evening.''

Once more I distrusted her. Perhaps she just didn't remember killing Jeremy, perhaps she'd blacked it out. Gone looking for him at his house, then came down to the shop and murdered him, came back later when Hadley and I were there, having forgotten already.

''How'd you know where he lived?'' I asked sharply.

''Phone book told me his address. When I got there I saw it was a house divided into studios and apartments. I just looked at the card at the bottom of the stairs. Then I waited.''

''What time was this?''

''It wasn't dark yet, but people were starting to come home from work.''

''Where were you waiting?''

''There were some back stairs, sort of an old wooden staircase, attached to the house. I went up those to the third floor, where his apartment was, waited in the corner by the railing.''

''Did he come home?''

''Yes, through his front door. He wasn't alone though, there were a couple of guys with him. In running suits.''

Hadley and I looked at each other. I couldn't help asking, ''What kind of state were you in?''

''Starting to sober up a little. More or less aware of where I was and what I was doing.''

''Who were the men? Could you see them? Could you hear anything?''

''At first I could hear. They all came in together, turned on the light. The window was open. I scrunched down on the back porch, heard Jeremy said, 'Did you get it?'

'' 'Yes,' someone said. Then some kind of mumbly thing, then 'Wait,' Jeremy said and then he closed the window. I sort of peeked up and over and saw one of the men handing him a package. Then there was a door closing. I figured it was the two men. I started trying quietly to open the door that led to the back of the house, but it was locked. I went down the stairs, and when I looked up again Jeremy's light was off. I was standing next to the side of the house when I saw him come out of the front door, get into his car and leave.''

''Alone?''

''Yes. At least I didn't see the two guys.''

"I wonder if they followed him down to the shop and killed him," said Elena, speaking for the first time since she'd returned to the room. "They were obviously FBI or something. What if Jeremy gave them the wrong information, or he knew too much?"

"It sounds like a dope deal to me," I said. "Everyone knew Jeremy did some dealing. Remember he asked, 'Did you get it?' But I thought he was strictly small time . . ."

Hadley broke into our conjectures. "Let's let Fran go on with her story. Okay, we're up to maybe six or seven on the night of the murder. What did you do then, Fran?"

She looked embarrassed. "Went and had another couple of beers. I guess I thought that if I didn't come down I could keep my courage up and not have to worry about what Elena or anyone else was doing, and what was going on with B.Violet. So I had some beer and felt better and somehow it occurred to me to go down to Best Printing and see if Jeremy was there. I still didn't have my car or my keys. I didn't remember what happened to them. So I took a bus. Walked into your shop and had the shock of my life, thinking it was Elena lying flat out dead there. And that's when I got scared—of having the cops come because he was murdered, and of having them ask me questions. I just had to get out of there."

I recalled her urgency very well. "Where did you go then?"

"I was going to go pick up my car, but I got kind of sidetracked. Went to a bar, had a couple, had a couple more, went home with some friends of mine and had a few more I expect. Then it was the next afternoon."

"That's when you called Elena and told her you thought Jeremy was an informer."

"Yes, I think so. It seemed important to tell someone. I don't remember much about that day. It was blurred. I was feeling pretty bad physically, shaky, just slept on and off. That night they were having a party . . ." She trailed off anxiously, looking at Elena's tight lips. "But that's all over, all over. This afternoon I called the woman at AA and now I'm back. I'm going to change, and I want to help any way I can. The bad part's over, it's really over, Elena . . ." Fran looked suddenly terribly vulnerable and sad, reaching over to her lover.

"It's over, I know," repeated Elena unconvincingly. "Let's go to sleep now, okay?"

Hadley and I sat outside in her truck for a while. "Is Fran off your suspect list?" she asked.

"I think so. Unless it's all some fantasy, some lie she concocted." I shook my head. "Two guys in running suits. . . ."

"There may be a way of confirming her story."

"What do you mean?"

"How are you at breaking and entering?"

"Going to Fran's apartment, looking for evidence?"

"I was thinking more of Jeremy's, actually." She faced me in the car. "Are you up for it, Miss Pam?"

"That's Detective Nilsen, and yes, I think I am."

20 ▼ ▼ ▼ ▼ ▼

I t was just after two in the morning; the sky was clear black with
stars, the air rose-scented. The temperature had dropped enough to
make a jacket necessary—and it was just as well we had something to
cover our tee-shirts: lavender and light blue weren't burglar colors. We
parked a block away from Jeremy's apartment and approached cautiously.

"Let's go the back way that Fran told us about," Hadley whispered.
"See if we can get inside."

I nodded and we crept around, then sneaked up the stairs. At the top
of the broken-down wooden staircase was a narrow landing that led into
the third floor hallway. It was open—after Hadley produced a knife and
jiggled the lock. She tried the same trick on Jeremy's door inside the hall
but without success. It had a double bolt. Hadley didn't seem surprised.
She motioned me out to the narrow landing again, gestured to a window
about four feet away. Jeremy's window.

"You're smaller."

I shook my head vehemently, then reconsidered. The window had a
wide ledge, and a sort of cornice over it. It might be possible to stretch a
leg from the railing of the back porch over to the ledge. You could hold
on to the cornice above and hope to God it wasn't as rotten as the rest of
this building looked.

"I'll try."

I stepped up to the railing and Hadley took hold of my ankle. I stretched and touched the ledge with my left toe, then my whole foot. I leaned up and grabbed hold of the cornice. It felt like it would hold.

"Let go," I told her, not daring to look down. The smell of early summer hit me with redoubled force, mixed with a thin, acrid odor of fear.

I was standing on the window ledge, with my left hand attached for life to the cornice above and my right blindly scrabbling with the window. I couldn't tell if it was unlocked or not. It might just have been painted shut. My left foot wobbled a little on something that felt like dried gum on the ledge.

"Is it locked?" whispered Hadley.

"Can't tell," I muttered, pushing with all my right-handed strength and feeling a sudden give. "No, it's stuck, but it's opening, it's coming."

I got it up about four inches then felt it stick again. "Wait." My hand that had held on to the cornice scraped as it slipped down. I crouched on the ledge, with both hands inside the window now, trying to push up with my shoulder, trying to keep my balance. It was no use. I twisted my head so I could see Hadley.

"I don't think this is going to work."

"That's okay. Can you get back to the porch all right?"

I considered the physical arrangement of my limbs. "I feel secure, but not exactly like I can move."

"I'll reach over." She stood up on the railing and stretched one of her long legs over. I had my entire left arm inside the room now and was still shoving; the other arm grasped Hadley's leg.

"I don't think there's room for the two of us."

"I know," she said. "Use my leg as a balance. I'm steady. And I'll give you a hand back."

"All right," I said, and then for some stupid reason I looked down. Instantly my stomach fell about two thousand feet and I blanched. Three stories is a lot higher than it seems from the earth. Instinctively I recoiled, and hit my head on the window.

"Pam, are you all right? What are you doing? Take my leg, come on."

My mother always said I had a head like cast iron, though that was possibly to excuse herself for dropping me on that knobby part of the body at some family picnic. At any rate, the force with which I had knocked back against the window had dislodged the frame enough so that I could slide it up.

"Hey, we're on," I whispered, a little dazed, starting to climb inside. "Go around to the door, I'll let you in."

I didn't dare turn on any lights, but fortunately it was just one room, with a kitchen and a bath, not difficult to negotiate in the dark. I stumbled and slid on some magazines or newspapers but managed to reach the door and unlock it. Hadley came in and turned on her flashlight.

"I always did have a hard head, luckily," I said.

"I guess you do! What a stunt. You should think about the movies."

"Yeah, too bad the Marx Brothers are no longer in business."

"I was thinking more of James Bond. I could be the love interest . . . Do you think the cops left us anything to look at?" she asked, sending her flashlight's beam on a trip around the room.

"*Someone's* been here, said the little wee bear."

"And it sure wasn't Goldilocks."

Jeremy's studio wasn't so full of junk as it was littered with stuff that belonged in drawers and closets. A certain amount of it was clothes and linen, but there were also ashtrays and beer bottles and coffee cups, and a smell of all three, mixed with the airless dirty scent of a closed-off room.

"I wonder what his family will say when they get here?" I said, lifting up a handful of socks strewn over the floor and staring at the magazines underneath: *Reader's Digest, Hustler, Rolling Stone, High Times, Newsweek.*

"Aren't you surprised that they aren't here yet?" Hadley asked, rummaging through the contents of drawers that had been dumped on the pulled-down Murphy bed. "I mean, it's been two days."

"Maybe that's partly why the cops were here, looking for their addresses. I'm sure Jeremy has family, he's talked about them often enough."

"It could have been the dope mafia here, looking for something, or the FBI, right?"

I had come to a pile of newsclippings stapled together. They were in a manila folder that had slipped down between the table and the sofa. Flipping through them quickly it occurred to me that Hadley still didn't know that Zee was staying with us, that there had been more than a casual connection between Zee and Jeremy. I had meant to tell her something about it, not all, yet still couldn't think how to begin without betraying Zee's trust.

But Hadley had discovered a stack of *Hustlers* and soft-core porn magazines under the bed. "That guy was sick," she said. "Poor June." She suddenly ripped one of them in half. "Christ, I'm starting to get the creeps in here."

I couldn't help shuddering too. June had deserved better than that. We all did. Reading porn had never been grounds for expulsion from a leftist collective, much less for murder, but if I'd know that Jeremy was a fan of *Hustler* I'd never have let him through Best's doors. And for a moment I was only sorry Jeremy was dead because I couldn't tell him so.

I was still holding the newsclippings and wondering if they had any importance. They were from different American dailies, *The Seattle Times*, the *New York Times*, the *Washington Post*, as well as some leftist papers. There were also several from Filipino papers, some in English and some in what I took to be Tagalog. They dated from about three years back, and virtually all of them concerned bombings and protests in Manila. When I turned the flashlight on them more closely I could see pencil marks. There were names underlined, some faintly and some with a check mark. Nothing else, no comments in the margin, nothing to indicate the agitators' interest to Jeremy.

Hadley had gone into the bathroom. "Yuck," I heard her mutter. She was opening the medicine cabinet. On an impulse I took the clippings out of the folder and stuck them in my jacket pocket.

Then I joined her. I'd expected her to be staring at a syringe or something, but apparently her comment had referred to the state of the toilet and the sink, which were obscenely filthy. She was now, for some mysterious reason, fastening a beautiful earring in her earlobe, humming. It was gold and turquoise and shaped like an S.

"It's too bad there's only one," she said. "I just found it in the medicine cabinet. I've always wondered what all those people with one hole in their ear do with the other earring."

"Jeremy didn't have one hole, he had at least five."

"Same difference. . . . I think I'll keep it." She laughed and turned me around, propelling me out of the bathroom. "There's nothing in here, let's try the kitchen."

Ten minutes later we'd finished our search. We found no dope, no incriminating letters, no mysterious tape recorder or tapes, no stashes of money, nothing that could link Jeremy to either organized crime or organized spying. Just a lot of dirt, a dozen porn magazines and the small pile of news clippings stapled together, with names checked or underlined in light pencil.

I wanted to get them home, take another look at them, show them to Zee. There was something about one of the names that seemed familiar. I couldn't remember where or when I'd heard it, but I thought it had been recently. Zee might be able to place it, or jog my memory.

"You want to do anything with the porn magazines?" I asked Hadley as we prepared to leave.

"Spare his family? Prove something to June?"

I shuddered. "No, let's just get out of here." I was feeling more and more paranoid. What if the house were under surveillance, what if we were met by plainclothes police outside, what if drug thugs accosted us on the way back to the car? Would Hadley's new earring and my newsclippings have been worth it?

We left by the back way again, being careful not to go too quickly and give ourselves away. We didn't go around the house again out to the street, but instead through the alley, just in case.

But nothing happened. There didn't seem to be a soul around, not even any frat boys on this warm, rose-perfumed June night. And we laughed as we got in the car, thinking we'd gotten away with something.

21

It was an idyllic sort of dream, an early forties movie about an island paradise where everybody wore sarongs and flowers in their hair, drank from conch shells and lay on green banks of moss under canopies of palm leaves.

I wondered what I was doing here. I was standing in the shallow water of the blue bay with cameras draped around my neck, a notepad in hand. I was wearing a straw hat, big sunglasses and bermuda shorts. The islanders laughed at me, collecting on the beach to point and wave.

Then their spokesperson, their queen, came to greet me, walking quickly and with shy dignity over the sand. She had very black hair and a red and gold sarong around her hips. The film orchestra began to play the overture from "South Pacific." It was Zee and she welcomed me, saying "The Revolution has begun." I noticed that she had a carbine over her shoulder and was now dressed in camouflage and khaki.

Fortunately I was dressed the same by this time, though I didn't have a gun, just my cameras. They were funny cameras, Polaroids, that kept spitting out pictures even when I thought I wasn't taking any. They were mostly action shots, of combat and death; some had people's faces — significant portraits of people I knew but didn't quite recognize.

We were climbing a mountain in the jungle. There were bright parrots in the lianas and the climb was very steep. Zee was leading the way, telling me about the customs and history of her people. I was very moved, I knew they were right to do anything they could to get their country back.

Then I realized that we were climbing a volcano. Zee was gone, everyone was gone, there was only me, with my cameras, again in my bermuda shorts and straw hat and glasses. There was a silence and then I heard it. The volcano was fizzing, it was hissing and spurting. It was mad, it was enraged, it was going to blow and cascade hot lava down on me. The light was suddenly blinding.

I woke to broad daylight and the sound of Hadley's espresso maker. She was bent over something at the table by the window. When I put on my glasses I saw that she was writing intently in a notebook. Her hair looked silvery in the morning light, pushed behind her ears. She was wearing a sort of discount store kimono that came only to mid-thigh. Her legs were bony and bare; her feet were enormous.

"I hope you're putting it all down," I called across the room. "Every single detail."

Hadley looked over and laughed, pretended to read: "Dear Diary, my orgasm last night measured 7.8 on the Richter Scale. And to think, Miss Pam had never been with a woman before!"

"Well, you'll never be able to say that again."

"Uh-uhn!" Hadley closed her journal and got up to fetch two cups. I wondered what she'd really been writing. I never kept a journal myself. I got up a little self-consciously, searched for my clothes, dressed and sat down at the table across from her.

Mornings after great passion can go two ways, at least in my experience. Either you remain connected, can't keep from touching each other, from continuing to want — or else you're embarrassed and constrained, wondering, 'What did I see in this person? Was that really us last night?'

I had a sudden sinking feeling that ours might be a morning like the latter. Hadley was quiet, her bright turquoise eyes preoccupied. She touched me on the arm as she poured my coffee, but didn't sit down.

"Got to go to the bathroom," she said. "Back in a minute."

I waited, anxiously, convinced now that this was going to turn strange. What did I know about her anyway? Nothing. What if she were involved with someone else? What if she'd had second thoughts about me, decided I was too straight, too stupid, too . . . something.

I sipped my coffee and stared at her notebook, square on the table. Had she left it there on purpose, so that I could read it for myself: "June 10. Made a terrible mistake last night . . ."

Well, I wouldn't. She'd have to tell me herself. Or I'd just leave, yes, maybe I should leave right now, before she got back. No, say good-bye at least . . . Good-bye Hadley, thanks for everything . . .

I heard the toilet flush downstairs and suddenly grabbed the notebook, flipped it open and read, "I'm in love, I can't help it." slammed it shut and was standing next to a hanging on the wall when Hadley came in.

I turned to her with a beaming face. "Tell me about your mother, Hadley."

She came over and gave me a long kiss. She had brushed her teeth. "Mmmm. Well. That's from Iran, where she was living when she met my father. She'd graduated in archeology, from Barnard, and was on a dig. It was before the war, late thirties. My father was from an oil family in Texas; they'd sent him over to check out the fields in Iran. I gather it was love at first sight. So my mother became a housewife in Houston. And my father went on making money and drinking. She was bored, bored, bored, and in the early sixties, when I was in high school, couldn't stand it anymore. She found out about some group, some organization where upper middle-class, educated, frustrated people like herself could pay lots of money to go on research expeditions to observe the flora and fauna of the Galapagos or chart the social customs of small French villages or dig around in Turkey. So my mother went to Turkey to help excavate something, and loved it, came back and started taking classes at the university for a graduate degree in archeology. She went again to Turkey the next summer, and finished her degree and went again the next summer and somehow never came back. They got divorced, which gave my father an even better excuse to drink, not that he needed one by that time." ·

"Do you see her very often?"

"Now and then. I've visited her in a couple of places. It's really been amazing to see the change. She was always a very competent person, running a big house, entertaining, all that kind of thing, but she was always a little cold and detached, bored, uninspired. Suddenly, seeing her supervise a dig in Turkey, wearing this straw hat and khaki shorts, and seeing her passion and how everyone paid attention to her and respected her — it was really amazing.

"But we're not really close. She doesn't understand my sexuality — in spite of the fact that she couldn't deal with my father and probably hasn't had sex herself for twenty years and sort of gives the impression that she has no time for men — she just doesn't admit the possibility of putting energy into human relationships, especially with other women. It's a form of wasting time, I suppose. And then, she's been disappointed in my career, I mean, that I don't have one. And I had all the breaks. Went to Sarah Lawrence. Studied economics, of all things . . . "

Hadley had gradually turned away from the Persian wall hanging and had gone back to the table. She poured herself a cup of coffee and her finger tapped gently at the notebook. "I always had the impression that to have a career you had to have something cold, very cold about you. And it was that coldness I could never muster. I always was too sympathetic, too . . . I don't know. I mean, it was fine, it was great for

BARBARA WILSON

her to break away. She'd taken care of my father for years. But he was left without anyone all of a sudden. I felt *responsible*."

She pushed her hair behind her ears again. "When she was doing all the beginning stuff, going to graduate school, I was still in high school. Then I went to college. It didn't take me more than one semester to realize I was a lesbian. It made sense. It was wonderful. I wasn't at all concerned about what to do in life after I made that discovery. I was beginning to feel for the first time, that's all I wanted to do. Then my mother left my father and he was all alone and I just went back there. Stayed eight years. In my father's house. In Houston."

I went over and put my arms around her neck. We remained like that for a moment, then she said, "Well, let's not get into all that right now. Tell me about yourself." She suddenly laughed and turned to me, pushed me into the chair next to her and cuddled close. "Tell me what it's like to be a twin, for instance. Did you use to play tricks when you were growing up?"

"Oh, of course, especially when we were really young, in grade school, and looked more alike. And later, too, in junior high, we'd sometimes take each other's tests. Penny was good in math and I was better at English. We either got bored or guilty about it after a while — Penny sitting through two algebra tests, me writing two English papers. And anyway, when you get older your interests separate. I remember in high school especially we had some serious fights. We'd try to find ways to act *extremely* different from each other, then we'd resent each other's behavior. I remember that whenever Penny went out with any especially repulsive guys that I hated it. I felt it reflected on me."

"Were you each other's best friend?"

"I suppose, in some ways. There was this underlying loyalty. You didn't gossip about your twin the way you would have about someone else. But otherwise, she had her friends, I had mine. After high school we each moved out and lived with different people. That was the most distant time . . . I missed her. But we were determined to separate ourselves. Actually, a lot of it came from other people — all the time, saying, 'Isn't it cute?' 'Twins, oh darling!' It was debilitating enough to be raised as a little girl in the fifties and sixties, but there's something about twins that really brings out the insipid worst in most people."

"But now you don't really look very much alike," Hadley said, beginning to stroke my leg with her hand. Prickles followed in her wake.

"I know. It's surprising sometimes. And a little sad. Because it was reassuring in the past to look over and know what you looked like."

"Maybe this is too personal, but what will Penny say about you getting involved with me?"

I shook my head. "I used to know what she thought about everything, or at least be able to put myself in her position. Now, it's harder, but we still don't judge each other much. She'll understand."

Hadley was still rubbing my leg. She pretended to yawn. "We had a late night last night — aren't you tired?"

I forgot that I'd meant to rush off; I forgot that I still had the clippings in my pocket, that I wanted to find out how Zee was and that I wanted to ask her some questions.

I yawned too. "I am, a little . . . Maybe we'd better lie down again."

"Good idea."

22

▼ ▼ ▼ ▼ ▼

B y the time I got home it was after noon, and though I felt relaxed I didn't feel particularly awake. Sam and Jude were still sitting over breakfast at the dining table, reading the paper and eating bran muffins and cheese. Or maybe they were having lunch.

"Just getting in?" Jude asked curiously.

"Mmmm. Where's Penny?"

"Out back. Working in the garden."

"Mind if I have one of these? Thanks."

I went through the kitchen and out the back door. In the morning the garden was partially shaded by a big apple tree, but now it was brilliantly green and sunny. Penny was hoeing in the corner, around the tomatoes and green beans.

"Hi," I said cheerfully. "Need some help?"

She gave me an unimpressed look. "So where have you been?"

I began to pull weeds by hand around the broccoli. "Give you two guesses."

"I never would have thought . . . " she began.

" . . . that I'd turn out gay?"

"You're not gay with one . . . encounter," she contested. Her hair was sticking straight up and, what with her red bandanna, she looked like a disapproving Bantam. "What I mean is that you hardly know the woman. Besides, the atmosphere's so hectic now . . . "

I hadn't meant to argue; I would have preferred to bask in her approval and share my good fortune over having discovered Hadley, sexuality and feeling of a new kind. I said coolly, "As I recall, you and Doug were in each other's pants about a minute after you were introduced. So how is this different?"

"But . . ." Penny said, then sighed and turned back to hoeing. "When it's B.Violet that caused this whole mess and everything," she muttered.

I felt like I'd been slapped. "What do you know about it?" I leapt over a row or two of cabbages to confront her. "Why B.Violet more than Best — because they're lesbian? But you've been playing Miss Don't Get Involved for days. A lot of things have happened this week and you don't want to know any of them. You're still part of the collective though; you've got to take some responsibility for the mess that Jeremy's created. You can't just shove it on to B.Violet. But no, you don't even want to deal with Zee . . ."

"Not so loud," Penny said. "She'll hear you."

"What I want to know," I whispered violently, "is why we never suspected Jeremy of anything. How was it that he fooled us into thinking he was this laid-back, spacey type with no thought in his head except how to get tickets to the Rolling Stones?"

"Look, Pam," Penny said. "Leave it to the cops. Don't go around getting mixed up in things. It was one thing at the beginning, but it's gotten more serious. Look, it's not you getting involved with Hadley that I mind so much as the idea of the two of you running around playing amateur detective."

A fleeting picture of myself clinging to Jeremy's third story window early this morning passed through my mind. I was glad Penny hadn't been a witness to that.

I said, "How can you — a progressive, a feminist, a leftist — be so certain that the cops will take care of everything? Especially if Jeremy was some kind of informer? For all we know he may have damaged the lives of a lot of people in some way. The cops aren't going to expose him, Penny. Wake up!"

"You wake up," she said, her hair fanning out like a halo of anger. "Just how do you think Best Printing is going to survive if you're spending all your time playing Nancy Drew? We've hardly gotten anything done all week. June and Zee haven't been in, Elena's a mess, Jeremy's dead and you're pretending like you're on a leave of absence or something. We were depending on that job from the city we had to turn down. I haven't known what to tell people who've called for bids. Call back next week when things have calmed down? Or next month? Or never? We've got to pay our bills, Pam. We can't afford to just stop. If it hadn't been for Ray . . ."

I was about to light into her for her capitalistic attitude — didn't she realize that one of our collective had been murdered and that meant that our entire political community might be threatened — how could she talk about work, about keeping going — but something in the way her voice had softened and her eyes had turned away slightly at the end of the sentence, gave me pause. A hideous suspicion formed in my mind.

"And where were you last night?" I said roughly, grabbing her shoulder.

Penny jerked away. "Leave me alone. You act like you have some right to him, and it's been almost a year, Pam. I've . . . cared about Ray for a long time. Besides, what does it matter to you anyway if you're a lesbian now?"

I was totally enraged, enraged and betrayed. My very own identical twin fucking the man who had broken my heart; it was too much. I didn't feel one bit like a happy lesbian who has just seen the light. I felt like a scorned and lonely heterosexual woman who's just about to hit her beloved sister with a hoe.

"I can't believe it." I finally found words. "After I told you what a creep he was to me. And what about Zee? She's his lover. It's incredibly disgusting to think that while she's hiding up in our attic you're messing with her boyfriend."

"Would you keep your goddamn voice down!" Penny whispered at a screaming pitch. "I told you before, Zee and Ray aren't lovers anymore."

"Since when?" I snarled back. "Since last night?"

"Since about a month ago," came the familiar accent of Zee herself from the attic window above us. She had shoved her head out and was peering down at us. I could see her smiling. "Besides, it wasn't so serious between us. Do you know, he told me he likes you, Penny. I'm so happy for you."

I was feeling more and more like a fool. I wanted to say something gallant and superior. Instead I began methodically to crush a small brussels sprout plant under my foot.

Penny was laughing up at the attic window. "Keep inside, Zee. Who knows who's watching? Pam's convinced this is all a dangerous plot."

Too much. Too fucking much. I turned and walked back through the garden and into the kitchen, up the stairs and into my bedroom. Why had I forgotten to tell Hadley the bitter truth about being the twin of someone who knew how to get under your skin in every possible way, on every possible occasion? As I lay on my bed, wretched memories of past tricks Penny had played on me came vividly to mind. That time in junior high when I'd been so crazy about David What's His Name and she'd pretended she was me and had gone up one day in front of a whole crowd of his friends and said, 'Will you go steady with me?'

I should have killed her then. I shouldn't let it have gotten to this point fifteen years later when she could make my life a living hell. The fact that Hadley had given me so much pleasure last night and this morning too, was immaterial now. Ray and Penny in bed together — it was incestuous, that's what it was. We might not look alike but we had exactly the same body build . . .but what if she were a better lover than I? What if Ray thought so?

Yeah, and there had been that time in grade school when Penny and I had both been enamored of the same little girl, a charmer from Morocco or Algeria, with big brown eyes and curly black hair. We had both asked her separately if she wanted to be friends with us. And she had chosen Penny. She had said Penny was nicer!

I wept miserably into my pillow. Oh, no one knew what it was to be a twin, to have someone around all the time who knew your weaknesses and could exploit them. Who was so much like you but better. It was like being compared all the time to your better half. It was hideous. We should never have tried to live together, work together, anything. Most twins lived separate lives, moved to different cities, had families of their own. They didn't keep jerking into each other like puppets controlled by the same hand.

I cried myself out and slept long and deeply. Once during the afternoon there was a knock at the door; Jude called out that there was a phone call for me.

I ignored it and buried my head deeper.

When I finally got up it was almost six and I was the only one in the house. Jude had left a message: *Hadley called. We've gone for a swim. See you at dinner?*

I made myself some iced tea and called Hadley. Earlier we'd talked about taking a picnic dinner to Lake Washington. No answer. Well, she wouldn't want to waste a nice day by waiting around for me to call. I had a headache and still felt out of sorts. I wandered into the living room, looked at magazines, did a few stretching exercises.

I was just getting ready to go up and visit Zee when Penny walked in the front door.

"Hi," she said, and looked uncertain. Then she came into the living room and sat across from me.

"Still mad at me?"

"I don't know," I said. "Remember that David in junior high? That was really a rotten thing to do, asking him to go steady."

Penny nodded. "I know. You got back at me though, remember. You told that slimy Roger that you, 'Penny', had had a crush on him for a long time. I had a hard time getting rid of him." She paused, laughed, and then when I didn't laugh back, said, "Are you planning to get back at me for this?"

Then I did laugh. "Like put a slug in your bed? God, Pen, we don't even look alike anymore—I wouldn't even know how to play a trick on you — not the same kind of trick anyway."

"If you cut your hair I bet you could."

"Actually I've been thinking of it . . . for other reasons."

"Do it," she said.

All of a sudden we were friends again.

"You don't really mind," she said. "About Ray and me? I mean, *really* mind? It's making me happy right now."

"I'll get used to it. Besides, he's about a thousand times better than Doug."

"You're not kidding. And Pam, I'm sorry if I was weird about you and Hadley . . . well, all I want you to know is that I like her, she's nice."

"Don't get any ideas," I said, then added, "It doesn't upset you, that I might become a lesbian?"

Penny shook her punk head. "I might even envy you. It's often seemed a far more sensible course."

"In that case, what do you think about dinner?"

"Anything but fresh vegetables," she said. "I'm getting sick of them. Can't we go out and get Chinese food, take it up to Zee? We could have a little party before Sam and Jude get home. I persuaded them not to come back for dinner, said you were in a bad mood . . ."

"Sounds good. Is that the door?"

"I'll get it."

I was close behind her when she opened it. On our porch stood two uniformed Seattle policemen, one of whom was holding a piece of paper.

"I have a warrant here, for the arrest of Zenaida Oberon Plaice," he said, self-importantly.

"What?" said Penny and I in shocked unison. "Who?"

"Mrs. Jeremy Plaice, wanted on the charge of murdering her husband." And when Penny and I still didn't respond, the cop added in a slightly more human voice that they knew she was here because they'd seen her just a few hours ago.

Hanging out the attic window.

23

The murder of Jeremy Plaice had merited one short paragraph on an inside page of the newspaper the day after it happened: "Man, 25, found dead of a gunshot wound at 9 p.m. in Seattle print shop. No immediate suspects." We'd wondered a little then how June had escaped a publicity blitz, but laid it all to the speed with which Marta Evans had acted.

This time there was no such luck. The main headline in the Sunday paper the next morning was something to do with unemployment, but the second headline announced in bold: **FILIPINO WIFE SUSPECT IN MURDER CASE.** And below it "Secret Marriage Revealed." The article went on to inform us of all sorts of new things. Jeremy Plaice had spent three years in the Navy at Subic Bay. His parents in California suspected his wife, Zenaida Plaice, née Oberon, of using their son to stay in the United States. There was mention of Zee's prominent "opposition" family, of her nursing studies and of her involvement in a local anti-Marcos group. No mention of forging and no mention of what the cops actually had on Zee, but plenty of insinuation. And there were our names too: "Penny and Pamela Nilsen, owners of Best Printing where the two were employed, were hiding the murder suspect in their attic."

"I wonder why we're not being charged as accomplices," I said.

"Employees!" said Penny. "Can't they ever get it straight?"

"I'm sure we'll have lots of opportunities to explain to the press just what a collective is," I said, glancing out the window. A man with a camera and notebook was walking up to the porch. "But I'd rather not bother."

We didn't answer the doorbell.

"In your attic?" Marta had said last night. "Pam, you haven't been playing fair."

"We never thought she'd murdered Jeremy," I protested. Of course we never imagined that she'd married him either.

"If you're suggesting that I defend her, a murder suspect," Marta said. "I'm afraid I don't have the resources."

"What about June? You were ready to help her."

"That was an emergency. And they hadn't charged her with anything either. It was procedural, a civil rights issue. This is different. His wife, they said? Now you're talking murder."

"Marta, I'm going to call you later. Think about it. We really need some help, your help."

I didn't have to call her back. She called us.

"Saw Zee at the jail," she said briskly. "She's all right. Don't talk to anyone and meet me at my office tomorrow morning. Jeez," she added. "How do you girls get into these things?"

There were others besides Marta and various reporters who wanted some explanation. Hadley, for instance.

When we got back from Marta's office Sunday morning she was waiting on the doorstep. She sputtered when she saw me, "Married! Attic! I've got to talk to you."

Penny gave me a reassuring look and passed into the house. Penny thought she understood — but she didn't really. Hadley had thought she and I were in this together. She felt betrayed.

"You could have told me, you could have *mentioned* that you knew a bit more than I did."

We'd started walking. I wanted to touch her but was afraid to. "I know," I said. "But Zee had asked us to keep her whereabouts quiet. And besides, I didn't really know anything. Zee came over in the middle of the night Thursday and said she needed a place to stay. It was Penny who figured out what she and Jeremy had been doing."

"What?"

"Forging documents for aliens. The cops or FBI must have been on to them somehow and when Jeremy got killed it was an easy deduction that one of his partners must have done it."

"But there was nothing about that in the paper," Hadley protested. She had her gray-blond hair behind her ears and was beginning to look interested rather than mad.

"The detectives are probably trying to put together the pieces and round up the suspects or whatever they do. They probably haven't said anything to the reporters — and the newspapers are making do with the racist angle: Filipino woman kills white husband after using him to stay in the country. Though they might start using the jealousy motive too if they find out about June. I bet they will . . . Christ, what a mess."

"But what about Zee — do you think she could possibly have done it? Have you seen her since she's been arrested? What are they charging her with? What's the proof?" Hadley was her old self again and walking quickly now; I had to jump to keep up with her long strides.

"The proof is just circumstantial, I think. The marriage, her disappearance after the murder, hiding — and of course, her being Filipina. No fingerprints or weapons yet, no witnesses, though you and I and Penny will all be on the stand, I'm sure."

We'd reached the point where the park dipped down into the ravine. Lush green trees carpeted the sides; down below on the path joggers ran back and forth like missionary ants.

"What about you?" asked Hadley in a low voice. "Do *you* think she did it?"

I stood staring down. "I don't want to think that," I finally said. "I'm afraid sometimes it's hard not to."

We sat down close together on the grass. I felt hopeless and depressed. I was remembering the sight of Zee being escorted down our attic steps and out the front door, handcuffed. I'd felt like we were handing over Anne Frank to the Nazis. And all because of stupid sisterly jealousy, stuff we should have given up twenty years ago. I had wanted to hug Zee, to at least touch her as she went by, but the cops quickly forestalled any displays of emotion. She was a dangerous murderess in their eyes, not our friend and co-worker. Zee had managed to smile though, as if she were thinking, So what? In the Philippines I'd be dragged off by my hair and mutilated.

She was in the King County Jail now, though tomorrow after the hearing she'd probably be out on bail. Marta hadn't been all that encouraging, could only say she'd do her best to help me and Penny to find a good trial lawyer for Zee. She'd warned us again not to talk to anyone but her right now; and then made us tell her and write down how we remembered the last week, starting with the merger meeting on Tuesday.

I'd left out a certain amount. Kite flying and softball and Sappho's — and breaking into Jeremy's apartment. Even so, there was more than enough. Marta had kept shaking her frizzy head.

"There are so many confusing things here. This sabotage, for instance — how can it be related? But it happened just before the murder. There must be some link."

But what link? Zee hadn't been involved in the wrecking of B.Violet. She'd hardly paid attention during the whole discussion of the merger. We had only Fran's word that it had been Jeremy who destroyed everything — the word of an alcoholic on a binge.

Hadley broke into my thoughts. "But if Jeremy *was* informing on someone *to* someone, spying . . ."

I interrupted her. "We have only Fran's theory that he was spying on us or on anyone. It's based on her seeing him give a package to two men. It could have just as easily been dope as secret papers." I was thinking, Fran again. Strange how someone so piss drunk could have been so many places and concluded so much.

Hadley was musing. "Who was Jeremy? Really? I still don't know, even after having been through his things. Porn, earrings, new wave music, dope — what else, Pam? Subic Bay, the Navy in the Philippines. Is there a connection?"

I remembered suddenly the small stack of clippings about demonstrations in the Phillipines. I'd forgotten to look at them as closely as I'd wanted to, to see if I could remember where I'd seen that one came from. I'd never managed to show them to Zee either.

"If this were a movie," I said, "We'd be on the next plane to L.A. to talk with his parents — and from there it'd be a quick cut to the swarming, steamy streets of downtown Manila." I sighed. "Real life is always so low-budget."

"If we went to California," Hadley said, "We could pretend we were sleazo detectives . . ."

"Seedy motels and luxurious estates . . ."

"Dazzling blonds answering the door in negligees . . ."

"Just trying to corrupt us."

"Yeah!" said Hadley enthusiastically. "What about the telephone?" she added in a more thoughtful voice.

"The telephone?"

"You know — long distance after five p.m., before eight in the morning . . . More our speed."

"Call his family? Find out more about him?"

"It's someplace to start anyway," she said.

We returned to the house to find June had arrived. She looked furious, holding the newspaper front page in her hand.

"This is true? They were jesus fucking married?"

"I think it was just convenience," I said. "To help Zee stay in the country."

"That motherfucking two-timer," June said, with some measure of wonder in her voice. "No wonder she offed him."

"Hey, keep it down, June," I said nervously. "Come inside." No telling anymore who was lurking around the neighborhood. The three of us went inside to find Penny and Ray sitting on the living room sofa.

"I didn't know we were having a collective meeting this morning," I tried to joke. "Or else I would have made some coffee cake." I still wasn't sure how at ease I could feel with the reality of Penny and Ray as a couple. In deference to my sister I could no longer malign Ray as an ex-boyfriend or even ignore him. I would have to start making some effort at friendly co-existence.

"Since we're all here," said Ray, "Maybe we should discuss this latest event." I noticed he was looking only at June, or possibly at my left ear, too. I wondered if Penny had told him about me and Hadley and what he thought. The idea of them discussing me made me flush, first with embarrassment, then with anger.

I said, instead, coolly and calmly, "We're not all here."

"But Zee," Penny began.

"I was thinking of Elena."

Penny looked almost blank for an instant and I thought how easily Elena had stepped back from the collective. Essential neither at work nor at decision-making.

"This is just informal," said Ray.

"Then you don't mind if Hadley stays too," I said smoothly.

There was a slight pause. Hadley obviously was supposed to back down at this point, to say, "Oh, I've got to be going, thanks anyway." But she didn't.

"It's fine with me," said June. And then Penny and Ray nodded too.

"Look," said Hadley. "I don't mean to be too obvious, but we've got a murder on our hands, and every one of us is under suspicion in some way. Every one of us is going to be questioned and every one of us has the chance of being called to the stand. June because she was lovers with Jeremy, Pam and I because we found him, Penny and Pam because they were hiding Zee, and Ray because he also worked at Best Printing and was the last one there that night. I know we all have a horror of getting involved, but it seems like we don't have a choice. At least we should get our stories straight and make some general agreement not to talk about ourselves to people who are going to use it against us. At best we might possibly work to help come up with a defense for Zee . . ."

"But no one here thinks that she actually killed him," Ray burst out of his black beard. "It's impossible. She's not that kind of person at all . . ." He stopped just as abruptly and looked around. "*You* don't, do you?" He asked June. "After your experiences . . ."

June bent her small, close-cut head. "Mistakes happen," she said, almost inaudibly. "They could have been arguing, maybe he pulled a gun and she . . . I don't know," she said. "Don't want to conjecture. People's reasons are their reasons, sometimes no rhyme or reason at all."

Penny also shook her head. "It's not important to me to know the answer. I'll support her either way."

"Pam," Ray said, almost imploringly, staring at me. I almost replied the way he wanted, for old times sake. But I said nothing. I just didn't know.

"Well, I don't think she did it," said Hadley firmly. "And I want to find the person who did."

24

An hour later we'd come to some decisions and divided the responsibilities in what seemed a suitably collective way. Ray would stay in touch with Zee's Filipino group, especially Benny and Carlos, and help rally support for her; Penny would be the link to Marta and the new lawyer and everything judicial; Hadley and I, with June's help, would keep conducting our private investigation into Jeremy's life, as well as X's motives for killing him. We also agreed that, for now, nothing was to be said publicly about the merger idea or sabotaging of B.Violet. That would only confuse things.

Although I agreed to this, I couldn't help feeling that Fran was getting off too lightly. Hadley and I would probably have to testify how we'd found Jeremy; Fran wouldn't. Fran had been the one who said she saw him destroying B.Violet, who'd supposedly seen him being passed a parcel by two men. But Fran wasn't being held responsible for any of this, by any of us.

Finally, we decided that we would start back to work tomorrow *for sure* and that, at least temporarily, Hadley would take over Jeremy's job in the darkroom.

"What about Elena?" June asked, standing up and stretching her compact body. Her round, hazelnut eyes looked tired; she yawned.

No one answered. Penny and Ray were halfway out the door to buy food for the barbecue here later this afternoon; Hadley was talking about going swimming, and I was thinking about Hadley in a bathing suit. I didn't know whether June meant we should tell Elena about our plans or to get her to start coming into work again too. Personally I felt that Elena had had more than enough to cope with lately; she wasn't really needed anyway.

"So you and Hadley are going to do some investigating," June said suddenly. "What kind of help do you want from me?"

It felt awkward. In dividing up the tasks, no one had wanted to acknowledge one painful fact: That until a few days ago June and Jeremy had been lovers. In spite of her anger she must have cared about him. Maybe a lot. Maybe a lot more than she was willing to let on.

June had dropped back into the chair and was regarding us. "Or do you want any help at all?"

"Of course we do," I said. "You knew Jeremy better than we did. How he spent his time, with whom, what kind of stuff he might have been playing around with . . . It's just a question of whether you want to talk about any of it to us . . ."

I trailed off. I had the sudden feeling that June had put up a wall against me, that I'd said something wrong. She was tapping a sneakered foot in a complicated rhythm on the carpet, containing something.

"You're just curious, that it? Think I might have the key, not even know it myself?" June paused, then looked directly at me and her look wasn't friendly. "Listen. I may not be proud of being with a guy who was screwing other women, a guy who was married to someone else. I may even think there was something pretty nasty about that guy — yeah, there was for sure — and I may want to find out why he was killed as much as you do, maybe more . . . But I don't want to be your negro doing your work for you. And I'm not about to go confessing my private life so you can figure out the mystery and take the credit."

"Christ, June," I said, shocked. "You know me better than that. I'm not interested in exploiting your private life, and I sure don't expect you to do my work for me."

"Don't you?" she said, standing up and going to the door. "Listen, Pam, I know you went around with Ray and maybe got some looks, but believe me, it was nothing like what Jeremy and I got. I mean, Ray can talk up a storm about racism; he's not joking when he tells that story about them practically kicking his ass out of town there in Utah when his car broke down — they didn't know if he was a chinaman or a chicano, but they didn't like either one — but you know as well as I do, Ray's got privileges most everybody else is just dreaming about."

What was she getting at? Her voice was no longer angry, just a little flat, a little dangerous. I realized she didn't know I was involved with Hadley now — and also that Hadley hadn't known I'd been involved with Ray. I stammered, "Well, I, we . . ."

June was leaning against the door. "Jeremy and I might have been black and white, but we did have some things in common, especially in your collective. Before he got there I was the youngest, before he got there I was the only one who'd never been to college, much less had some kind of graduate degree. We'd been around in ways you can't even imagine. Sure, your politics impressed me; I didn't know beans about no revolution, girl," she laughed shortly and opened the door to go. "I guess I still don't."

"But we need your help, June." I wanted to explain: Look, I've fallen in love with Hadley and that's part of what's happening here, that's maybe why we seem like some kind of team, but I couldn't find the words. I mumbled instead, "Penny said you *wanted* to help . . ."

"Yeah, but you and Penny are two different kettles of fish," June said, hand on the door knob. "She's not afraid to jump out of an airplane, for one thing."

"So, does this mean you don't want to help us?" Hadley asked calmly.

"I mean to follow some leads on my own," said June. "We'll see who gets there first." She gave us a curious smile and disappeared out the door. "See you later!"

When Penny came back from the store I told her what had happened.

"It's not my fault I'm too chicken to skydive — and now June thinks I'm being racist."

In spite of her concern Penny seemed amused. "Don't forget ageist and classist."

She was peeling fruit for a salad, and Hadley had taken a hand in hulling the strawberries.

"I can't help feeling that June is hiding something," Hadley said. "Are you sure she didn't know anything about the forging? I mean, who was printing that stuff, anyway?"

"June's no murderer," Penny said. "She's been hurt and now she's pissed at being offered some minor role in something that's still a big emotional thing for her. You want her to share her information, but you don't want to share anything with her."

Ray had been outside getting the charcoal fire going in the rusty old barbecue. He came in looking for the grill. "Maybe the collective method doesn't work so well when it comes to solving crimes," he said. "But I'm interested in what June said about what she and Jeremy had in common. It makes sense that they'd be drawn to each other and against us. A class issue, why didn't I ever think of that before?" he wondered, pulling at his black beard.

"You're so goddamned theoretical all the time," I exploded. "June has practically accused me of being a plantation mistress and as usual

BARBARA WILSON

you've totally missed the point."

For answer Ray threw a convenient banana in my direction and slammed out the back door.

"Not again," groaned Penny and went after him.

"Now I think I see why you didn't tell me about this previous relationship," Hadley said. "Still a little rocky, eh?"

A cookout that was actually cooked-out — what could be more unique and thrilling in the Northwest? Although most of our backyard was taken up with the garden, we still had a patch of grass and a rectangular courtyard our family — hauling flat rocks from the beach — had built many summers ago. The evening had that northern slant of light that seems to last for hours without fluctuating. A golden evening fringed with green leaves, smelling of roses, sounding of children, with hamburgers and sourdough rolls and baked beans and buttered corn on the cob and five kinds of salad: fruit, spinach, pasta, carrot and potato. It was rare to be able to sit outside like this, without a sweater anyway, in the evening during a Seattle summer — though year after year we bundled into our jackets and blankets at eight o'clock and huddled around the barbecue, pretending we were in San Diego.

Sam and Jude came back from a day hiking; phone calls brought neighbors and friends. June returned in an apparently chipper mood with her daughters Amina and Ade.

Penny greeted her as if nothing had happened; she got June husking corn and she herself played a game of tag with the girls. To Amina and Ade she was Auntie Penny, though four-year-old Amina thought it was pretty hilarious to call her Auntie Nickel, Auntie Quarter or sometimes even Auntie Million Dollar.

I couldn't help noticing, in my present guilty mood, that there were no other Blacks here — though there *was* Ray's friend Bill Asuka and his new Korean-American girlfriend, Evelyn, and Maggie Chin, the Taiwanese student from next door, and Ray himself . . . but what was wrong with me, anyway, counting like this?

I remembered suddenly what Penny had said to me one day, "You know, Pam, you worry about being called racist as if it were syphilis or something. Like you were accused of carrying some dread, disfiguring, incurable disease. But I think it's more like telling someone or being told, 'Hey, you've got snot hanging out of your nose.' You say thank you and wipe it off. Though that doesn't mean the snot's not going to ever drip again."

"Gross! You're always so disgusting, Penny!"

But it was true. I worried much more about racism than she did, resisted the charge, would do anything to avoid it . . . No wonder June felt more comfortable with Penny than with me. Penny treated her like a human being; I treated her like a symbol of something I was terribly afraid of not pleasing — or just plain terribly afraid of.

June seemed ready, at any rate, to put the afternoon behind her.

"About this, this investigation stuff," I said, sitting down on the step above her and her children on the back porch after dinner.

"No problem, Pam. I've been thinking about it and I decided that what you and Hadley have going for you is objectivity. I've got a lot to deal with on my own. I don't want to be getting much more involved than I already am."

Surprisingly I wasn't relieved. "But you could tell us a lot . . . we could tell you, too . . ."

"Probably not much more than you could find out on your own. Jeremy was a closed-up guy, remember. Anybody who could keep a marriage secret didn't go around spilling any other kind of beans."

Could it be true, as Hadley suggested, that June was hiding something? She didn't look one bit secretive at the moment. Ade and Amina were sitting on either side of her, quietly figuring out what half-eaten corn cobs could be made to do.

"What about your leads — you said you were going to follow up some leads?"

June shrugged her small strong shoulders. She was wearing a tube top that showed them off to perfection. "I guess I just had too many sunbeams this afternoon." She changed the subject.

"So, what's this Penny tells me about you and Hadley?"

"Oh . . . just one of those things . . ."

"Well, I wish you luck." She looked a little doubtful. "Just kind of happened, huh? Just like that?"

I couldn't say I'd always been a lesbian. Some of it definitely had to do with Hadley.

"I like her a lot, you know."

We watched Hadley throwing a ball with some kids in the alley. Her long arms flew around like the hands of a large clock; her silvery hair whirled around her plain face. She was having a great time.

"Well, she's tall, anyway," June said charitably.

Later the full moon went up like a handheld prop in a cheap stage production, far too decorative to be anywhere out in space. Our guests lingered on and on, even though it was Sunday night, Monday morning tomorrow. They had to marvel over and over at the magical weather, feel the warmth and moonlight on their bare skins.

I looked over and saw Amina and Ade sleeping on June's lap, and Penny talking to her in what seemed a serious manner.

"We're just talking about the possibility of June going away for a while," Penny said, when I joined them a little hesitantly. "There's still

BARBARA WILSON

a good chance that the press could pick up on her initial arrest. I'd like to spare her that."

"Go where?"

"Well, my sister lives in California, Oakland . . ." June didn't sound too sure. "I don't know . . ."

"I think it's a great idea," insisted Penny. "A change of scene would do you good. Don't worry about the shop. We'd call you if we felt we couldn't handle it."

"You wouldn't be trying to get rid of me?" June asked mildly. She glanced from Penny to me.

"If anyone deserves a vacation," I said, "it's you."

"Deserving ain't always getting." She stretched and stood up. "But what the hell. I'll leave tomorrow."

25

▼ ▼ ▼ ▼

Hadley and I slept together again that night. Not at my house—I still wasn't quite ready to deal with Sam and Sapphism together at the breakfast table—but in Hadley's bed under the skylight. We drank some tea and then a little wine and lit a candle and made love. It wasn't the full display of fireworks as the first time, when I'd wondered what was going to happen next, but it was still just fine. More play and perhaps more satisfaction. My orgasm poured down into my toes instead of up through my cortex and out the top of my head.

Afterwards I asked her to tell me about her father.

"Now? Why?"

"I want to know about your life. You were close to him . . ."

"This is always the time when I want a cigarette," she interrupted. "And I never smoked in my whole life. I'm sure I saw too many French films as a teenager and they did permanent brain damage."

"Have a candle instead," I offered, passing it to her.

"The wax makes such a terrible mess of the sheets, you know—when it drips. Besides, you nasty little Freudian, if you think I'm going to talk about my father with a stubby pink candle in my mouth . . ."

We tussled a minute, laughing, then Hadley asked, with a shake of her silverstraw hair, "Do you know how attractive money is? Sure you do. Money is very attractive. And so kind and charming as well. It can afford to be. Yes, he got drunk, but even then he was charming. When I was small he'd sit me down beside him and hold long conversations with me, always treating me like an adult woman. 'Your mama doesn't understand me,' he'd say. 'But you do.' He was tall and well-built with funny eyes like mine. And there were presents and trips and everything nice for his little girl . . . who didn't understand why her parents didn't get along, just like Shirley Temple, but who couldn't do anything about it . . .'' Hadley broke off, pulling up the sheet with a sudden movement to her bony shoulders. She had soft warm freckles on her chest and upper arms, and a streak of white scar tissue from a broken arm.

"Didn't his work suffer because of his drinking?"

"Money doesn't have to work, don't you know that? Besides, he was more or less just a figurehead. He and his older brother, Uncle Bob, had inherited the business, but Uncle Bob ran it. Dad was a superfluous vice-president with a fancy title. As long as he didn't cause problems he had an office in the main building in Houston—later the polite term was 'working out of the house.'"

"He stayed home then?"

Hadley just nodded. Eight years she'd spent in Houston after college, taking care of him. What had her life been like, what had happened to make her leave? I didn't know how to ask those questions. Instead, I asked something that had occurred to me several days ago.

"Hadley, it's not just your family . . . I mean, *you* have money too, don't you?"

She looked at me for a moment with her clear turquoise eyes and, though she didn't move her leg away, I could feel her skin physically lifting off mine. Instinctively. Her voice didn't lose its detachment, however.

"Rolling in it," she said, and blew out the candle. "Goodnight."

We were quiet the next morning. Zee was to be arraigned at ten in open court. It was only on the way down to the courthouse that Hadley broke the silence. She said, as if to herself,

"I always dread the moment when the money comes up. I hid it for a long time, still hide it from most people. I never know how they'll react."

"Why?"

"Like I said, money is attractive. Complicated. In the women's movement especially, where everybody is so goddamned poor."

"But you don't act like you're rich."

"A crash course in radical feminism. I trained myself into—well, not exactly poverty, that would be impossible—but into not acting on desires. *Not* automatically picking up the phone to call long-distance . . . choosing the $5.95 lasagna instead of the $10.95 chicken cacciatore . . . *not* offering to pay the tab, or to loan money, or to give expensive presents . . . It makes me a little nervous sometimes, that you don't expect anything like that, that you seem self-sufficient, that you can take care of yourself. In my worst times I believe I'm a born Mother Theresa, only at home with the needy."

"But Hadley, does this mean that you don't give yourself anything you want, that you *never* eat chicken cacciatore?"

She just smiled, the curious half smile that didn't quite make it to her eyes. "It's not really the same problem that it was a few years ago. I've given away a lot over the last three years and the rest is temporarily tied up. I don't live on it anymore. I live on my wages . . . so I do feel able to spend that money."

"Who'd you give it to?"

"I gave a certain amount anonymously around Houston and here too, to women's groups I thought were decent. But it was hard—most of them were so poor and the women had no experience budgeting—the money wasn't always spent in the most useful ways. It led to quarreling among them and I ended up feeling very judgmental—though it wasn't *my* money anymore. And of course there were all sorts of rumors. You know, that *Playboy* was co-opting them or something. So I tried giving to out-of-state groups and national organizations—publishers, journals, music groups. And some to political campaigns and to peace groups and to international groups. My name was on every mailing list and the fund raisers were always calling me . . . It all got pretty complicated. I spent hours doing research trying to figure out who deserved what and how much. I could have done it full-time and not felt any better, though. It wasn't making the whole issue any easier. I realized I didn't want to spend the rest of my life counting out stacks of coins and pushing them to various outstretched hands around a table."

I was a little taken aback by her matter-of-fact tone. The King County courthouse loomed up before us.

"I heard of groups of wealthy people, mostly well-off leftists who'd inherited, who had come together to form non-profit organizations to give the money away. They stayed out of it, hired some people to give it away for them. There was a local one I joined, but then I decided I only wanted my money to go to women. So now it's tied up with a national group—same type of thing. We meet once or twice a year."

She busied herself parking while I thought about all this. When the engine was off she didn't move to get out however. She motioned me to stay a minute.

"There's something else I haven't told you, Pam," Hadley said. "I've been through this money stuff with three other lovers. It taught me a lot, but I'm not ready to do it again. I mean, get guilt-tripped. I know, at least, I think I know, that you're not the type, but . . ."

I tried to look like I was not the type. Who knew? My life had been lived within the puritanical but comfortable boundaries of the small business family, until my consciousness began to change. But both Penny and I still had the American ethic close to heart—work and you will succeed. I was probably as awed by and as disrespectful of unearned riches as anyone.

"And another thing," said Hadley, as if she were determined to get it all out at once, "because you'll hear this from someone sooner or later. I was lovers with Fran for a year or so. It ended six months ago—around the time she met Elena."

"You and Fran?" I couldn't help bursting out in horror.

"You've never had a chance, or probably the inclination, to see Fran's good sides," Hadley said. She was still holding on to the steering wheel, gazing out the window. I knew was this making us late for the hearing, but it was too important to drop. I'd had enough trouble understanding the connection between Fran and Elena, but Fran and Hadley . . . and did that mean Fran had dropped Hadley for Elena?

"She's really quite gentle underneath. She has this bar dyke exterior, this working class attitude, and it's true she is working class—she grew up in Shelton, her father was a logger until he got his foot crushed . . . And she worked too, worked from the time she was fifteen, delivering pizzas, gardening, odd jobs. And then she joined the Army when she was eighteen. She was in for ten years, she was a sergeant. She's been all over the world, you know. That's just it. She's really extremely cultured. She speaks a couple of languages, reads, her apartment is filled with books and things she's collected . . . And then she got political, you know she helped start Mobi-Print, she's really done a lot, Pam, she's . . . ."

I wanted to shout, I don't care. But I felt too numb. Hadley was still in love with Fran, it was obvious. And it was obvious too that she'd been protecting Fran all this time, giving her the keys, making sure she didn't have to talk to the police, pretending to believe her stories about having seen Jeremy at the shop, having seen Jeremy with two men . . . all this time, she'd been keeping me from getting at the truth because of a misplaced loyalty to Fran.

"I'm not sorry it's over," Hadley was saying. "I feel sorry for Elena. I don't think she used to drink so much before she met Fran. She seems so unhappy now."

"You didn't drink with Fran?"

"Me?" Hadley startled me with an ironic smile and a flash of her turquoise eyes. "Haven't you figured me out yet? I'm the rescuer, the one who tries to ignore it, who pretends everything's all right, that I can help."

"But you didn't help Fran."

"Actually, I did. For a while. It was very satisfying. It was the same satisfaction I used to get after an emotional encounter with my father, when I sent him off to yet another sanitarium . . . maybe this time!"

"What made you give up on your father?"

Hadley shrugged. "I had to live my own life finally. One day it just got to be too much."

I didn't think somehow that it had been that easy, the same as it couldn't have been easy with Fran.

"One more thing and then I'm finished confessing," said Hadley. "Three years ago, when I was giving my money away here in town, before I even knew Fran, before I worked at B.Violet, I gave my old friend Margaret $10,000 to replace the equipment in her typesetting collective."

"Uh-oh."

"It was a mistake," Hadley said flatly. "Fran and Margaret have been fighting about it for years."

"Fran never knew you were the one . . . ?"

"No," said Hadley. "She didn't."

But I wasn't so sure. I remembered Margaret's strange look of satisfaction as she inspected the damage done to B.Violet that morning. She must have realized that Fran had finally carried through with her threat to get back at Hadley.

We got out of the truck and started walking to the courthouse. I took Hadley's hand. I felt it had cost her a lot to tell me all this, but that she didn't have a clue as to how much she'd explained. She didn't realize that one more piece of the puzzle had fallen into place.

26

The arraignment was briefer and less exciting than I had expected. It certainly had nothing on Hadley's revelations in the truck. Or perhaps it was Hadley's revelations that made it difficult for me to pay too much attention to the proceedings. I kept think of Fran, the working class enigma, and of Hadley's mysterious eight years with her father in Houston and of a dozen things unconnected to Zee's fate.

We were late too, which made it more confusing. We slipped into seats on the side row in back and I watched more than I listened for a good ten minutes.

The courtroom was fairly crowded, mostly with Filipinos, twenty-five or thirty of them, and a few whites, most of them probably reporters. The Filipinos were wearing summer dresses or loose barong shirts; the whites were wearing utilitarian shirts, slacks and skirts, except for Penny, up in front, and Hadley and me, all of whom were wearing jeans.

Ray was sitting with Penny, and Benny and Carlos were next to them. Benny was barrel-chested and muscular, with a hooded intelligent look to his black eyes and a slight moustache on his smooth ochre-brown face. Carlos looked younger, more sensitive; he had a beautifully shaped mouth and a full-cheeked cozy softness. Everything about him was warm and brown. They were both paying close attention to the arraignment but while Benny had a suave almost contemptuous air, Carlos merely looked eager and worried. I could see him constantly giving gentle, reassuring glances over at Zee.

Who, in spite of being dragged out of the attic in her least glamorous clothes, without jewelry or make-up, and in spite of having spent the night in jail, seemed poised and intent, listening to the charge ". . . that on the night of June 8, 1982, you killed your husband, Jeremy Maurice Plaice."

Maurice?

I suddenly saw Marta Evans up in front, plump, with glasses and frizzy orangish hair that never quite settled, wearing a suit with padded shoulders and some sort of political button on her lapel. There was always something a little frowsy and comfortable about Marta, as if she were the mother of nine kids who somehow managed to have enough time for each one. The kind of mother who bustled and scolded and then turned on you a dazzling smile of understanding. Then went back to her work or put on glasses, picked up the paper, off in another world. A little like our mother had been, in fact.

But Marta was forty and married to a man who worked with Indochinese refugees and as far as I knew she didn't even have a cat. She was talking in a low voice to a man next to her, a thin young man wearing a dark lawyer's suit. That he was Zee's defense lawyer became apparent when he stood up and went to the lectern, to move that the indictment be dismissed on the grounds of insufficient evidence. It was a dramatic move but not a dramatic moment; somehow it sounded like he was asking the judge to hold the mayo on his BLT. I decided I didn't like him or the judge either.

I spaced out again, staring around at the audience—did you call people in a courtroom an audience? I wondered how many had had papers forged for them, what their lives had been like back in the Philippines, what they thought of the white women in the room, Hadley, Penny and I, so easy in our privilege, and actually the cause of all this. . . But then, Zee couldn't have gone on hiding in our attic forever. The cops were on to her; they must have found a marriage certificate, some record, something. Was that why Jeremy's apartment had been a mess? Had the cops been looking for something like that?

Or had Zee herself?

The judge denied the motion to dismiss the indictment as if he were the waiter muttering "no substitutions." There was sufficient evidence for a trial, he felt. He read the murder charge again in a flat, calm voice and asked Zee how she pleaded.

"Not guilty." Her voice was just as calm, steely even. After she spoke I saw her turn infinitesimally towards the crowd, as if looking for someone. I smiled, in case it was me, but she didn't smile back. Whoever that person was, he or she wasn't in the courtroom.

The judge set her bail at $75,000, based, he claimed, on Zee's disappearance after the murder and her "foreign connections." There was

BARBARA WILSON

a rumbling of disgust in the courtroom; everybody knew who was supposed to be foreign here. If you're not white, it doesn't matter how long you live in America, you're still an outsider. Of course no one was particularly pleased at the amount of bail either. Penny nodded over to me; I knew she meant she wanted to put our house up as collateral, and I nodded back firmly.

The judge adjourned the proceedings. Zee was taken off until bail could be arranged, and we all rose as the judge retired to his chambers. The court didn't clear immediately. Penny began talking excitedly to Marta and the other lawyer. Ray turned to Benny and Carlos; three black and brown heads bent close.

Then I saw her.

"Mrs. Reyes," I called to the woman at the back of the courtroom. "If you have a minute . . ."

Zee's aunt was, like Zee, a startlingly beautiful woman. She was simply dressed in a straight white crepe skirt and a red silk blouse with a floppy bow at the neck. Her eyes were heavily made up and as black as the dyed hair that had been pulled into a soft bun at her nape. She wore a red hat.

"Hello Pamela," she said as we sat down beside her on the bench, recognizing me at once but without any apparent interest.

I introduced her to Hadley. They shook hands. Mrs. Reyes' was practically gold-plated with rings and bracelets.

"I thought you were on vacation," I blurted.

"I was," said Mrs. Reyes. "I got a phone call and came back. I am Zenaida's closest relative here in Seattle."

She sounded as if she were talking about the funeral of someone who'd died unexpectedly.

"Did you know . . . about she and Jeremy being married?"

"I knew—after they'd done it." She was composed but bitter. "She shouldn't have done it, an irreversible thing like that. He wasn't even Catholic. But what could I say? It was done, she was in love, she . . ."

"She was in love?" Hadley repeated, incredulously.

Mrs. Reyes stared at her. "They were married, of course they were in love." She paused and added cautiously, "At least in the beginning."

"Why didn't they live together then?"

"It was his family," said Zee's aunt. "He was afraid of what they might say. I always thought that was the cause of some problems between them. They went down to California to meet his parents—not to tell them they were married exactly but just to introduce Zenaida and start getting them used to the idea. Zenaida came back first and wouldn't talk about it. After that Jeremy would still call sometimes but he didn't come over and they didn't see each other so much."

"When was this? When did they get married?"

"Well," said Mrs. Reyes, considering. "It must be, well, yes, August,

September, it must be almost two years ago now.''

"Two years ago! But that was before Jeremy started working with us.''

"I believe she told him about the job," said Zee's aunt, moving down the bench to the commiserating embrace of another Filipina.

" 'She sat there in shock,' " said Hadley. " 'Mind reeling with a thousand possibilities, a thousand questions.' " She shook me gently. "Hey, snap out of it.''

"But Hadley, don't you see? This means that . . .'' I stopped, mind reeling with a thousand possibilities, etc.

"It just means that it's more complicated than we thought.'' She paused and said, "I think it's about time for that phone call to Fullerton, don't you?''

Had Zee and Jeremy been in this together? Had Zee been informing on the Filipino community as well? Two years they'd been married and not a whisper of it to anyone. Zee had told him about Kay quitting and he'd just been able to stroll in and say 'Got anything for someone with camera experience?' How stupid we'd been to believe it was a wonderful coincidence. But who would have thought otherwise? Certainly not from the way Zee and Jeremy had acted. Jeremy friendly and vague, Zee so preoccupied with politics. Had Jeremy been blackmailing her? Had he been jealous of Ray? Had she been jealous of June? Maybe she had killed him. Who knew what had gone on in that darkroom before Hadley and I arrived? Maybe she really had killed him and was lying to all of us, using us as a cover . . .

We were suddenly in front of a phone booth and Hadley was being very efficient in finding the Plaice family phone number from the directory operator and charging the call to her home. Too efficient. I hadn't had time to prepare my story when Hadley handed me the receiver and a woman's querulous voice came on the line:

"Yes, yes, can I help you? Who is this?''

"This is Pamela Nilsen, a friend of Jeremy's from work. Is this his mother?''

"Yes.'' The voice went tentative. "Yes?''

"I worked with Jeremy,'' I repeated. "At Best Printing. I just wanted to tell you how sorry I am.''

I heard her begin to cry and felt a hypocrite. How did these hard-boiled-egg detectives do it? I couldn't possibly get any information out of her without feeling like a heel. I saw Hadley outside the booth look at me inquiringly and I turned my head away, deciding only to sympathize and to offer help and to hang up.

''. . . I knew the first time I saw her that that girl wasn't right. A Philippines girl, how could Jeremy marry her without telling us. It isn't right for two different races to get involved, I told him. I told him the problems the kids have in school, being mixed-like, how they'd get laughed at. And then you get all their relatives asking for money and wanting to come to America too. And you can't get a good job when they find out you're married to a foreigner. But Jeremy just said, don't worry, Mom, it'll all work out. But he never mentioned another word about her after they left, so . . . It was him being in the Navy did it. It's disgusting the way they let those young boys go to prostitutes—he was only eighteen— and then they develop a taste for it that spoils them for nice American girls . . .''

I thought, if this is what she told the reporter, then the account in the paper was mild.

"Mrs. Plaice," I interrupted. "When was this, when did you meet her?"

"It was Christmas," she said. "Christmas before last and Jeremy called down and said he wanted to come home and could he bring his girlfriend and of course I was just tickled pink, he'd never brought a girl home for the holidays before, and of course I was worried about him, I was working again, his brother and sister were married and there was just Jeremy. I used to worry about him and then he just up and joined the Navy, gone three years . . . so it wasn't like we were used to him bringing girls home . . .''

She paused for breath and her voice took on a tone of betrayal.

''. . . And then we went to pick them up at the Ontario Airport and you know he hadn't said one word about her being a Philippines girl, he could have at least said something. Well, we're not rich people but I'd decorated the house up something special and cooked a ham and a turkey and there were all kinds of relatives and some of the neighbors . . . oh, it was downright embarrassing.''

"How long did they stay?"

"Well I just asked her what they did in the Philippines instead of Christmas and she said they celebrated the birth of Christ, they were Catholic there, but how was I supposed to know that, they look like Japanese practically, over there in Asia somewhere with those slanty eyes I thought they had Buddha or something. I was just trying to be friendly and so I started telling her about Uncle Joe being stationed there during the war and somebody else said something about the Philippines always wanting to be the fifty-first state and someone else said they thought it was better with just Hawaii, though the Philippines people made really nice baskets, she'd bought some on sale . . .''

"And Zenaida left."

"They both left, first her, in a huff, then Jeremy. Then Jeremy came back and we told him it was all for the best, a girl like that could have never fit into American life, he'd be feeding all her relatives before he knew it . . .''

"Well, thanks, Mrs. Plaice," I said in as neutral a voice as I could manage. "I just wanted to say I was sorry."

"My husband and me we'll be coming up there when the trial starts," she said. "I want to make sure justice is done, that everybody knows what a good boy Jeremy was to be murdered by that little . . . ."

I hung up and turned, shaking, to Hadley. "I'm sure glad we didn't fly down to Fullerton," I said. "Or I think there could have easily been another murder. By strangulation."

BARBARA WILSON

27

Late that afternoon Zee was released on bail. Hadley and I were waiting for her when she and her aunt arrived home.

"I see you want some explanations," said Zee tiredly when she saw us sitting on the front steps.

"This isn't the right time," Mrs. Reyes said, unlocking the door and making a kind of sweeping movement as if to drive away flies. "Go away now, girls, can't you see Zenaida is exhausted? She has just spent a night in jail."

"Come on in," said Zee. "We'll have some tea. And a talk. I enjoyed talking to you, you know, Pam, up in the attic."

"We didn't come just to interrogate you, Zee," I admitted. I was recognizing for the first time how very bad the situation was for her and how well she was taking it. She couldn't be guilty, I knew that. I knew it. "We also wanted to ask what we could do to help."

"Thanks," she said, catching my hand and pressing it. "But I guess I need to tell you some things, things I didn't tell you before." She sat down in the living room and brushed her thick black hair with both hands. Mrs. Reyes went into the kitchen without another word.

"When did I marry Jeremy and why? Is that what you have been asking yourselves? Well, I have too, you know. For months. I knew Jeremy first from his interest with one of the Filipino groups. He was liked, at least he was accepted. No one could very well understand what he was doing with us, but he explained that he had been in the Navy in the Philippines and that was making him completely anti-Marcos. We all said okay to that. If you believe in something so much yourself you don't need so much convincing that other people believe it too. And well, you know, this was all around the time I was quitting the nursing school and trying to switch into graphics. My English still had some problems— Jeremy offered to help me—just as a friend. I thought he was a very good kind of person in some ways. And then I was having trouble with the immigration, you know, and suddenly he says to me, I will marry you if you want to—to help you—it won't be serious.

"I don't know why it seemed like such a good idea. I guess I had known some other people who had done it, mostly political men who did not want to be deported, with white women. And it seemed like a permanent solution. No more forms and waiting in lines, and always being afraid of having to go back to the Philippines. This time if I went back I would be the wife of an American. I would have some *rights!*"

Zee laughed scornfully. "That is the state of things there, you know, no rights as a Filipino, every right as an American. I had to ask myself how I felt about Jeremy and the answer was he seemed very kind and anyway I never planned to marry anyone else—not me! So we did it, without anybody but a few people knowing. And then it was funny, I don't know, maybe just the fact of being married made us fall in love a little bit. There is so much *solemn* attached to it, this marriage thing, you can't help but feel. Ah, we were sleeping together then and Jeremy wanted me to meet his family. That was when—his family weren't so very nice to me. And I came back feeling like I could have nothing to do with a white man again, you know? There is always some way they try to make you feel dirty . . ."

I almost asked her about the porn magazines and if he'd ever . . . but Zee looked so uncomfortable already that I didn't push it.

"I came back from Fullerton," she repeated, "and I fell in love with Benny for some months. Then I didn't want to say a word, a word about being married. And later, with Ray, the same. Now Carlos, but of course he knows . . . Jeremy was okay about it, I was surprised. He said he understood, he wanted only to help me and be my friend . . ."

I didn't believe it had been so simple. "And he never pressed you . . . ?"

"No," said Zee quickly. "Never like that. We were friends."

Like what? I wondered, but said only, "And so you told him about the job at Best Printing."

"Yes," said Zee, embarrassed, explaining, "He didn't have a job right then so when Kay quits, quit, I just called up and tell him."

"But you never told us you knew him."

"I know . . . it was just a funny situation. And then, pretty soon, I didn't like him so much anyways."

"How do you mean?" Hadley asked.

"He wasn't always that way," Zee burst out, "that spaced-out way. It was only something he did, maybe to make people to trust him, I don't know. But he could be different."

"How different? Calculating, threatening . . . ?"

"Just different." Zee retreated.

I said, "Jeremy started about a year ago at Best. When did the forging start?"

"Six months ago."

"And it was his idea."

"Yes."

"He didn't force you?"

"No."

"I know you did the camera work at Best, but who did the typesetting, who did the printing?"

"Some people, another place," Zee looked panicky. "We don't need typesetting, we just get a form and copy it. And . . . some people, they've got a little press in their garage, they can run it."

Suddenly Zee had become guarded, distant. I hesitated to push her, but I wasn't satisfied.

Hadley spoke up, "I don't believe you killed him, Zee. But do you have any idea who did?"

"I've thought and thought," said Zee, looking down, not at us. "But it gets so complicated. Somebody maybe whose papers were wrong— who gets caught. Maybe they killed Jeremy and make it so I'm punished."

"But if Jeremy were informing on Filipinos in the community," I said. "And if someone found out . . . ."

I pulled out the newsclippings I'd found in Jeremy's room. "Do any of these names look familiar to you?"

Zee regarded them closely. "But yes, there's Rodrigo Villaron, and Maria Gallego too, listed as members of the student group from some years ago, they're in San Francisco now . . . And Amado, that's Benny's brother I was telling you about—the one who was killed when he went back. Where did you find these?"

"Jeremy's apartment."

"I didn't want to think it, Pam, that he could really do this to us."

"But you did think it, on occasion."

Zee's voice sank low. "The questions he asked me sometimes—like personal questions about people. I didn't understand why he wanted to know."

"Did you know he had hundreds of dollars in his pocket when he died?"

Zee just stared at me.

"He wasn't blackmailing anyone, was he, Zee? He wasn't blackmailing you?''

"No!''

"Threatening to talk to the authorities about what you were doing?''

"No. No. No.''

"I think,'' said Mrs. Reyes, appearing at the kitchen door without the tea we'd been promised. "That this is enough.''

"Guess you watched a lot of *Perry Mason* as a kid,'' said Hadley as we went down Mrs. Reyes' driveway to her truck.

"Was I that bad?''

"No, you were rather good, in fact. It just seemed hard on Zee. That style of questioning, I mean.''

"Well, we found out a few things,'' I said, stung. "Do you really think I was too brutal?''

Hadley paused. "You know, she didn't exactly admit to anything you were asking.''

"Nope. She denied everything I suggested. Very convincingly. But I'm sure now that Jeremy was informing on them and that he was probably blackmailing Zee and possibly others to keep quiet. That doesn't mean that's why he was murdered of course . . .''

"So how're you going to find out?''

"I think we should start with Benny and Carlos tomorrow.''

"You don't think you're getting a little too carried away with this?''

"What do you mean? I thought you liked being a detective?''

"I do—sort of. On the other hand, have you noticed that car down the street with the two men in it, watching us?''

"Jesus Christ,'' I said, breaking out in a sweat. "Let's just act normal, get in the car and . . .''

We jumped into the truck like star athletes and roared off down the street. The car stayed parked where it was.

We were still shaking by the time we pulled up in front of my house. All the thrillers I'd ever seen were playing in technicolor in my brain: shoot-outs on the freeway, free-falls from the forty-ninth floor, bombs under the car . . . We'd better get some guns if we were going to continue this investigation. But I didn't want to shoot anyone!

"Hey, we haven't had dinner yet,'' Hadley remembered.

"You can *think* about eating?''

"I can always think about eating.''

"I want to call Zee and tell her there's two men watching her house.''

"Okay, and then we'll go out to eat. Maybe a pizza—do you like pizza?''

There were some people in the living room when we came in: Penny,

Ray and a couple I didn't recognize.

"Pam," called Penny.

"Just a sec." I ran to the phone and dialed Zee.

"She's in the shower," said Mrs. Reyes.

"Mrs. Reyes, there's a car with two men parked near your house. They may be watching you. I just wanted to tell you."

There was a pause while she looked out the window. "Oh, yes, thank you, Pamela."

"You're not worried?"

"It's Benny and Carlos," she said. "Keeping an eye on things."

"Oh," I said. "Well, that's good, just checking . . ."

"Thank you, Pamela. Now good-bye."

"Benny and Carlos," I muttered to Hadley.

"Our latest suspects," she said. "Maybe we should go back and invite them out to dinner."

"No way. Tomorrow's soon enough."

"Pam," called Penny impatiently from the living room. "Come on."

I went in, followed by Hadley. The woman on the couch looked vaguely familiar, though I couldn't place her. Blond curls and pretty like Elena, though with a considerably pudgier figure. She looked like the housewife Elena had never become—kindly, cheerful, a little martyred. The man next to her was probably her husband, a blue-collar worker with thick arms and a hardbitten face.

"This is Jeremy's sister and brother," said Penny. "Karen and Don."

"Oh."

From the way Jeremy had talked about his older siblings I'd imagined them looking like Jim Morrison and Janis Joplin. These two were obviously down-to-earth regular types whose favorite group was probably the Beach Boys.

"Nice to meet you," I remembered to say and introduced Hadley. "Jeremy used to talk a lot about you."

"We came up to collect the kid's stuff," said Don, as if he hadn't heard me.

"We thought you might have some things you could tell us," said Karen apologetically. "Seeing you worked with him and everything. I guess you were the ones who found him—maybe you've got some idea who killed him." Her voice turned pleading. "He was such a good kid." She pulled out a photograph of a seven- or eight-year-old boy on a horse. Jeremy with a smile of sweetness and pride. "I've always kept this . . . Jeremy was the youngest, you know, he was really the pet. I got married and moved away when he was eleven but I always thought of him."

"I know," said Don gruffly, "that I didn't always treat him seriously. Hell, I was eight years older and who wanted a little kid tagging along everywhere? But I liked him too, took him to his first baseball game."

A mood of melancholic nostalgia was palpable in the room, as if a funereal hymn were playing softly somewhere overhead. Hadley snapped us out of it.

"We think Jeremy might have been into drugs, maybe a dealer," she said matter-of-factly. Did we? I stared at her.

But Karen and Don didn't look that surprised; embarrassed and defensive maybe, but not surprised.

"We knew he had a drug problem in the Navy," Karen said. "Over there in the Philippines. It was so easy to get stuff there, you know. A lot of people took drugs, I guess."

"But Jeremy got caught," said Hadley, in the same matter-of-fact tone, as if she knew the whole story and was only asking confirmation.

"But he didn't get punished or discharged or anything," said Karen eagerly. "He just got a reprimand. He knew somebody, you see . . ."

"Karen," warned Don. "This is just family stuff, we don't want to tell them Jeremy's life story—because he finished with that drug business a long time ago. He learned the hard way."

Karen looked less convinced but she kept silent. I was thinking—a reprimand? In exchange for what? For supplying information? It was a far-fetched idea. How could they have known he'd be useful?

"When did Jeremy move to Seattle?"

"Well, pretty soon after the Navy," said Karen. "Couple, three years ago I guess."

"And you've seen him since then?"

They both looked uneasy.

"Once or twice," said Don. "I don't live in Fullerton anymore."

"Don lives in Riverside. I live in Ventura," Karen explained, once again apologetic. "We have families." She paused. "We never met the girl he married. Heard about her from Mom. Course no one ever knew he got married."

Don's face had turned dark red. "She's the one behind all this. And now she's going to pay for it."

"She's not guilty," Ray spoke up. "It's some kind of mistake, man."

Don looked at him as if Ray had just crawled out from under the sofa. "The cops don't make mistakes," he said contemptuously.

The magnitude of this error silenced us all temporarily. Then Karen spoke up, with quiet urgency, "But if you think, if he was a dope dealer or something, that maybe one of his customers . . ."

"These people are the ones who are probably dope dealers," said Don. "Come on, Karen—they don't know what they're talking about, they're the ones who hid that girl in their attic."

Karen looked further apologies at all of us but got up and followed him out of the room and out the front door.

"Anyone want a good deal on some really fantastic Colombian?" asked Penny.

"They're going to be great in court," I said. "I can see it now. They'll blow the photo of Jeremy and the horse up to life-size. 'Of course I haven't seen him for fifteen years, but I know in my heart he was the same sweet boy he always was.' "

"Do you really think he was into dope dealing, Hadley?" asked Ray. "Is that the explanation?"

"Anchovies," she said. "Black olives, tomatoes, onions."

"*Half* anchovies," I amended.

"We haven't had dinner either," said Penny enthusiastically. "Don't forget the green pepper and pepperoni."

"And sausage, chorizo if they've got it," said Ray. "But do you really think that, Hadley?"

I noticed that for the first time he was addressing her as a real person.

"I think I'd better get two pizzas," she said. "That's what I think."

28

Hadley stayed with me that night, or rather, with us. It didn't feel to me that I was alone with her in the house where I'd grown up and where I'd come back to live. Too many ghosts. Ghosts of my parents who wouldn't like it; ghosts of male lovers who would be titillated but disapproving; even the ghost of Ray, who was now a live presence on the other side of the upstairs hall.

I was overly conscious of every sound louder than a murmur that Hadley made. She was all bones and joints and she couldn't seem to touch me in the right way. She herself came with about a fingertip of pressure and immediately went to sleep.

I lay there, itched and brooded.

The name of Fran hadn't come up again, but it was in the air, less a ghost than a scent of something wrong. Hadley had said that money was attractive, but swaggering, working class toughness was attractive too, at least to women who'd grown up with money like Hadley and Elena. I thought about Fran's strong, bulky build, her handsome face with its light hazel eyes fringed with black, her black white-streaked hair. I wondered what it would be like to be with a woman that big who didn't (I glanced over at Hadley) sometimes feel like a barely carpeted staircase. Not that I was attracted to Fran. I'd never seen her in anything but the worst light. But I wanted desperately to understand what Hadley had seen and still saw in her.

She saw enough in Fran to want to protect her, to *have* protected her throughout our little investigation. Had she stopped to consider the real possibility that Fran was more involved than she let on? Why should Fran be immune from questioning? Why shouldn't she be pressed to give up any information she had? *She* was the witness to Jeremy's sabotage of B.Violet; *she* was the one who'd come up with the spying theory after seeing him being passed something by two men. Those were the only two motives possible. Either Jeremy had been murdered in revenge for what he did to B.Violet or his killing had something to do with the forging and possible spying ring he'd set up within the Filipino community.

Probably that was why Hadley was so keen on linking Jeremy's drug problems in the Philippines with his eventual role as a forger and probable agent in Seattle. If she could establish that the FBI or some other secret group was involved in Jeremy's murder, then Fran would be clearly off the hook.

The only problem with the two widely different motives is that they didn't rule each other out. Jeremy the forger, the spy, could have still been killed because he destroyed B.Violet. It was that simple.

Needless to say, I didn't sleep too well that night.

In the morning there was a lot of polite traffic in the bathroom and the kitchen. It was strange to see Ray in his kimono again, after all these months, making huevos rancheros for breakfast; it was probably just as strange for him to serve them up to his ex-lover's new lover. At one point he and I exchanged a wry look of complicity that was just this side of forgiveness; it gave me a little hope that we'd all be able to like each other sometime not too far in the future.

It still somehow didn't make the morning go any easier. Penny and Sam got into an acerbic exchange about some economic issue in the morning paper: prime rate, interest, the Federal Reserve, the International Monetary Fund—it escalated rapidly and ended with Penny denouncing Sam as a closet Republican and Sam counseling Penny to go back and do a little homework. Jude meanwhile was trying to interest Hadley in every conceivable kind of food and beverage, as became the self-appointed hostess of the household who was not going to be put off by some glum lesbian saying over and over, "No thanks, I'm not hungry."

"For Christ's sake, Jude," I said finally. "She doesn't eat a lot of breakfast."

Jude looked at me with eyes that accused, So why didn't you ever tell me you were getting involved with a woman, huh? I'm supposed to be a good friend of yours, one of your best friends, I even live in the same house, but no, I have to find out like this, in front of everybody, no explanations, just expected to go along with it . . .

I excused myself from the table and went out to the garden for a little vegetable relief. After five minutes or so Hadley joined me. By common, unspoken agreement we did not discuss murders, roommates, former lovers or sex. We went over the pros and cons of organic gardening, for instance what to do when the tomato bugs used your supposedly lethal hot chili solution to make enchiladas. Did you have to go right on to DDT?

After a while the house got quiet; everyone had gone to work. I knew we should head out for Best as well—there was a lot to do there—but I didn't feel too motivated. I was tired, the sun was hot, and the earth was giving off rather suggestive vibrations of fertility and fecundity.

We necked instead.

I was just about to suggest that we go inside to remove a few of these bothersome garments, when footsteps came crunching up the gravel drive and around the side of the house. Goddamn reporters, I thought, hastily straightening my clothes and hair.

"We rang the doorbell," said Benny, and Carlos nodded. They were both wearing cool white shirts with rolled up sleeves, and chinos. Their hair was freshly combed and they both smelled a little of aftershave. I felt Hadley and me to be panting, disheveled sex maniacs in comparison. I hoped they didn't notice.

I invited them in for some iced tea.

"It's about the news clippings you have," Benny said. "Zenaida said you found some clippings at Jeremy's room that have some familiar names underlined."

"Yes. Would you like to see them?" I pulled the stack out of the pocket of my jacket hanging in the hall.

Hadley brought out glasses and a pitcher of tea. It wasn't exactly cold, because it had evidently just been made up before Jude or Penny left, and there were no ice cubes, but it would have to do. We all sat down at the dining room table.

Benny's hooded, intelligent black eyes skimmed the clippings quickly. A slight but sharp intake of breath told me he'd found his brother Amado's name. Carlos read more slowly, his round, sweet face bent worriedly over the newsprint. He said something in Tagalog, something that sounded like a long curse.

"Did you ever suspect Jeremy of spying on you?" Hadley asked.

"Not a white boy, no," Benny said, pulling out a cigarette and lighting it. I wanted to trust him, because he was Zee's friend, if nothing else, but I felt a certain ruthlessness about him, under his suave manner. I didn't like him smoking in my house either.

"We know there's been some infiltration in the city," said Carlos. "Seattle is a place where there would be. It's where decisions get made about hiring for the Alaska canneries; there are a lot of Filipinos here.

We naturally think there are Marcos agents around." He spoke English more slowly than Benny but with a better accent. I recalled Zee telling me that he was studying physics at the university. Somehow that didn't fit with his youthful plumpness, though why it shouldn't, I didn't know.

"We knew Jeremy as Zee's friend," said Benny. "Then later she told me her secret, that she'd married him to stay in the country. It's not uncommon."

"*I* didn't know about the marriage," Carlos added, looking a little wounded. "But I did not have anything against Jeremy. It was a good idea it seemed like he had, about making the documents."

"Were you part of it?" I asked.

"No. Yes. Only to help some people. If we knew a name we would tell Zenaida. She and Jeremy did the work, she said it was safer for her."

"So it all went well at first," Hadley said. "Then things began to happen. A few people caught, deported . . ."

"Yes," said Benny. "And then my brother. He was so determined to go back to the Philippines. He took precautions, he had some forged papers to go back under a different name, because before, he had been known, he was known as a student leader, as you see here." Benny stabbed a finger at the pile of newsclippings. "But as soon as he got home, they knew. They found him and took him; some days later my family got a phone call, 'Go to the trash dump and see what you find.' His body was there, broken up, the fingers gone, and the toes, no penis anymore." Benny clenched his fist, his mouth tightened. "If Jeremy was here in Seattle to watch us, if he knew about my brother, and he did know because he helped with the papers, he could have told them."

I had the same feeling of unreality I'd experienced up in the attic with Zee. For these people the torture and death of those they loved was a fact of life, something that had to be understood, even if it could not be understood.

The question was, were Benny and Carlos only now beginning to think of Jeremy as an agent, after seeing the newsclippings, or had they realized it last week, or even long before, and made the decision to kill him because of it? And if they had killed Jeremy because he'd caused Amado to be tortured and murdered, who was I to be investigating and looking for justice? Perhaps justice had already been done. Not by the sweet-faced Carlos, who would never let Zee take the rap, but by the more ruthless Benny, smooth, moustachioed, wreathed in smoke.

"Any possibility Jeremy was blackmailing anyone?" Hadley asked. "He had a lot of money in his pocket when he died."

"If he was, we never heard," said Benny. "He wasn't blackmailing us, he wasn't blackmailing Zenaida."

Carlos looked less sure. "I had felt a change in Zee just lately. A little like she was maybe afraid of Jeremy, or maybe a little afraid of what they were doing. It was after Amado was killed this spring. She said she was worried about the documents, that maybe it was too dangerous for us to be involved in."

"Zenaida would not have killed Jeremy," Benny stated categorically. "It would neither do her nor the Filipino people any good. It is not doing us good this stuff in the newspapers. The trial will be a farce. It's a racist plot to pin the blame on her."

Hadley had risen and wandered over to the mantle. She suddenly turned and said, "Both of you were seen in Jeremy's apartment on the night of his murder, handing him a package. What was in that package?"

It was a bold stroke. If it had been me, if the idea had even occurred to me that these might be the two men Fran had described, I probably would have flubbed it by asking them if they ran and what had they been doing running in the U District when they lived in the South End?

Benny's hooded eyes took on a darker, more threatening cast. "What do you think?" he asked scornfully.

"I think it must have been money. Money to keep Jeremy quiet about what he knew, money not to turn any more names over to the Marcos goon squads. I think that after your brother was killed, that Jeremy came to you and told you just what would happen if he didn't get regular payments from the illegal aliens and the rest of them whose names he knew."

"You're crazy," said Benny. "We would never let ourselves be blackmailed."

"Benny," Carlos said urgently, "let's . . ."

"It was dope, if you want to know," Benny continued, lighting another cigarette with a steady hand. "Good strong marijuana, grown by Filipino farmers in Eastern Washington. If you knew anything about Jeremy you knew he was a dealer; he had a deal going with us. So much marijuana in return for so many documents. No," he said, with a sarcastic twist to his mouth and faint moustache, "We wouldn't let ourselves be blackmailed. It was purely an economic exchange, the kind the U.S. government has with its client states—international capitalism, the exchange of natural resources and profitable agricultural products for pieces of paper. Tit for tat. Tit for tat," he repeated, as if the phrase gave him pleasure.

I couldn't figure out Hadley's tactic. Far from challenging the meaning of his sarcasm, she was fiddling with her hair and looking into the mirror above the mantle in a very uncharacteristic display of vanity. Then I saw that she'd inserted the gold S-shaped earring with the turquoise stone, the same color as her eyes.

"But that's Zee's earring," Carlos burst out. "Where did you find it?"

Benny stood up and went over to Hadley. He was about five inches shorter but he seemed to look her right in the eye. Or the ear, to be more precise.

"Oh, yes, that used to be Zenaida's earring, but she lost the other one

BARBARA WILSON

and gave this one to Jeremy. I remember. I suppose you found it in his apartment."

"As a matter of fact, we did," said Hadley. "Do you think she'd like it back?"

"Not without the other one. It's lost, you know, it's been lost a long time."

"Well, we'll have to keep looking for it then, I guess."

Carlos rose as if he couldn't stand it anymore and started for the door.

"Do you mind if I take these clippings?" Benny asked me.

I didn't feel like looking at him. "Sure, go ahead."

When they'd gone I turned to Hadley. "And you talk about my detective techniques. Christ! You should be on TV . . . you should have your own show . . . Do you think they did it, Hadley?"

"I think we know now that Jeremy was recruited in the Philippines to do some spying or passing on of information here in the States. I don't know by whom. The CIA, someone in the military working with the Marcos government? We'd have to find the officer who gave him a reprimand for his dope possession instead of a discharge, and we'd have to find out what the conditions were. But I think it's clear that Jeremy was up to a lot of things. Maybe he started small, just attending the meetings and the demonstrations, and then got lucky. Marrying a Filipina activist must have been a great cover. By the time Zee realized what was going on it was too late. He was working at Best, involved in the forgeries, which he himself had suggested, he knew the names of everyone. Of course he was blackmailing Benny and anyone else he could. Money, sex, drugs, he could have asked any of them as payment. He was running a little empire out of your darkroom until they got him . . ."

"Until Benny got him?"

"Well, we don't know that for sure, do we?" Hadley remained at the mirror, swinging the S-shaped earring back and forth with a finger. "Yet, anyway."

29

The next morning, exactly one week after the murder, Elena met me outside the shop door as I was arriving to open up.

"Elena! You've come back to us."

"Well . . . not . . . look," she said. "I'd hoped you would be the first person here. I need to . . . Look, how about a cup of coffee?"

"Well," I hesitated. I'd gotten down here at seven-thirty this morning precisely because I wanted an hour to get things ready for a big job we were starting today. But Elena didn't look well. Her skin was, in the glowing light of a summer morning, the color of a beige pair of pumps, and her curly blond hair looked like she'd removed it from a paper bag and clamped it on askew. Her jeans no longer clung to her, but were all folds and wrinkles. What had happened in the four or five days since I'd last seen her?

"Sure, Elena," I said, putting the keys to Best back in my pocket. "But just for a half-hour or so . . ."

She didn't seem to hear me at all.

We started off to the local trattoria. I kept waiting for her to speak, but she didn't say a word until our caffé lattés had been ordered. Then she mumbled so that I almost didn't catch it:

"I'm moving back home to Indiana."

"What?"

"I can't take it anymore," she said in that same low, tense monotone.

"Everything is just too hard. Always too hard. I can't stand up to it any more. I can't give the kids anything they need, emotionally or financially. They put up with a lot from the two court cases already and now this . . ."

"Is Fran drinking again?"

"She may be," said Elena. "I told her last Friday night after you and Hadley left that I didn't want to continue our relationship any longer."

"But Elena, you were so worried about her last week. And now she's going to AA and everything." I stopped. What did I know? Perhaps Fran had only said that, perhaps that was something she said all the time.

"She's got to help herself," said Elena. "I can't help her anymore. I can't help anybody anymore. No one ever helps me." She was crying now, just as the caffé lattés arrived. The waitress, who was barely awake, looked as if she couldn't imagine anyone being that emotional this time of day.

I had a feeling that it might not be morning for Elena though, but the end of a long hard night. She smelled of alcohol and her eyes were wet and feverish. I reached out and took her hand. It was surprisingly cold and shaky. I rubbed it between my own hands.

"You've had a difficult time the last couple of years, Elena. But are you sure going back to your parents is the best thing to do?"

"I guess I can't think what else to do now," she said, withdrawing her hand and wiping her eyes. "You know, Pam, I'm so goddamned tired of sisterhood," she said almost violently, and then laughed. "It's really a joke, feminism. When I think back on it, I was a hell of a lot happier as an oppressed wife and mother."

"Oh, Christ, Elena."

"No, really. Was it so bad? As long as I didn't know anything different . . . I think back on those years with a kind of longing sometimes. Like right after we were married, when he was in graduate school and I was teaching in the local high school. We'd meet in the same little restaurant after work and he'd sometimes have flowers, or I'd have a book to show him, we'd both be full of stories about our classes . . . And even later, when I was home with the kids, I remember feeling a kind of peacefulness in the midst of the boredom. It was nice some days to realize I didn't have to get up and go to work, that I didn't have to be ambitious. I know I couldn't go back to that, but . . . was it really such a bad time? I don't know if I think so anymore."

"What about your parents, I mean, going back to your parents?"

"I had such a secure life as a kid, you couldn't believe it. A little pink and white room, swimming and dance lessons. Good in school, played the flute, lots of friends . . . it seems like a dream."

"But Elena," I tried to reason. "It wouldn't *be* like that if you went back. I mean, your parents know about you being a lesbian and how political you've been and how you've lived . . ."

"You'd be surprised," she murmured, sipping at her coffee. "They wouldn't care, I bet, as long as we didn't talk about it. As long as the word never came up in conversation or my life in Seattle was never referred to—and you don't have any idea, Pam, what a relief it would be *not* to talk about it. I feel like I've done nothing but talk for the last three years. Talk about my life, my relationships, my oppression—as a daughter, a wife—about compulsory heterosexuality, about biological determinism, about homophobia, racism, classism, anti-Semitism, sado-masochism, battering, incest, rape, spirituality. I'm tired of talking. I don't have another word to say!" she burst out vehemently and even banged the glass-top table.

But she did. She said, "I've come to the conclusion that lesbians aren't one bit better than anyone else. There's been this huge amount of propaganda about lesbians being so much more together than other women. *They* don't put up with any male bullshit, no, *they've* made the right decision. You don't like the way men are—and who in their right mind does?—become a lesbian, that's all you have to do. And if you don't, if you continue trying to work things out with your husband or your boyfriend or your son or your father, well, then you're a jerk, plain and simple."

Elena's raised voice was attracting attention from two young women executives in another corner, one of whom seemed to be nodding her slickly coiffed head in agreement.

"But I'll tell you, Pam, I've seen more fucked-up women who are lesbians and even more who are lesbian-feminists. They're jealous, they gossip and lie, they're promiscuous, they drink, they fight, they hurt people, they don't live out any feminist ideals in their own lives, they think they can judge everyone but themselves. They're nothing but goddamn hypocritical bitches!"

The women executives were getting worked up too, I could see out of the corner of my eye. "Now, Elena, come on . . ."

She stared at me, laughed darkly. "I forgot, you've become one of us now. But wait until you're out of the honeymoon stage. You'll see."

"Elena," I said. "What really happened between you and Fran?"

Elena looked down at her empty but still foamy cup. "When Fran sobers up, she doesn't need you," she said at length.

"But she needs your help to stay sober."

"That's a little harder. Especially if you're used to the dramatics. Especially if you drink yourself—are you just supposed to stop overnight, too? What if you can't? Besides," she added, more and more bitter, "no one ever helps me. They expect me to be the strong one."

"Look," I said. "Don't make a final decision. I mean about moving to Indiana. Why don't you just visit? Take the kids and see what it's like there, but don't decide now, here."

"My parents want me to come. They'd pay everything, the moving expenses . . ."

"But Elena—what would you do there? Could you teach? Wouldn't the court case and everything follow you there?"

Elena started crying again, tears glittering then dripping. "It's not fair. Why is it *my* life that's been wrecked? Other people live as lesbians and don't get punished. Why did I have to lose my job, everything?"

"But you're fighting back, Elena. I know it's hard, but if you win, it will make a difference to all of us."

Through her tears Elena's face turned sad, distant. "It's not that easy, Pam. And anyway, I don't have the strength anymore. Not again. Three years ago I had a lot of strength." She twisted and tore at her napkin. "I was full of great discoveries: Women are oppressed. Lesbians are oppressed. I wanted to stand up and tell the world to go to hell. I told my husband to go to hell anyway. That was the big mistake. It was too fast— all of it—for him. He got freaked out and went vindictive. I shouldn't have moved so fast, I shouldn't have . . . I just shouldn't have . . ." she repeated over and over and burst into tears again.

Impatience was gaining on sympathy. My watch said it was near eight-thirty. Everyone would be arriving at the shop wondering where I was; the paper company would be delivering, we had a big day ahead of us and here was Elena regretting that she'd told her ex-husband to leave.

"Like I said, don't make any big decisions now, Elena. You're upset, but it will pass. Visit your parents, remember what it's like and come back. The shop can wait."

"Sure," she said bitterly. "The shop could wait twenty years before I'd ever be any use there. I know I'll never be any good as a printer, it's no use pretending otherwise. Oh yeah, I thought it would be so great, a printshop. Working class feminism, hahaha . . ."

"Elena, I'm sorry. I just can't stay to talk any longer. I can call you up later, but we're really busy today and . . ."

"I heard Hadley's working with you now."

I nodded.

"Fran is really pissed, you know. She thinks it's betrayal. She thinks Margaret and Anna are going to start a typesetting business on their own and then she'll be left out in the cold."

"Oh, for godssakes, Elena," I got up to go. "I really have to leave. I'll pay the cashier."

"No, wait, Pam," she said, pulling at my sweatshirt. "I mean, I didn't even ask you about Zee and everything . . ."

I paused unwillingly. "She's out on bail, the trial is set for the end of next month and we still don't know how they can prove it."

"But they were married."

"I can't believe that had anything to do with it. She's having to take the rap for someone else, probably someone who found out he was informing, or maybe one of his own circle, some other agent. I don't have any idea how we can find out, but Hadley and I are trying.''

Elena's face had changed. ''Then you *don't* think that Fran had any-thing to do with it,'' she murmured under her breath.

I stared at her. Could that be the real reason she'd called it quits with Fran? From a fear that Fran had really knocked him off?

I bent down, hugged Elena. Her body was light and stiff as a styro-foam board. ''I'm sure you don't have anything to worry about, Elena.''

She didn't look up at me. ''Thanks anyway, Pam.''

The morning was ruined. Everyone was there when I arrived back at the shop.

''I thought you were coming in early to get ready,'' said Hadley.

I didn't say anything. I didn't feel like explaining about Elena. No one ever asked about her, and anyway, what *had* happened between Hadley and Fran, and maybe I wasn't a lesbian anyway, a lot of what Elena said was probably true. They were a mixed-up bunch of women really, not Hadley so much, but who knew? It would probably come out sometime or other, you couldn't grow up rich, a lesbian and with an alcoholic for a father without having a lot of problems.

Hadley seemed annoyed by my silence. ''Suit yourself,'' she said and moved off to ask Ray something.

''Lovers' tiff?'' asked Penny, with what seemed like a sneer.

I suddenly walked out the door.

Lesbians were no better than anyone else; lesbians were terrible people. What Elena had been trying to tell me had finally sunk in.

I found her about a block away from the trattoria, sitting at the wheel of her car, staring straight in front of her.

I went to the window, bent down. ''You did it, didn't you, Elena? But why?''

She shook her head, didn't even look surprised. She motioned me to get into the car. ''I was angry, angrier than I could have imagined—crazy, I guess. I told you lesbians, women were no better than anyone else.'' She leaned her head on the steering wheel, started laughing eerily. ''It was really funny when Fran saw me and thought I was Jeremy, smashing up B.Violet—even she would have never imagined that a woman, her own lover, could do something like that . . .''

''What are you talking about, Elena?''

''What you're talking about—you know now, don't you? I was the one who did it, who wrecked B.Violet. I did it because I wanted to get back at Fran and because Hadley paid for everything and Fran still loved Hadley and I was drunk. I'm a goddamn drunk too and I'm scared.''

''But I'm talking about Jeremy. You killed Jeremy, you killed him, didn't you?"

"It wasn't me, I didn't, I saw him but I didn't . . ."

Someone leaned over the car and cast a shadow on my side of the windshield. Elena jerked back and almost screamed. I shuddered myself, then realized it was Hadley. I rolled down the window.

"I was going to make a joke about your meter being up," she said, subdued. "But I guess it's not appropriate . . . Are you guys okay? Are you coming back to work, Pam, or what's going on?"

"Get in, Hadley," I said. "You might as well come along. In fact, I think you'd better."

"Sure," she said, getting in the back seat. "I didn't feel like working anyway on such a nice sunny day. Where to?"

"To Fran's."

30

I don't have anything more to say to Fran," Elena said, refusing to start the car.

"That's okay," I said. "I can do the talking."

"What's this all about, Pam?" Hadley leaned forward and put a hand on my shoulder.

"Did you have any idea that it was Elena who wrecked B.Violet?"

"Oh," said Hadley and sat back. "Well, it makes sense."

"I'm sorry, I'm so sorry," wailed Elena. "There's no way I can apologize enough."

"Fran doesn't know? Is that why we're going to Fran's?" Hadley asked. She sounded a little dazed.

"That . . . and other reasons," I parried. "Come on, Elena, start the car. Unless you have any other big revelations to make. Like what you meant when you said you saw Jeremy but you weren't the one who killed him. Who was? It was Fran, wasn't it?"

"I don't know, I don't know," Elena cried.

"I don't think we're going to get anywhere if you keep browbeating our chauffeur, Pam," Hadley suggested.

"Well, you drive then. Or I will."

She didn't move. In fact, we all remained sitting exactly as we were. After a few minutes Elena's sobs died out. She took her keys from her pocket, put them in the ignition.

"You're right. We've got to ask Fran, once and for all."

We still weren't moving. I didn't say anything. I was starting to feel ashamed of my 'browbeating'; what did I think I was in, anyway? A fucking TV cop show?

"Why don't you tell us what happened, Elena," said Hadley gently. "Just as much as you want to right now. As much as you feel okay about telling."

"It's all so weird," said Elena, calmer now but with a snuffle in her voice. "I don't expect anybody to believe me, especially after what I did."

Hadley stroked her shoulder. "I know, I know, but just try, Elena. We're not going to judge you."

That wasn't true, but I let it stand. I avoided Hadley's eyes.

"Well, after the meeting about the merger and after the fiasco at the bar, Pam dropped me off at home. I tried to be calm but I just got madder and madder. I went over to Fran's apartment but she wasn't there, and all the time I was thinking about the idea of the merger and how maybe it wasn't the right idea—it had been Fran's idea and it wasn't based on knowing anything about Best really—and Fran and I had had this stupid fight earlier and she'd said she was still in love with you, Hadley, and that's when I found out that you'd given all the equipment to the shop. . . . And I was drinking—God, you don't have any idea about my drinking, Fran's drinking. I couldn't get drunk in a bar like her, no, I'm too nice for that, but I can sure put it away by myself, at home. . . . And I just had this idea, well, I found myself going over to B.Violet and starting to do some damage. And the more I did, the better I felt. I can't explain it, I've never felt anything like it. That urge to destroy. It never even occurred to me that I might get caught, but the next thing I knew, Fran was standing in the doorway, shouting 'Jeremy,' and then she kind of clunked over. Obviously she thought I was Jeremy. I was luckier than I thought. I was scared she might have hurt herself and went over but she was just asleep . . . she'd cut herself a little on that piece of glass. And then it was like everything was finished for me. I looked around and everything was a mess and I didn't understand what I'd done. At all."

Hadley was still stroking her shoulder, but I couldn't seem to manage any gesture of comfort. I felt revolted. There was too much in the story I couldn't digest. I kept sticking to the essential point—that Fran *had* thought Elena was Jeremy. The key to the whole thing was the identity issue after all. Not that Fran thought the dead Jeremy was Elena, but that Fran thought the living Elena was Jeremy.

"But what happened next is the hard part to tell," Elena said. "I've wanted to tell somebody all week, it's just that I couldn't figure out how, not without admitting what I'd done to B.Violet." She paused and then said, "I was sitting there, in the midst of the shambles and the door was open the way Fran had left it and all of a sudden Jeremy and Zee were standing there, just looking at me.''

Hadley and I were too astonished to say anything. Elena continued, ''I told them I'd just gotten there myself and found things like that. I said I thought Fran had done it in a drunken state and passed out. Fran was okay, I told them, just passed out from drinking. I remember Zee went over to her and lifted up an eye and felt her pulse. She said I'd better take Fran home. Jeremy just kept shaking his head and looking around.''

''But what were they doing there?'' Hadley asked.

''Just passing by, it was the worst luck,'' said Elena. ''But the next day it was even worse. I'd ended up just leaving Fran lying there, because I couldn't wake her and felt too weak to move her. So I went home, then came back later. You know the rest, I called everyone, pretended I didn't know anything. Fran was gone by then, you know. . . But later, in the afternoon, the phone rang. It was Jeremy. He said he and Zee wouldn't say anything about Fran wrecking the place or me being there—they understood how these things happened and they didn't want to stop us from claiming a loss to the insurance people. All I had to do was turn up at Best that night at eight o'clock and give them a hundred dollars and the case would be closed. . . .''

''Shit,'' I said. Could Zee be a blackmailer too?

''Did you go?'' asked Hadley.

Elena nodded, bending her face low over the steering wheel. ''I didn't have all the money. I had about fifty, but I hoped that would be enough. I hadn't wanted to go. I'd wanted to find Fran and explain everything. I thought if I could explain it to her then I could explain it to everyone. But I didn't find her, and so I felt like I had to go to Best . . . it was a little after eight when I got there. The door was locked and the red light was on in the darkroom. I went in—and he was lying there, dead.''

''Zee wasn't there?''

''No. There was no one. I just ran out. I had this terrible fear that Fran had had something to do with it.'' She stopped and then said, without lifting her head, ''I guess I still have it.''

''Well, then,'' said Hadley. ''I guess we *had* better go ask her.''

Fran came to her apartment door wearing an indigo blue man's dressing gown, luxuriously curvaceous in a way she had never appeared in her flannel shirts and jeans. The white streak in her black hair waved up and spilled over her smooth forehead like seafoam; her hazel eyes were clearer than I'd ever seen them.

''Well, if it isn't the famous detective duo and their latest suspect—or witness?'' she said jovially. ''Come to confront me about my testimony? Well, come on in.''

It wasn't the reaction I'd expected at all. Hadley and Elena said nothing and I began to feel a little foolish. Here we were, at nine-thirty in the morning at Fran's, at my insistence. What did I expect to find out and how?

We went in. Fran's apartment, in spite of Hadley's description of her as a closet bon vivant, was still a surprise to me. Rows and rows of books along one wide wall. An old Persian carpet on the polished wooden floor; an enormous stereo set-up, framed photographs and several original paintings; fresh flowers on the table. I'd expected clutter; there was none; had been sure I'd find a revealing lack of taste—plastic, velour, lesbian kitsch. Nothing like that.

Fran was looking at me in amusement, as if she knew exactly what I was thinking. "Coffee?" she asked and went to make it.

We were all subdued, though Elena's desperation seemed to be giving way to the remorse of the hangover. She crawled into an armchair and covered her eyes with her hands.

"Didn't I tell you that Fran had a nice place?" Hadley tried. "She took those photographs herself. Aren't they good?"

"Yeah, great." I wanted to say something more, something cutting, but I felt too nervous. Fran had some kind of power—over them, over me—that I hadn't begun to fathom. I only knew that she could be nasty, she could be persuasive, she could be out of control, she could be orderly and elegant, she could be vulnerable, and she could probably be very violent.

Those who are unpredictable always exert more influence than those who can be counted on to do the expected thing. That was definitely something to remember when dealing with Fran.

Hadley looked disappointed at my response. Well, what did she expect? I hadn't come to admire Fran's photographs, but to make her admit what she'd done to Jeremy. Hadley was supposed to be my sidekick, not Fran's art agent. I wondered if I was falling out of love with her so soon.

Fran came sweeping back into the room like some robust bordello madame, carrying a tray of cups and a pot of coffee. One thing for sure, ever since I'd been with Hadley I'd started to really look at women's bodies, or at least admit to myself that I was looking at them. And Fran was built like a lavish Victorian love seat with velvet pillows. It didn't help that she went right over to Hadley with her tray, and that Hadley half-smiled into the deep V of Fran's cleavage as she bent over.

I decided I was in love with Hadley after all.

Elena had begun to twitch and shiver, with jealousy or shame, it was hard to tell. Her soft face was as creased with emotion as if she'd been lying on a bed of horsehair and nettles. Misery in tied bundles around her eyes; thatches of worry and anger on her forehead; and two long, bitter marks, like painful parentheses, around her mouth.

"It wasn't Jeremy you saw at B.Violet that night," she said hoarsely. "You obviously don't know what I look like if you could make a mistake like that."

Fran didn't do anything rash. She carefully put down the tray and advanced on Elena.

"You? You? You?" was all she said, in ever deeper tones of disbelief.

Elena got hysterical, even as she shrank into a kind of ball in her chair. "You've never cared about me, you just wanted a drinking companion because Hadley wouldn't. You got me drinking with you and all fucked up. It's not my fault. You shouldn't have told me about Hadley and that she bought you that equipment, it wasn't fair. I never knew I'd be that angry. I never used to be that angry."

For a moment Fran looked like a large blue bear about to smash a gnat, but suddenly she started stroking Elena gently on the face and head. Her voice was full of pity.

"You're right, Elena. I did fuck you up. And I'm sorry. It doesn't matter about B.Violet, really. You know I asked you a few days ago if you wanted to come to AA with me. I'm asking you again. . . . Do you want to change?"

Elena just sobbed.

I remembered the first time I'd seen Elena, long before she began to work at Best. It was at a rally over abortion rights; Elena was speaking out for the rights of lesbians as well. She stood on the raised platform in Westlake Mall, on a cold day in March, in jeans and a lavender sweatshirt, a beret slanted over her blonde curls. She was glowing with health and power and righteousness; her ringing voice cut through the crowd with the conviction of an evangelist, and at the end of her speech she lifted her arms in a victory salute, silhouetted against the back wall of Bartell's Drugs, shouting, "We *will* survive!"

The scene here in Fran's living room was far too dramatic to be a private moment between them, but it was still effective. Fran standing there like Aimee Semple McPherson in her indigo robe stroking the head of a fallen sister, promising her salvation. How the hell was I supposed to insert the accusation that it didn't matter if it had been Elena or Jeremy at B.Violet; the point was that Fran had thought it was Jeremy who sabotaged the shop and that she had killed him because of that.

I glanced at Hadley, but she looked supremely touched. She'd never suspected Fran, never, and never would.

All of a sudden it came over me that I didn't either. It just didn't fit, I couldn't see it. I started thinking again about what Elena had said in the car and the truth slowly dawned on me. It was very depressing.

"Come on, Elena," Fran urged. "I'll take you to AA tonight. You'll be surprised who you meet there. It'll be like old home week."

Elena struggled out of the chair and for a moment I thought she was going to kneel down at Fran's slippered feet, but instead she gave her former lover a good kick in the shins.

"Whatever I do about changing my life, it's going to be because I want to. You can't make me do anything anymore. It's my life, god-damnit, get out of the way!"

And in a wild leap of energy Elena flew from the room and out the door. I congratulated her silently.

After a moment Hadley said, "How long have you known that I was the one who gave the money to Margaret, Fran?"

Fran was looking somewhat dashed, rubbing her leg. She sat down in Elena's chair. "Not too long. Margaret told me when I started talking about a merger with Best. I don't know what her point was, because she only undercut her own position. She used to have a certain mystique in the collective, remember, as the one who'd been given thousands of dollars. I should have guessed it was you, Had. You always were so adamant about never giving B.Violet a thing."

A bitter but complicit look passed between them. Hadley bit her lip but Fran said, "It doesn't matter now . . . everything's gone. I don't know, if you and I had been able to work it out. . . ."

"If you hadn't started drinking again," Hadley had to say.

"If you hadn't been so moralistic all the time. Shit, your idea of a good time is a soyburger and a glass of milk. When you could eat filet mignon every night."

"I don't like filet mignon," Hadley said stubbornly, but with the beginning of a laugh in her voice.

"Oh, let's forget it. You've got someone else"—she glanced at me with a magnanimous sneer—"It's all water under the bridge. . . . You know, I've been looking at that one earring you've got on. Was it Jeremy's?"

"Sort of."

" 'Cause I found one like it."

"Where?" Hadley was thrilled.

"It was weird. I don't know where. It was sticking to my sweater, like it got hooked on somehow. Couldn't figure it out. Do you want it? It'll look good. Match your eyes."

She went out of the room cheerfully. All of a sudden I was remembering Fran's body half-covering Jeremy's, in the instant when she'd thrown herself down, thinking he was Elena. Had the earring gotten caught on her sweater then?

"Excuse me a minute," said Hadley and got up and followed Fran into the bedroom. They seemed to be there an uncomfortably long time, and when they came out, Fran was dressed in her normal, heavy-duty dyke clothes and was far too pleased with herself.

Hadley didn't look at me at all.

31

F ran dropped Hadley and me off at Best Printing, where Ray and Penny seemed to have formed a mutual pact not to discuss our absence. I didn't care, I was feeling pretty low. I hadn't liked the way Fran kissed Hadley good-bye, not one bit.

Later in the afternoon I asked Hadley what she planned to do with the earrings. She told me, and then I explained to her what I had in mind.

"Oh, that's much better," she said. "It's more dramatic."

By this time I was quite sure I'd lost her back to Fran, but I couldn't stop to think about it yet. As she left the shop, she gave me a good strong hug that reassured me slightly.

"So, see you later then." She winked one of her iridescent turquoise eyes.

After dinner I told Penny that I was going to visit Zee for a while, see how she was doing.

"I should go too," Penny said. "But I'm too tired." She was flopped on the sofa with the comics, her starchy hair in every direction, her big purple-rimmed glasses down over her nose. I felt a strong wave of affection for her, and sadness too.

"Ray coming over later?"

"Nah. I want to be by myself for an evening. I'm glad Sam and Jude are at the movies.''

I hadn't thought I'd say it in quite this way, but I did.

"I'm thinking of moving out, Pen. By myself.''

She looked at me from under the comics. "Is it Ray? We don't have to come here, you know.''

"No . . . it's more. . . . You know we've lived in this house twenty-five years almost? I've never lived alone, had my own place. For one thing, I'm curious to see what kind of place I'd even choose to live in, if I could choose.''

"We should just get Sam to move out, that's what we should do. He is *so* obnoxious sometimes.'' She looked at me suddenly as if she were really hearing what I said. "Is it because of Hadley? You don't feel comfortable bringing her here?''

"It's not just Hadley . . . if I am a lesbian, and I *am*, Penny, you know my life is going to be different. It's got to be. I've got to find out . . . what it all means.''

I thought, And I'm not going to find out living here with two couples and Sam never saying an encouraging word and Jude talking too much and you and me knowing each other far too well. Even if it's not Hadley I end up with, even if it's not.

Penny nodded. She understood me better than I thought. "We're just regular twins, you know,'' she said. "Not Siamese.'' She pretended to feel the back of her head. "It still kind of hurts though.''

"Yeah,'' I said. "It's bound to.''

Zee answered the door herself when I knocked.

"Oh, it's Pam,'' she said, a little too loudly. "Come on in.''

Whoever she'd alerted was just slipping around the corner of the hallway opening when I came in. I thought I caught a glimpse of Benny's dark head, but I wasn't sure.

"Just wanted to see how you were doing,'' I said, sitting down in a chair.

"Tea? Or would you like a drink? My aunt's working tonight. She won't wrinkle up her nose if we have some of her expensive Scotch.''

"Just a light one,'' I agreed, wondering why Zee was in such a wrought-up state. I doubted it had anything to do with the pleasure of my company. What had she and Benny been discussing?

Zee fetched ice cubes and the bottle of Chivas, put them down on the coffee table in front of us. She was dressed up: designer jeans, high heels, a royal blue silk shirt. Six gold chains hung around her slender neck, matched with gold earrings and gold rings. Her heavy black hair hung in a solid mass around her delicate face. She didn't look much like the woman who'd lectured me about the Philippines up in our attic, and, for many reasons, I was disappointed.

"Everyone says to say hello—Penny, Ray . . ." I stopped. Was that really everyone? "Have you heard anything from June since she went to Oakland?" I asked. "No? She's probably busy, having a good time."

I sipped some of my Scotch, racking my brains for more to offer. Why was I so put off by Zee's glamorous appearance tonight? I'd felt genuinely close to her only a few days ago, felt as if we might be going to be friends. And now?

"I heard Benny and Carlos visited you," Zee said.

"Yes." I was cautious; I didn't want to discuss Benny if he could hear us. But what was she doing with him anyway? Carlos was much nicer. Benny had the eyes of a criminal.

"You showed them the newsclippings."

"Yes."

"And you see now, Jeremy was spying on us." She said this matter-of-factly. "He was the cause of the death of Amado."

I nodded. Was she going to claim that Benny had done it? Was Benny going to appear in the hallway opening and gun me down because I knew too much?

"It's funny," I said finally. "How many people I've suspected in this case. Margaret and Anna to begin with. It was just too much of a co-incidence the murder happening right after B.Violet was vandalized. And then, for a long time, I thought Fran had done it. She had seen, or thought she'd seen, Jeremy at B.Violet. She was drunk enough to have killed him in revenge and then to have made up a wild excuse about Jeremy being an agent in the Filipino community.

"I thought it was crazy at first, thought that Jeremy had just been doing a drug deal. Well, in fact, he was. But with Benny and Carlos, and with people's lives at stake. Fran had only made a guess, but she turned out to be right. Jeremy was an agent—someone who was involved in the Filipino community, who knew names, who knew cases, who knew enough to blackmail. That was when I forgot about the sabotage of B.Violet. It had only thrown me off the track of the real murderer of Jeremy, the obvious murderer, the one who had done it for justifiable reasons. No, I decided, the destruction of a women's typesetting business had nothing to do with Jeremy's murder.

"But I was wrong." I stopped for a moment, but Zee didn't say anything. She was staring down at her carmine-polished fingernails. She hadn't touched her drink. Whatever excitement had been present at my arrival was gone now. She was merely quiet, waiting.

"There's only one person who links the two events together, only one person who was at both places, only one person who is the obvious suspect."

"You rang?" said June, standing in the hallway opening. "Or maybe it isn't really that obvious."

She came into the room, sat down next to Zee and poured herself a drink.

"When did you get back?" I asked.

"I never went. You think I've got money to go to Oakland, when my car needs fixing and my kids need a trip to the dentist? It's typical of you all that you're trying to protect me and say get the hell on out of here, girl, before you get in the papers, but you don't ask me how the fuck I'm going to get there. Nope, I just stayed right here. Keeping an eye on things."

"You are not going to tell me you murdered Jeremy, June. I won't believe it."

June was standing again, drink in hand, walking around the room easily but ominously. Her dark skin glowed under Mrs. Reyes' soft lighting arrangements. "Why the fuck shouldn't I murder Jeremy? Even when I think about him now I feel like murdering him. Do you have any idea what he had me doing? He had me in his game just like the rest of them, just like you too. He had that whole goddamn collective wrapped around his little finger and you didn't even know it. Who the hell do you think was printing that stuff for him anyway? Who was staying up all night running the press for little Jeremy's projects?"

June thrumped her strong thin chest. "This fool here. This fool who didn't suspect a thing except she was helping her man somehow. Aw, but you white girls are even bigger fools. You're so liberal you can't even see straight half the time. Oh no, June couldn't have done it, June's our good friend. Yeah, right. It's a terrible tragedy her husband got himself killed, but she didn't do it, she didn't kill Jeremy.

"And then you go around acting like detectives, you and that Hadley girl, pointing the finger here and there and here again. You maybe hide Zee but you give her up without a word when the time comes. You say, we're going to find out the truth, and you, June, get your ass to California. We don't need you around making any complications. You go around and then you settle back on Zee with any speck of proof."

"I don't care what you say," I said. "I know you didn't do it. I know it. I know it."

"Why are you so blind, girl? Look in front of your own eyes. The man did me wrong, so I shot him. Isn't that the way the song goes?"

"If you really killed him, how come you haven't turned yourself in yet?"

"Not because I didn't want to give you the pleasure of detecting my crime—only you were too stupid to do it—but because," June paused. "I really don't feel like going to jail, you know."

All through this Zee had said nothing. "It's true, jail is not too good a place to be," she commented now, quietly and absently, as if remarking on the weather.

I felt somewhat at a loss myself. I suddenly wondered why it was all so important. What did it matter if Zee had done it, or if June had, as she claimed? Jeremy had been a dangerous person, missed by no one except his family who remembered him the way he used to be at seven or eight, blond, sweet, sitting on a hired horse.

"June, do you really think I'm so liberal? That that's the reason I didn't suspect you . . . assuming you are guilty?"

"Honey, you are so liberal you don't even know how liberal you are. It truly blows the mind." She sat down on the sofa again as if exhausted. "Though now you're a lesbian there may be some hope for you."

Zee was still not saying anything, not admitting anything one way or the other. She fished for one of the ice çubes in her drink and sucked on it, like a small, sad child trying to pass the time.

It was suddenly as if none of us knew what to do or say anymore.

Then the doorbell rang, and it was Hadley.

32

▼ ▼ ▼ ▼ ▼

S he was supposed to make a stunning entrance; we'd had it all figured out. But no one noticed.

Hadley sat down, looking from me to Zee to June, all of us slumped, wordless. "Oh well," she said. "So how was California?"

"That big earthquake got there just before I did, everything was gone, it was a tragedy. You didn't hear about it? Hmmm, that's strange. There must have been too much going on here."

"Yeah," said Hadley. "It's been hectic all right."

A further silence, and then Zee spoke softly. "You have my earrings on, Hadley."

If I'd had any doubts at all concerning June, they were gone now. She didn't have the slightest idea what was happening, while Zee appeared to understand it was all over.

"Benny told me you found one . . . I hoped you would think it was Jeremy's," Zee paused and sighed. "I was in Jeremy's looking for some marriage certificate. I thought afterward that it would be best to find the paper and get rid of it, I couldn't find it . . . I had lost one earring earlier, in the darkroom . . . I thought if I put one in Jeremy's bathroom, they would think it was his too. . . . But you found both. . . ."

"You don't have to tell them anything," said June. "I told you, we'd figure out a way. They're not the cops, you don't have to tell them anything."

"I know," said Zee. "I guess that's why I want to tell them, to see if they understand." Her black eyes sought mine briefly and then looked away. She had trusted me and I had tried to trap her, Hadley and I both had.

She sighed again. "Okay, where to start. We knew he was an agent, we couldn't do anything about it. We have known for some weeks now, when Amado was killed. It was like you told Benny, he came and said, if you don't want this to happen anymore, pay up. And we paid, we paid with dope, we paid with money, we paid and paid. I didn't want to do the documents anymore, but he . . . he made me. That night, we went to B. Violet's. Jeremy said he wants to look at their equipment for himself, in case we really do merge, if we can use it for our work.

"Elena, she was there, standing there like a crazy person. Of course she wrecked and messed everything, you could see it. But she pretended Fran had done it and we pretended to believe her. Afterwards, Jeremy says he is going to blackmail her. He thinks it's so funny, you should have heard him laugh. He says, the way she acts in meetings, and now he will make her pay. He called her up, he made some time for her to come to the darkroom. I heard him, I decided to go, to try to talk him out of it.

"Now, you have got to know this—Jeremy had got a gun. He always carried it. He had it in his jacket pocket, a small one. I don't know what kind, I never used a gun before. That night I went there, before eight. I was trying to talk to him. He was saying he had asked Elena to bring him a hundred dollars, but maybe he wouldn't make her pay. He said he would tell her that if she fucked with him that he would forget it. He had never fucked with a lesbian before, he said. He was telling me the things he would like to do with her. . . . I don't want to say, but then, I don't know, I took the gun—he had the jacket hanging on the hook behind the door—I just took it and shot it. I didn't know about guns, how to shoot, I wasn't thinking, knowing anything. I don't know but he fell and that was the end. I ran away outside, I still had the gun, in my hand. There was nobody around, nobody came out and looked.

"Like in a dream I put the gun inside my jeans and then I walked to the ferry. I waited a little bit and then I went out to Winslow. On the way I put the gun over the side. It fell, I saw it fall in the water, they won't ever find it."

"So now's your chance," said June. "Which side are you on? Are you going to say anything?"

"How long have you known?" I asked her.

"I came over here yesterday, mad as hell, when I should have been in Oakland, to find out the truth. How Zee could have been married to the fucker the same time he was with me."

"We were talking," said Zee. "We had some common things we were feeling about Jeremy. I told her what he had done to me and to everyone."

"He never tried any of that blackmailing shit with me," said June. "But it was probably only a matter of time. He was sick."

"I knew he was sick," said Zee. "He was sick about the Filipino people. He hated us. I don't know why."

"I think Jeremy hated a lot of people," said Hadley. "He was a weak man who needed a sense of power. The more he got the more he used it. I wonder if we'll ever know who was paying him for his information?"

We sat in silence. June had an arm around Zee and Zee was looking at her lap. They were united in a way they'd never been before, a way that was good to see, even if it made me feel excluded. June's sense of direction had been as keen or keener than ours, but she hadn't pursued Zee like a detective, she'd confronted her like a woman and stayed to comfort her like a friend.

"It seems so strange," I said. "It was Elena who wrecked B.Violet and Elena who was really the cause of Jeremy's death. You protected her from Jeremy, Zee, and she doesn't even know." I suddenly realized who Zee had been looking for the other day in the crowded courtroom.

"Yeah, Elena, the big feminist heroine," muttered June.

"I think it's funny, somehow, you know, Pam, you and me were talking in the attic. And I said I wanted you to understand about women in the other parts of the world and how you had to learn to care about them to be a feminist. And now maybe I'll spend the rest of my life in prison because of a white woman in America."

Zee said it quietly, as if it didn't concern her, but her black eyes burned into me, asking for something that I was finally ready to give.

"No," I said, "You *can't*."

"No," Hadley repeated firmly. "The weapon's gone, they've got nothing on you other than that you married him. You're going to be trusting a few too many people with your secret, but I swear you're not going to jail. Not for Jeremy Plaice. You've got too many things to do to be spending your life in prison."

And June, without letting go of Zee one instant, said, "Amen to that."

Hadley and I walked out to our separate cars, stood under the streetlights talking like strangers. The weather was changing; purple clouds moved against the smoked glass sky, there was a taste of rain in the air.

"Somehow I always thought the solution of the case would hinge on you and Penny being twins," Hadley said. "It never even came up."

"You made a great entrance anyway. . . ." I paused. "I guess this means our detective story is kind of at an end, doesn't it?" I was giving her another chance, a way not to break my heart.

Her long legs kicked at the tire of her truck. Under the streetlamp her hair was silver and her eyes like cool blue stones.

"I can see you know what I'm going to say," she said. "But believe me, it's not usually a practice I make, to bring women out and then. . . ."

"Just don't tell me you want to be friends."

"What about starting our own detective business. Amazons, Inc. Have labrys, will travel."

"What did we ever really solve? Nothing that we can ever talk about to anyone."

"Hell, Pam, please don't be mad. I like you, I've always liked you. You're uncomplicated, nice, it's been . . ."

"*Nice* . . . give me a break. I'm sorry I'm not a violent drug addict or something. Would you like me better then?"

"Listen, I told you I'm the rescuing type. And you've never needed rescuing. Fran needs me right now, to keep going to AA, to change her life."

"You don't have to keep rescuing her! You stopped rescuing your father."

"And maybe I'll leave Fran again too."

"What about Elena? Or is that just twice as good? Two people to save now?"

"They're through with each other. I can tell. If Elena knows what's good for her she'll go back to Indiana."

I was silent.

"If I thought you could handle a triangle . . ."

"Forget it."

"I bet, in a few months, I could get her out of my system."

"I'm not waiting."

"And you don't want to be friends?"

"No!"

"Look. I want to show you something. Maybe it will make it easier."

She turned away, bent over, put her hands to her face, as if pulling out eyelashes. When she turned back her face was strangely different, colorless under colorless hair.

"They're blue contacts, the strangest blue I could find," she said, handing them to me.

Her real eyes were pale green and unfocused under the glow of the streetlamp. The two round turquoise blue drops glittered in the palm of my hand. Like tears. I handed them back.

"It didn't make it any easier," I told her.

"I thought it might not," she said, kissed me and started walking away.

I waited until her truck had started up and she was pulling slowly away down the block.

"I didn't just like you for your goddamned turquoise eyes, you know!" I screamed, beginning to run after her. "Hadley, come back here. I'm warning you, if your car turns the corner, I'm never talking to you again. You'll never see me again."

Her truck turned the corner.

I've always wondered if she heard me.

ABOUT THE AUTHOR

Barbara Wilson is the author of several novels and short story collections. *Sisters of the Road,* her most recent murder mystery featuring Pam Nilsen, was published in 1986. She has also translated two books from Norwegian, *Cora Sandel: Selected Short Stories,* and a novel by Ebba Haslund, *Nothing Happened.* She is co-founder of Seal Press, where she works as an editor.

Other Selected Titles From Seal Press:

Fiction & Women's Studies

Girls, Visions and Everything
by Sarah Schulman
$8.95

Sisters of the Road
by Barbara Wilson
$8.95

Ambitious Women
by Barbara Wilson
$7.95

Walking on the Moon: Six Stories and a Novella
by Barbara Wilson
$6.95

The Things That Divide Us
edited by Faith Conlon, Rachel da Silva and Barbara Wilson
$7.95

Every Mother's Son: The Role of Mothers in the Making of Men
by Judith Arcana
$10.95

Women in Translation

To Live and To Write: Selections by Japanese Women Writers, 1913-1938
edited by Yukiko Tanaka
$8.95 pb. $16.95 cl.

Nothing Happened
by Ebba Haslund
translated by Barbara Wilson
$7.95 pb. $14.95 cl.

Two Women in One
by Nawal el-Saadawi
translated by Osman Nusairi and Jana Gough
$7.95 pb. $14.95 cl.

Egalia's Daughters
by Gerd Brantenberg
translated by Louis Mackay
$8.95 pb. $16.95 cl.

Cora Sandel: Selected Short Stories
translated by Barbara Wilson
$8.95 pb. $16.95 cl.

Early Spring
by Tove Ditlevsen
translated by Tiina Nunnally
$8.95 pb. $16.95 cl.

An Everyday Story: Norwegian Women's Fiction
edited by Katherine Hanson
$8.95 pb. $16.95 cl.